ONCE A SOLDIER

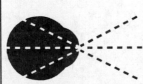

This Large Print Book carries the
Seal of Approval of N.A.V.H.

ONCE A SOLDIER

MARY JO PUTNEY

THORNDIKE PRESS

A part of Gale, Cengage Learning

GALE
CENGAGE Learning·

Farmington Hills, Mich • San Francisco • New York • Waterville, Maine
Meriden, Conn • Mason, Ohio • Chicago

GALE
CENGAGE Learning®

LIBRARY OF CONGRESS CATALOGING-IN-PUBLICATION DATA

Names: Putney, Mary Jo, author.
Title: Once a soldier / by Mary Jo Putney.
Description: Large print edition. | Waterville, Maine : Thorndike Press, 2016. |
    Series: Thorndike Press large print romance
Identifiers: LCCN 2016030142 | ISBN 9781410492524 (hardcover) | ISBN 1410492524
    (hardcover)
Subjects: LCSH: Large type book. | GSAFD: Love stories.
Classification: LCC PS3566.U83 O53 2016 | DDC 813/.54—dc23
LC record available at https://lccn.loc.gov/2016030142

Published in 2016 by arrangement with Zebra Books, an imprint of
Kensington Publishing Corp.

Printed in Mexico
1 2 3 4 5 6 7 20 19 18 17 16

*I haven't mentioned lately how much I
love libraries and librarians. . . .*

CHAPTER 1

Portugal, 1809
Chaos, the screams of women and children floundering desperately in the water. An absurdly tall nun with a rifle slung over her back as she tried to save a gaggle of school-girls. Brutal French soldiers closing in. . . .

"Is he dead?"

Hard fingers pressed into Will's throat. He tried to shake them off, and was rewarded with stabbing agony in his head. The pain cleared his wits a little and he realized that someone was checking his pulse.

"Not yet," a vaguely familiar voice responded. The fingers disappeared. "Bashed on the head. Not sure how serious it is. I recognize him, though. The name's Masterson."

"Let him sleep," another voice said gruffly. "If he's not awake, he won't want a share of this deplorable brandy."

Thinking he had a fierce-enough headache

without drinking bad brandy, Will opened his eyes to find that he was in a damp, dark place, a cellar maybe, with cluttered racks covering most of the stone walls. A lantern hanging from a ceiling beam cast enough light to show the face of the man leaning over him. Tangled blond hair and a scruffy beard several shades darker. Shabbily dressed, but alert, wary eyes.

Will squinted at him. "I know you, don't I?"

"The name's Gordon. We went to the same school long, long ago. How is your head? You took quite a blow."

Will touched his aching temple, wincing at the pain. There was sticky blood, too. But his brain seemed to be working. He now recognized Gordon, though that wasn't the name the fellow had used when they were students at the Westerfield Academy. Given his bad behavior then, it wasn't surprising if he'd decided to change identities.

"Where am I?" Will's voice was rusty.

Gordon sat back on his heels. "Vila Nova de Gaia, in the cellar of a house overlooking the Douro River," he replied. "Do you remember the bridge of boats? People drowning as they tried to escape from Porto to Gaia and the improvised bridge breaking up under them?" His voice turned dry. "You

8

were very heroic. Led the charge to rescue a group of nuns and schoolgirls from being raped and possibly murdered."

The tall nun. Frantic, wide-eyed girls. Remembering now, Will asked, "Did they escape?"

"Yes, at least for the moment." The reply came from a dark-haired, hard-featured man who leaned wearily against the opposite wall, his arms crossed over his chest. "No idea what happened once they were out of sight."

Hoping that at least one group of innocents had managed to survive the carnage, Will shakily tried to push himself up. Wordlessly Gordon helped him sit against the damp stone wall. Every inch of Will's body ached, but he didn't seem to have any major injuries.

No uniform. He was dressed like a Portuguese man of modest means. Since he was fluent in Portuguese, Spanish, and French and he'd spent time in Porto, his commanding officer had sent him to learn what was going on in the city. Nothing good, he'd discovered.

He surveyed the shadowy room, which contained three men besides himself and Gordon. All looked as battered as he was.

Gordon made a courtly gesture. "Allow

me to introduce our fellow English spies. That's Chantry against the wall, Hawkins swigging from the bottle of brandy, and Duval to the left."

"I dislike being grouped with you English spies," Duval said in a languid voice with a faint accent. "I'm a French royalist."

"But a spy?" Will asked.

"I might be considered that by narrow-minded French officers," the Frenchman admitted. "In truth, I'm merely an irredeemable rogue."

"Irredeemable? This is a good time to talk about redemption," Hawkins said thoughtfully. He was the man with the gruff voice whose shaggy brown hair half obscured his face. "If we weren't going to die in the morning, would we attempt to make up for our past sins? Or shrug and return to them?"

Gordon frowned. "I think I'd try to be better. I've always assumed that there would be time to become an honorable man. I didn't expect to run out of time so soon." He took the brandy bottle from Hawkins and swallowed deeply, then passed it to Will.

"I don't know how to be good," Chantry said, his voice edged. "I'll go to hell no matter when I die. Which is going to be in a few hours."

Will wondered if he'd misheard. "What's

this about dying?"

"We're all to be shot at dawn," Duval explained. "So say your prayers and hope that *le bon Dieu* is in a merciful mood." His mouth twisted. "I expect no such mercy. But given the chill of this cellar, roasting in hell is not without appeal."

Will tasted the brandy warily. Wretched indeed, but he welcomed the throat-scorching kick as he tried to absorb the knowledge that he was about to die in front of a firing squad. He'd faced death in battle often enough, but the cold-bloodedness of an execution was . . . disturbing.

After a second swallow of brandy, he handed the bottle back to Gordon. "There's no way out of this cellar?"

"We searched. At the least, we hoped to find more drink on one of the racks, but there was nothing useful, and the only way out is that door." Hawkins gestured. "That very heavy door, which is locked and barred from the other side."

"There are also two armed guards out there," Duval added. "Not such bad fellows. They gave us two bottles of brandy because they thought a man shouldn't go to his death sober." He smiled crookedly and reached for the bottle. "They apologized for the quality of the brandy, but, in truth, I no

11

longer care. We finished the first bottle while you were unconscious, so we're all ahead of you in drunkenness."

" *'In vino veritas,'* " Hawkins murmured. "As I look at the rapidly diminishing moments of my life, I think of all the people I hurt being careless or selfish." He retrieved the brandy from Duval and took a swig. "If by some miracle I survive this sentence of death, I vow to do better. To pay more attention. To . . . to be more kind."

"That's a good vow." Gordon frowned. "If I survive, I swear not to sleep with any more married women. They're nothing but trouble."

That produced a couple of chuckles. "If you're not going to sleep with married women, you might as well be dead," Chantry pronounced. After a few moments' thought, he continued, saying slowly, "But if I chance to survive, I vow to take up the responsibilities I've been avoiding. A safe promise that allows me to greet the firing squad gladly."

"What about you, Masterson?" Gordon asked. "Unless you've changed greatly, your soul shouldn't be imperiled by death in the morning. At school, you were damnably well behaved and good-natured."

"Don't confuse good manners with blameless behavior," Will said dryly. "I've been working on redemption for my sins for years, and I'm nowhere near balancing the scales in my favor." He wasn't sure if redemption was even possible.

Hawkins sighed gustily. "Unfortunate that the guards didn't give us more brandy. A bottle each would have been welcome. Even with only two bottles, we'd have had half a bottle each if you hadn't woken up, Masterson."

"Sorry to deprive you," Will said apologetically.

Hawkins regarded the bottle solemnly, then leaned over to give it to Will. "In fairness, you should finish this bottle, since we all had a head start."

Dreadful though the brandy was, Will accepted the bottle and emptied it with one long swallow. There was nowhere near enough to become drunk, alas.

He hoped again that the nuns and schoolgirls had escaped to safety. That would give some meaning to his death. God knew he'd seen enough meaningless deaths.

In a burst of fury at the brutality of war, he hurled the empty bottle across the cellar. He meant to strike a section of plain stone wall, but instead the heavy bottle crunched into a rickety upright supporting one of the wall racks. The rack collapsed with a dusty crash as shelves of old crockery and unidentifiable objects pitched to the floor.

"Jesus, Masterson!" Chantry said indignantly as he dodged back, his head clipping the lantern so that it swung wildly. "Are you trying to kill us prematurely?"

The dust sent Will into a coughing fit before he managed to choke out, "Sorry. My aim was off."

As he looked at the dust rising from the collapsed rack, the erratic light of the swinging lantern briefly illuminated straight lines gouged in one of the stones that had been concealed by the shelving. The lines were very faint, but the pattern looked familiar. Frowning, he levered himself up and lurched across the cellar. "Does anyone know who owns this house?"

Duval shrugged. "I heard that it belongs to British wine shippers who've operated in Gaia for a couple of generations, but I don't know the name. Does it matter? The current owner and his household fled when the French confiscated the house."

"It appears that a Freemason built the house." Will reached the wall and traced the angular lines with his fingertip, confirming his guess. "Freemasonry evolved from medieval stonemasons' guilds, so their

14

symbols are based on the tools of a mason. This is a compass overlaying a square, a Masonic symbol."

"So?" That was Hawkins's gruff voice.

"Freemasons aren't always popular. Some have been known to build escape routes from their homes in case rioters came after them. Maybe that's what this one did."

The dusty mortar around the block looked like all the other mortar in the foundation, but the side seams were a little wider. If Will's guess was right . . . On a hunch, he looked at the collapsed rack. It made sense for the builders to have the necessary tools convenient if the escape route was needed.

Yes! One of the uprights had separated into two pieces, and both looked like hardened metal. He lifted a length that tapered to the shape of a narrow chisel. Perfect for gouging. He dug into the mortar on the right side of the stone, and it crumbled away like sugar icing.

"The devil you say!" someone exclaimed as the other men scrambled to their feet and gathered behind him. The tension was palpable.

Silently Hawkins picked up the other piece of the broken upright and started gouging on the left side of the block. Gordon bent over and began clearing away the

15

wreckage of the collapsed rack so the area under the work space was open.

Duval asked, "Are you a Freemason to know so much about them?"

"I'm a part-time engineer," Will explained. "The Royal Engineers corps never had enough men, so line officers like me are sometimes seconded to work with them if we have engineering experience. Very educational."

"If there is an escape tunnel . . ." Hawkins's voice broke for a moment. "Do you have any idea where it might lead? This house is full of French soldiers and there are guards all around."

"My guess is the tunnel comes out among outbuildings where it won't be obvious," Will replied. "There's no point in going to this much trouble just to be captured outside."

With most of the mortar chipped away, Will said to Hawkins, "Step back." Then he carefully shoved the wider end of his tool into the gap he'd made between the stones. The temptation was to use full force, but he didn't want to damage his lever.

The stone shifted. Releasing the breath he didn't realize he'd been holding, Will worked at the block until it was far enough out from its neighbors to get a grip on. He tugged and the stone moved toward him. Hawkins grasped the other end and they both pulled. Abruptly the stone jerked free and crashed heavily to the dirt floor of the cellar, narrowly missing Will's left foot.

And behind it was a tunnel large enough for a man to crawl into.

"Well, hallelujah!" Chantry breathed.

The tunnel was lined with damp stones and the part Will could see in the dim light slanted upward with horizontal grooves on the bottom to provide traction to anyone crawling through. His eyes narrowed as he evaluated it. An average-sized man could fit in there, but Will was broader than average. Keeping that thought to himself, he said, "Now it's time to discover if this goes all the way to the surface."

"And if there are rats, scorpions, or dead bodies," Duval said dryly. "I'll go first. I'm not so large as you great hulking Englishmen, plus I speak the French of a native if I emerge outside and encounter a soldier."

"Those are good reasons." Will gestured at the tunnel. "Good luck!"

"I don't envy you going blind into that tunnel," Gordon said as he offered the Frenchman a curved, broken piece of pottery. "This isn't much, but it might be useful against those rats or guards."

Duval accepted the impromptu weapon with a nod of thanks. "I shall return to tell you what I find."

Will was sure that he wasn't the only one praying for success as Duval climbed into the tunnel and began to crawl forward on his belly. The four remaining men waited in silence, listening to the faint sounds of Duval inching upward. He muttered a French curse or two at different times, and then the sounds faded away completely.

"It must be a long tunnel," Gordon said. His gaze was on the floor, concealing his expression.

"The longer it is, the better chance we have of leaving safely." Chantry rubbed at his side. "I've cracked a rib or two. I didn't think it was worth binding them when I was going to be shot, but I'd better do something or I won't be able to crawl."

Gordon stripped off the shabby greatcoat he was wearing. "I'll cut this up for the binding." He used another piece of broken pottery to saw the heavy fabric into strips.

They all worked together to bind Chantry's ribs, the activity a welcome distraction. Will had just tied off the last bandage when they heard sounds in the tunnel.

A few moments later, Duval's head

18

emerged. "We are saved!" he said jubilantly. "The tunnel ends in an old stone shed that is one of a cluster of outbuildings. When I looked out, I saw no soldiers near. It is raining, so wise men stay inside."

As Will helped the muddy Frenchman get his feet safely on the ground, Hawkins said tersely, "Then it's time we made our escape. Chantry, will you be able to make it up there with your cracked ribs?"

"What's a little pain compared to fast-approaching dawn?" Chantry replied with a twisted smile. "I'll make it."

"The rest of you go first," Will said. "If the tunnel is too narrow for me, I don't want to block anyone else from getting away."

Duval frowned as he studied the width of Will's shoulders. "It will be difficult but not, I think, impossible. Perhaps you should remove your coat and shirt. A small difference might be enough. I will carry your garments up the tunnel for you."

"Good idea." By the time Will had removed his coat and shirt, Gordon, Chantry, and Hawkins were crawling toward escape. Chantry gasped with pain as Hawkins helped him up into the tunnel, but he didn't complain, just started inching doggedly upward.

Duval wrapped Will's garments in a tight, flat bundle, then used his cravat to tie them to his lower back. "The tunnel is tight and somewhat damaged in places, but I do think you will be able to get through. I will not be far ahead. If you get into trouble, call. We will find a way to bring you to freedom."

Will had his doubts that would be possible, but he appreciated the sentiment. "If I become impossibly stuck, for God's sake, get away! There's no point in all of us dying."

"I am not so easily dismissed, Masterson," Duval retorted. "I shall see you on the surface." He climbed into the tunnel and began working his way up again.

Will took a deep breath, then followed. He was not fond of confined spaces at the best of times, and the climb out through stifling blackness would haunt his dreams for years, assuming he made it out. Even without his coat and with his bare torso slick with water and mud from the damp, there were times he thought he was lethally stuck. He learned how tightly his shoulders and chest could be compressed, and it was barely enough.

The tightest place was the very end, where the tunnel opened into the shed. After two attempts, Will grimly accepted his fate. "I can't make it," he said flatly. "Leave without me."

"You damn well will make it!" Gordon retorted. "Back up a couple of yards and cover your head while we widen this hole."

Will summoned enough strength to back down a few feet and wrap his arms over his head before debris began falling on him. It took only minutes before Gordon said, "All clear!" Then he extended a hand into the tunnel.

Grateful for the help, Will managed to crawl the short distance out onto a cold, muddy floor. He lurched to his feet, then pulled on the shirt and coat Duval had carried for him, grateful for any slight warmth.

"Quickly now," Chantry said. "The night is almost over and we must get away. We're in luck. The building to our right is a stable and Hawkins has liberated five horses. I know roughly where we are and can lead us to open country. As soon as we step outside, we must be swift and silent. Ready, Masterson?"

After Will nodded, Chantry opened the door of the shed. The heavy rain made the darkness almost impenetrable, but Will could make out the shapes of the horses just outside. Hawkins had managed to bridle and saddle the animals, after stealing them.

The men swiftly mounted, Hawkins helping the injured Chantry into his saddle. They saved the largest horse for Will. Chantry led and set the pace, a slow walk so as not to attract attention. Will was sure the other men shared his desire to gallop away at full speed, but he knew Chantry was right to be cautious.

Occasional lights started showing in windows as people rose to begin morning chores. But the houses thinned until finally they were out of the city. Chantry increased their pace to a trot, then a canter. Cold, wet, and uncomfortable as the ride was, Will much preferred it to the escape from the cellar. If he was shot now, at least he'd die free.

By the time they'd put several miles between themselves and Gaia, the sun had risen and the rain had ended, though it was still heavily overcast. Chantry led them into a protected thicket and came to a halt. With effort, he dismounted, one hand rubbing his ribs. "Time for us to go our separate ways, gentlemen."

The other riders also dismounted, gathering in a circle as they held their horses. Looking up at the sky, Gordon murmured,

"I never thought a wet, cold day could be so beautiful. Knowing I should be dead adds savor to the morning."

"We all contributed to our successful escape," Duval said pensively. "Facing death creates an interesting bond of brotherhood, does it not?"

Indeed it did. As Will looked at the faces of his companions, he realized how unselfishly they'd worked together. He knew almost nothing of any of them, yet he truly did feel a sense of connection from shared danger. "Though we may be self-proclaimed rogues, you're all men I'd like at my side in any future tight places."

"Rogues may be more useful in tight places than honorable men," Hawkins said, amused. His voice turned serious. "Facing death was simple, but now we face hard reality again. How many of us will attempt the redemption we discussed? I intend to."

Gordon gave a twisted smile. "I'll make a start at it."

Chantry looked gray-faced from pain, but his voice was firm. "I said I would take up my long-neglected responsibilities, and I like to think I'm a man of my word."

Duval sighed. "What is done can't be undone. Perhaps there can be reconciliation, if not redemption. I should make the attempt."

After they had shared a dark night and imminent death, it was strange to think Will would not see any of these men again. Strange and wrong. "If this war ever ends," he said tentatively, "perhaps those of us who survive may meet again in London and exchange lies about our heroic deeds and redemptions."

"The Brotherhood of Rogues Redeemed!" Duval said grandly. "I like the idea, but we shall need a point of contact in London for sending messages so we might find each other."

Will thought a moment. "Hatchard's bookstore in Piccadilly. I know the owner." In fact, Will was a major customer. "I'll ask him to keep any letters he receives that are addressed to the Rogues Redeemed, and that they can be read by any of us that call at the store. I'll give him the names we're all using tonight."

Chantry grinned. "Because we might be lying about our identities? I like your suspicious mind." Wincing from pain, he stretched a hand into the center of the close circle of riders. "May we meet again in more auspicious times!"

Will clasped Chantry's hand. The others did the same in a five-way handshake that made their agreement somehow more real. When they released their grips, Will swung back into his saddle, thinking he was grateful to have met these men in these circumstances.

He hoped they all survived to meet again someday.

CHAPTER 2

Southwestern France, outside Toulouse, April 1814

News of the emperor's abdication triggered riotous celebrations in the army camp. Since Will Masterson didn't enjoy feeling drunk, he'd stayed mostly sober and spent the night strolling among the tents to ensure that none of his troops killed each other in their exuberance.

By morning, the revelers had run out of drink and were sleeping off their excesses. Will caught a couple of hours of sleep himself, and awoke to the knowledge that since he hadn't managed to get himself killed, it was time to go home. War was damnable, and he'd had his fill. In his heart, he was no longer a soldier. He was ready to settle back into the civilian life he'd been born to. In fact, he looked forward to it. For years, he hadn't believed that would ever be possible.

He was writing a letter to his brother in London to announce his return when his batman, Sergeant Thomas Murphy, scratched at the canvas beside the open tent flap to catch his attention. "The colonel wants to see you in his tent, Major."

Will sanded his last sentence, then set his lap desk aside and got to his feet. This would be a good time to tell Colonel Gates that he would be resigning his commission as soon as possible. His admittedly varied skills were no longer necessary now that peace had arrived.

The camp was generally quiet as Will made his way to the colonel's tent, though a couple of indefatigable young Irishmen were holding a donkey race on the edge of the camp. Will wasn't sure he'd ever been that young.

The colonel's tent flap was up, so Will ducked inside. "Good morning, sir. Is this a good time for me to tell you that I will be departing the army with all due speed?"

Colonel Gates grinned and waved toward a camp chair. "Have a seat, Will. Glad to hear you're selling out. With Boney defeated, the army will be cut drastically and fewer officers will be needed. The more dilettantes like you who leave, the more space there will be for career officers like

27

me. Care for a cup of coffee?"

Will laughed. "I'm glad my departure pleases you. Coffee would be welcome." He settled into a camp chair. "Do you know the terms of the abdication? I'm assuming the emperor is not going to be shot, or he wouldn't have agreed to go quietly."

"He tried to abdicate in favor of his son with the empress acting as regent, but the Allies weren't having any of that." Gates filled a coffee mug and handed it over.

Will swallowed appreciatively. He'd developed a taste for coffee in his army years, though he was still English enough to enjoy tea equally. "Impossible to imagine a regency with Napoleon lurking in the background waiting for a chance to take over France again."

"Exactly." Gates topped up his own coffee. "He's to be exiled to Elba, a little island off Italy. He can have a court and his own guard, but it will all be in miniature."

Will's brows arched. "Is it safe to cage him so close to Europe? I'd prefer to see him sent to Botany Bay."

"The Royal Navy will patrol the island, which should keep Boney from causing more trouble." Gates raised his mug in a toast. "To the end of an era!"

Will clinked his mug against the colonel's.

"For better and for worse. I'm not sorry for my army years, but I'm ready to go home."

"And so you will, Major Masterson." The educated English voice belonged to a lean, dark man who stepped into the tent. "May I join you?"

"Of course." Gates swallowed the last of his coffee and got to his feet. "Will, Colonel Duval is the main reason I called you here this morning. He's army intelligence, and he wishes to speak with you about a special mission. I know the general outlines, but I'll leave you to discuss it privately."

Will stared at the newcomer for a moment, wondering if memory was playing tricks on him. No, he'd never forget the men he met that night. He rose and offered a hand. "Unless you have a French twin, I believe we've met."

"So we have." Duval's gaze glinted with amusement and he spoke with no trace of a French accent. "A memorable night."

After shaking hands, Will reclaimed his chair. "You didn't mention that you were in the army, and you seem rather more English today."

"Half French, half English," Duval explained as he helped himself to a cup of the coffee. As he stirred in chunks of sugar, he continued. "I didn't mention the army, and

29

you didn't mention that you were a peer of the realm, Major Lord Masterson."

"Titles don't seem relevant when one is about to be executed." Will studied the other man, thinking that Duval must have interesting tales to tell about the intervening years. "Should I be concerned that you have a special mission in mind for me?"

"Nothing too alarming," Duval assured him. "Are you familiar with San Gabriel?"

"A tiny country in the mountains between Spain and Portugal. It's the smallest kingdom in Europe, isn't it?" Will replied. "But I've never been there, nor do I know anything else about it."

"The Gabrileños have been staunch allies in the war against Napoleon," Duval explained. "They contributed first-class troops to the Anglo-Portuguese Army under Wellington. Now they want to go home."

"What sane man doesn't?" Will said. "I assume there is some problem with this, or you wouldn't be talking to me."

Duval nodded. "Their infantry units were in the thick of the battle for Toulouse and took a lot of casualties, so they won't be fit to march back to San Gabriel for some weeks. But there's a small troop of Gabrileño cavalry, and they're ready to leave now. They need an officer to take charge and keep them out of trouble on the way back."

"Why me?" Will asked. "I speak Spanish and Portuguese, but I don't even know what the language of San Gabriel is."

"It's a dialect that falls between those two languages. You won't have a problem with it," Duval assured him. "The Gabrileño commanding officer, Colonel da Silva, will have to approve you, but he will."

"And? Surely, there's more to the matter."

Duval frowned. "We're concerned over the condition of San Gabriel, and I'd like firsthand information. It's never been a rich country, but under the Alcantara family, it has been stable and well run, and as I said, they've been solid allies in the fight against the French. Then last summer, the French general Baudin crashed through San Gabriel, looting and destroying. He also captured the ruler, King Carlos, and his son, Alexandre, the hereditary prince, when they rode out to parley under a flag of truce. Baudin appointed a senile old uncle, Prince Alfonso, as regent for the young Princess Maria Sofia, who managed to escape."

"Has the country collapsed into chaos or banditry with the rulers gone?"

"I really don't know," Duval said. "There has been very little news out of San Gabriel. My guess is that the country has serious problems. As British allies, they deserve our aid in rebuilding. I hope you're willing to lead the Gabrileño cavalry back and spend a week or two evaluating the situation."

"Aren't the king and his son on the way home? Surely, French political prisoners are being released."

"We don't know what happened to them," Duval said, his expression grim. "I fear they're dead, but I intend to learn the truth. In the meantime, San Gabriel has no effective leadership. Now that the war is over and the Spanish guerillas haven't got the French to fight, I'm worried that a band of them might take over. The Alcantara residence, Castelo Blanco, is a formidable medieval fortress. If a gang of marauders move in, they'll be very hard to dislodge."

All true. Will hesitated. With the war over, he yearned to return home as quickly as possible. Accepting Duval's mission would delay him for weeks, perhaps months.

But he'd never forgotten the question of redemption that had arisen during that long, tense night in Porto. Taking on this task wasn't redemption, but it would be a service he was well qualified for. And though he'd prefer a speedy ship home, the long ride across Spain and Portugal would be a way of saying good-bye to his army life. He'd also be able to visit his friend Justin Ballard before leaving the Peninsula, possibly forever. "Very well, if the Gabrileño commander approves, I'll lead his men home."

Colonel da Silva was a wiry man with silver streaks in his dark hair and bandages on his right arm and leg. He was sitting in a camp chair in his tent and looked as if even that was too much effort, but his eyes sharpened when Duval introduced Will. "Major Masterson. Colonel Duval said you might be willing and suitable to lead my caballeros home." He spoke in fluent but accented English.

"That is for you to judge, sir," Will said in Spanish. "How many men, and will they resent a British officer?"

"Your Spanish is good," da Silva said approvingly. "Duval said you speak Portuguese as well, and that you know how to fight. Those abilities ensure acceptance. There are only two dozen men fit to ride. The wounded will stay here until their injuries heal well enough for them to go home." A shadow crossed his face. "Many of my men have been lost over the years. More would be alive if news of the emperor's abdication had reached Toulouse before the battle for the city."

"God willing, there will be no more such unnecessary battles," Will said quietly.

Da Silva crossed himself with his left hand. But years as a soldier taught men not to brood over what couldn't be changed, so he continued, "None of my surviving cavalry officers are fit to ride home, so the men are under command of the senior sergeant, Gilberto Oliviera. He understands the need to maintain good order on the journey across Spain. His father is the chamberlain at the Castelo Blanco, so Sergeant Oliviera knows the royal household well."

"How is San Gabriel faring without King Carlos?"

Da Silva hesitated. "Not long after Baudin ravaged my country, a courier brought a message from Prince Alfonso. He said there was much destruction of property, but most of the people had survived and he would stand watch over San Gabriel until by the grace of God, King Carlos returned safely home to his people."

"That sounds promising."

"I doubt the letter was written by Prince Alfonso." The colonel chose his words carefully. "The prince is very old and . . . infirm.

Perhaps it was written by Princess Maria Sofia in his name."

"Will the princess rule well if the throne comes to her?" Will asked bluntly.

"When I left San Gabriel, she was a sweet, pretty little girl, a close friend of my daughter. Her brother, Prince Alexandre, was very capable and there was no reason to suppose his little sister would ever inherit. In normal times, if she came to the throne, she would have strong advisors to help her. Now . . ." He shook his head. "I don't know enough about the situation there. If I could ride out tomorrow, I would. Since I can't, I pray that Duval is right to recommend you."

Will wondered just how dire the situation in San Gabriel was. "Soon the princess will have the advisors she needs. Perhaps, by the grace of God, King Carlos and his son have already been released from prison and are on their way home."

"Even the grace of God has its limits, Major Masterson," da Silva said bleakly. "How soon can you leave? Tomorrow morning?"

That quickly? Very well, then. "I'll need to consult my commanding officer, but if he has no objections, yes, tomorrow," Will replied. "I assume your men are well mounted?"

"Very well mounted, thanks to the defeated French." Da Silva's teeth showed in what was not a smile. "I also ask you to take messages to my wife, and to assure her that I and our eldest son are well. He is one of my captains and was wounded in the recent battle, but he is recovering. Soon we will both be home again."

"I'll be happy to carry such news," Will promised.

As quickly as that, the matter was settled. Colonel Gates approved Will's departure, so Tom Murphy immediately started packing, organizing, and disposing of things that were unnecessary.

That night, Will made his farewells to his friends in the camp. Though he would not miss the war, he would miss the intense camaraderie developed under shared dangers and privations. He wondered what, if anything, would replace that closeness.

At dawn the next morning, Will led out his small troop for his last ride through Spain.

CHAPTER 3

The Kingdom of San Gabriel, April 1814
The news raced across Europe like a summer storm. The emperor has abdicated. Napoleon is gone! The long wars are finally over!

And as the initial euphoria faded, the more thoughtful wondered, *What happens now?*

Athena Markham was at work in her small study in the Castelo Blanco, wondering how the devil this small, war-ravaged country would get the money to survive and rebuild, when Princess Maria Sofia del Rosario de Alcantara — and several other less important names — burst into the study, so excited she could barely speak. "Athena, the war is over! Napoleon had been forced to abdicate!"

Athena looked up from the account books, anxiety vanishing at the good news. "Well, glory be! The end has been coming for some time, but Bonaparte is so tricky and ambitious that I half expected him to pull another tiger out of his hat. Has a Porto courier just arrived?"

"Yes, as soon as the messenger announced his news down in the courtyard, he was mobbed by people wanting to hear him repeat it over and over. When he breaks free, he'll call on Uncle Alfonso, then come by here." Sofia chuckled. "Inviting the couriers to stop in San Gabriel for food and lodging as they travel to and from Porto and Lisbon was one of your better ideas."

"In uncertain times, staying well informed is vital." Athena just wished that the summer before they had been warned in advance that General Baudin and his troops would sweep through San Gabriel as they retreated east from Wellington's army.

Unable to hold still, Sofia danced across the study like a butterfly. Petite, dark-haired, and beautiful, she looked seventeen rather than twenty-four years old. "Will Papá and my brother be home soon, now that the emperor has fallen?"

Athena sighed and leaned back in her chair, absently petting Sombra, Sofia's gray tabby cat, who was relaxing on the desk. "I don't know, Sofi. We haven't heard a word since General Baudin burned his way across San Gabriel and took them away. I would think there will be a general release of political prisons such as your father."

"Unless they're dead," Sofia said, her dance ending. She gazed out the window, her shoulders rigid. "They must be alive, Athena. It was not like Napoleon to kill the ruler of a country, even a tiny one like San Gabriel."

"That's true of the emperor, but his general was a brutal man, and your father and brother were not the sort to cower before anyone," Athena said gently. "It's not a good sign that we haven't heard a word about them since they were taken prisoner."

"You think they are dead," Sofia said flatly.

It was the first time Sofia had admitted the possibility. Until now, she'd spoken as if they would return to San Gabriel as soon as the war was over.

If they were dead, Sofia would become the ruler of San Gabriel. Knowing it was time for plain speaking, Athena replied, "It is not beyond hope that they will return, but there is a strong chance that they will not."

"I'm not strong enough to rule San Gabriel," Sofia said in a low voice. "There is so much I don't know!"

"A deficiency we've been working to correct ever since I arrived here," Athena pointed out. "You've made great progress in learning how to govern, and since Gabrileño custom says a female who inherits can't take the throne until she's twenty-five, you still have a year to learn while Prince Alfonso is your regent."

Sofia turned from the window, her expression wry. "The official regent, poor dear uncle. He tries, but San Gabriel would fall apart without you. A pity that you can't carry the title of regent, since you're doing the work."

Athena laughed. "Nonsense, I'm merely the too-tall and too-English companion to Her Serene Highness, Princess Maria Sofia. Your people love you, Sofi. You're the one they look to for guidance. You will rule well if the task falls to you."

"I wish I had your confidence." Sofia fidgeted with her bracelet. "It's very selfish of me, but the worst part of taking the throne is knowing that I must marry for political reasons. That's what princesses do. But Papá always promised that I would be able to choose my own husband, within reason. Instead, I'll have to marry some horrid, pop-eyed royal duke who will want to push me aside and govern my country as he sees fit."

"You're a long way from having to do that, Sofi!" Athena said firmly. "No need to worry about such things today. The war is over and we should be celebrating. Your father and brother may be on their way home already."

"I wish I believed that." Sofia collected Sombra from the desk, then held the cat close for long moments before she raised her gaze, her dark eyes stark. "Promise you won't leave me while I still need you, Athena! Please."

Athena hesitated. She'd never intended to stay so long in San Gabriel. Her heart yearned for the green fields and peace of England. But she could not abandon Sofia, or San Gabriel.

Wondering if she'd ever return to the home of her heart, even though she'd never been very welcome there, she said quietly, "I'll stay, Sofi. For as long as you need me."

CHAPTER 4

The road through the mountains from Spain to San Gabriel was ancient and worn deep into the earth. Will wondered if Roman troops had marched through these stony hills and passes. Perhaps not, since Roman roads were usually wider and smoother.

As his small group of Gabrileños emerged from the sunken stretch of road, Sergeant Gilberto Oliviera spurred his horse forward. "San Gabriel! *Home!*" he called, his voice vibrating with emotion. Then he pulled his mount back as he laughed. "And our beloved homeland is drowning in fog so we cannot see it!"

Will and the rest of the riders joined the young sergeant and looked down the road ahead. Sure enough, the long, oval valley below was filled with white clouds. Toward the far end, a rounded hilltop just barely broke through the mist.

Oliviera explained to Will, "This happens sometimes, though usually only in winter. If it was clear, you could see all of San Gabriel from here. The river that runs through the valley, the royal castle, the villages, the fields and trees and vineyards." He released his breath softly. "Home."

"I look forward to seeing my own home." Will chuckled. "We have mists much more often." Raising his voice, he called out, "I know you're impatient, but have a care. Your families will be really angry if you break your necks on their doorsteps, and I don't want them to blame me!"

With a ripple of laughter and excitement, the troop started down the track at a reasonable speed. There was enough width for a wagon or two riders, so Will fell in beside Oliviera. The sergeant had run away from home to fight the French at a ridiculously young age. Though still young, he'd seen almost as many years of war as Will. He kept his men under such good control, Will suspected that his own services as a commander hadn't been needed. Duval's real interest must be information about how San Gabriel was faring.

Will asked, "What do you look forward to most after greeting your family?"

Oliviera considered. "After my family,

Gabrileño wine! It is the best wine you will ever drink, Major. One swallow and I will truly know I am home. You shall share that wine because you must stay with my family. My father is the chamberlain to the royal castle and we live within the walls. There will be ample space for you and Sergeant Murphy."

Living in the castle would be a good way to learn the country. Wondering what he'd find, Will said, "Thank you, I accept most gratefully."

Martinez, the lead rider, called out, "The shrine of Madonna de las Rosas is ahead! We must give thanks to Our Lady for our safe return!" He spurred his horse forward eagerly.

Squinting, Will could see the faint shape of a tower through the mist. The outlines of the small structure solidified as he drew nearer. Ahead, Martinez halted in front of the shrine and gave an anguished cry.

His fellow riders responded to that anguish at top speed. As Will pulled up, he saw that the building was in ruins. The front wall had collapsed and there was just enough of the stone structure left to support the battered tower. Behind were the remains of a small building that had been totally destroyed.

Oliviera made a low, pained sound as he swung from his horse. "The shrine was built to offer welcome to travelers coming from Spain. There was water and a small shelter for rest. And now . . . !" He spat. "May those French swine rot in hell for this!"

The other Gabrileños stared at blackened stone and charred rafters, their expressions stricken. Will guessed that this destruction brought home to them the reality of what San Gabriel had suffered. If a shrine could be destroyed, what, then, their homes and families?

Will dismounted as he studied the exposed interior. This close, he could see that some effort had been made to clear away the burned rubble and restore order. "The enemy could damage the building, but they could not destroy the sacredness of this place," he said quietly as he recognized a familiar shape inside the ruined structure.

He stepped inside and laid his hand on two charred rafters that had been nailed together in the shape of a cross as tall as he was. "Your countrymen have done what they could. Soon there will be the time and labor to rebuild completely." He gestured at a small, crudely carved wooden figure in front of the cross. "A cross, and a statue of the Madonna and child. What more does a

45

shrine need?"

Oliviera swallowed hard. "You are right. Those godless brutes did not destroy the holy spirit of this place." He knelt and crossed himself. Will stepped back as the other members of the troop did the same. One of the older soldiers spoke a prayer of thanksgiving for their safe return home.

But when they rose, one by one, their expressions had lost the earlier jubilation. They were steeling themselves to face what other damage their country might have suffered.

The mood of the Gabrileños was grim as they rode down into the valley. Dusk was starting to fall. The gathering darkness combined with the fog made Will feel as if he was riding through a haunted land.

The track led into a grove, and vicious oaths rang out at the sight of the blackened trees. One of the men snarled, "They torched the cork trees, the bastards!"

Another man said, "Cork trees recover from fire better than any other trees. Look, there is new growth coming." He spat. "But may the Frenchmen who did this pay the price for their sins by never having a decent bottle of wine again!"

Will smiled a little. In this wine-loving part of the world, that curse was more fero-

46

cious than rotting in hell.

A quarter mile farther along, a young man called Ramos said tensely, "Soon we will come to my family home. I pray God they are safe and well!"

Ramos spurred his way to the head of the group. When he reached a lane leading to a farmhouse, he turned onto it. The house at the end looked abandoned, with no lights or other signs of life.

As the troop followed Ramos, Will saw that the structure was solidly built of local stone, but one end was charred and the roof in that section had collapsed. Ramos urged his horse into a gallop, crying, *"Mamá! Papá!"*

Grimly Will loosened his lightweight, accurate carbine in its saddle holster as he approached the farmhouse. Though the house looked deserted, a soldier who wanted to survive learned to take nothing for granted.

The shutters in a window opened a little, showing parallel bars of light from inside. A woman shrieked, *"Julio, mi hijo!"*

As people rushed from the house, Ramos vaulted from his horse, calling, "Mamá! *Mamá!*"

As soon as the young man touched the ground, he was engulfed in family. Will sighed with relief and settled back in his saddle. This was one story that wasn't ending in tragedy.

Ramos's father gave his son a long, bone-crushing hug as silent tears ran down his cheeks. Then he stepped back so other family members could greet their returning son.

Will led his horse over to the patriarch, saying, "I'm glad to see this reunion, Señor Ramos. We saw some of the marks of war on our way down the mountain. How is San Gabriel faring? Your soldiers have had little news from home."

The older man turned and recognized Will's scarlet uniform with a nod of respect. "It has been difficult since the French pig Baudin stormed through our valley. Very difficult." He gazed at his son, his heart in his eyes. "But with our young men returning, surely we will rebuild and grow strong again."

That sounded more like hope than optimism. Will said, "This is only the beginning. In a few weeks, the rest of your soldiers will also be home."

He took his leave of Señor Ramos, then returned to his horse and collected the other riders to resume their journey. Since the mountain night was growing cold, he tugged on his greatcoat, which was warm and many-pocketed and designed for riding.

He and that coat had gone through a great deal together. With luck, he wouldn't have to sleep in it tonight. But as he guided his mount deeper into the misty valley, he wondered what he would find at Castelo Blanco.

Weeks had passed since news of Napoleon's abdication had reached San Gabriel. Unfortunately, it had not been followed by any news about the captured king and prince. There were occasions when no news was good news, but this wasn't one of them.

Unable to sleep, Athena rose and donned her robe and sheepskin slippers against the cold. Though her room had a fireplace, fuel was in short supply and not to be used without good cause.

She opened her notebook, which grew larger by the day. She had lists of things that must be done, broken down by their urgency, followed by more notes about possible solutions.

There were other, shorter lists of resources. Isolated in the mountains, San Gabriel has always been largely self-sufficient. There were no reserves of money in foreign banks. Much of the country's treasure had gone to outfitting the troops sent to war. General Baudin had stolen anything of value he could get his greedy hands on. There wasn't much money left here.

Plus, having so many men go off to war had created a severe shortage of labor. Those Gabrileños left — women, children, young and old — had worked hard, but there weren't enough people to do all the planting, harvesting, and maintenance.

She frowned at her notebook and wished she knew when the surviving soldiers would return. While fighting the Corsican Monster was no doubt brave and noble, Athena, as a woman, couldn't help thinking that staying home and doing the unglamorous work of raising food and running the farms and vineyards would have been more useful.

Where did one seek help for a damaged, remote little kingdom that most Europeans had never heard of? Her annual allowance was enough to provide her independence and the freedom to travel, but it didn't go far in a place with so many needs. She'd used a whole year's income in advance to buy food over the recent winter.

Her mouth tightened when she thought of her father. He could help if he wanted to, but he'd never want to. That had been established long ago.

If San Gabriel's soldiers returned home soon, might some of them bring loot that could benefit their family and friends?

She was smiling wryly at the thought when a scream brought her to rigid attention. It was followed by more shouting, barking, and cries as if a battle was raging right here in the castle. Could bandits have broken in? The castle was virtually impregnable; but in these quiet days, the only guard on the gate was a twelve-year-old boy, Señor Oliviera's youngest son.

Athena reached for her rifle, sure the disturbance was in the Olivieras' apartment. She checked swiftly to see that the weapon was properly loaded, slung her ammunition bag over one shoulder, and raced from her room to the stairs.

Sofia emerged from her room, blinking awake and looking worried. "What's happening?"

"I don't know," Athena snapped. "But stay back, and be prepared to run if necessary!"

She hurtled down the first flight, spinning around a corner to the second flight down. Athena wasn't much of an army, but she was the closest thing to it in the castle.

By the time Will and his two remaining companions reached the Castelo Blanco, he'd been witness to numerous joyous reunions, but even they paled compared to

Sergeant Oliviera's welcome. When they reached the gate in the curtain wall that led into the castle courtyard, they were greeted by a very young Oliviera brother who was standing guard. The boy had peered out through the small window in the middle of the door, then flung it open, crying, "Gilberto!" in a voice so high-pitched it almost disappeared.

Laughing, the sergeant leaned from his saddle and pulled his brother up onto the horse with a fierce hug. "I hardly recognize you, Albano! When we leave our horses in the stables, can you feed and bed them down while I take my friends inside? We've all had a long journey."

"Oh, yes!" Grinning ear to ear, Albano bounced on his brother's leg as they rode their horses halfway around the castle to the stables behind.

Will was glad to dismount, and he looked forward to sleeping in a real bed in a real building. After tending to his horse, he slung his saddlebags over one arm and took his carbine in the other hand; it was not something one left in a stable. Then they all headed inside, the sergeant leading the way.

The Olivieras occupied a ground-level apartment with an entrance opposite the stables. Since Albano was outside, the door hadn't been locked and Gilberto led the way into a sizable hall. Half a dozen candlesticks with glass chimneys were set on the table, but only one was lit. The candle produced hardly enough light to reveal heavy doors in each of the three walls, and a barely visible stairwell in the shadowed far-right corner.

Gilberto strode across the room to fling open the door in the left-hand wall, revealing a large, well-lit kitchen. He called, "Mamá, I'm home!" as if he'd been gone for the day rather than years.

His announcement triggered a response that made the earlier reunions Will had witnessed pale in comparison. A mob of Olivieras poured into the kitchen and boiled around him in noisy waves. There were ancient aunts and grandparents and a couple of knee-hugging toddlers. A woman who must be his mother gave an earsplitting, wordless scream of joy when she embraced her son as if she'd never let him go.

Others echoed his mother's scream. If Will hadn't known better, he'd have thought a massacre was in progress. A large gray-muzzled dog joined in, barking frantically as he stropped Gilberto's legs, almost knocking him over. The Olivieras were a handsome lot. One young woman who was probably a sister was so beautiful that Murphy just stared at her, his jaw slack.

The delirious happiness in the room was as exhausting as it was exhilarating. Murphy followed Gilberto into the apartment, his gaze still on the girl, but Will stayed back in the hall. He'd wait until the tumult subsided before introducing himself.

He strolled across the room to stretch his legs, admiring the intricate patterns of the tile floor. He had not known how beautiful tile could be until he came to the Peninsula. But the furnishings were spartan. Apart from the refectory table, there was only a pair of creaky-looking chairs that might collapse if he tried to sit down.

The tile medallion in the center of the hall floor had a coat of arms, likely that of the country or the ruling family. He was admiring the artistry when he heard swift footsteps from the stairs. When the steps ended, he looked up — and saw that the candlelight illuminated the barrel of a rifle pointed at his chest from the shadows. "Drop the gun!" a voice snapped in the Gabrileño dialect. "Very, very carefully." The command was repeated in French.

Will said peaceably in Gabrileño, "I mean no harm. Sergeant Oliviera has returned to his family, and I'm a British officer who accompanied him." He let his saddlebags fall to the stone floor and slowly leaned over to set the carbine on top.

"You're certainly not local," the voice growled. "Say something in English."

"As you wish," he said in English. "If you allow me to remove my greatcoat, I can show you my uniform."

The rifle barrel didn't waver. "Take the coat off slowly," the voice said in crisp English. "If you move your hand toward a weapon, I'll shoot you."

Not making any sudden moves, Will peeled off the greatcoat. His uniform was shabby and mended in places, but unmistakably British red. "My name is William Masterson and I'm from Oxfordshire."

After a taut silence, the rifle was lowered and a magnificent Amazon stepped from the shadows. Now that Will didn't have a weapon pointing at him, he realized that the rich, low voice belonged to a female.

Tiny sparks of energy tingled through him and long-dormant parts of his body began sizzling to life. He stared, entranced. The Amazon was close to six feet tall and she had the fair complexion of a Northerner. Even swaddled in a dark, ankle-length robe, she was strikingly attractive, with strong, regular features, a braid of warm brown hair falling down her back, and dangerous hazel-gold eyes.

And she handled the rifle with the ease of an expert. Not just an Amazon warrior, but the Amazon queen in person. He drew a slow, deep breath before saying, "I gather you're English also?"

"Athena Markham of no particular place, but yes, English." Her low voice had a well-educated accent. "Sorry I was so threatening, but it's been a difficult year, and the screaming sounded like an attack."

"I thought the same thing." He glanced to the door that led into the Olivieras' apartment. The noise had abated some. "I'm grateful you held your fire."

"Learning how to shoot is easier than learning when not to." She studied his uniform. "A major in the Fifty-second Foot. As part of the Light Battalion, you've probably seen just about every major battle in the Peninsular Wars."

"Yes, and more skirmishes than I can remember," he agreed. "With Napoleon defeated, I'm heading for home, and San Gabriel is on my route. You live here?"

"For the last five years." Her eyes glinted. "And you're the largest man I've seen in all those years."

Will laughed. "The Gabrileños I've met

tend to be wiry and compact. I feel like Gulliver in Lilliput."

"I've felt like that since I arrived. I'm sure I'm the tallest woman in San Gabriel."

"Are you a palace guard?" he asked half seriously.

"No, Lady Athena is my companion," a light female voice said in English with only a faint trace of accent. "Or my governess. Or the acting regent of San Gabriel."

A petite, strikingly pretty young girl with dark hair and eyes stepped from the stairwell behind Athena Markham, a pistol gripped in both hands. Unlike her companion, she didn't look skilled with firearms, but she did look determined. Luckily, the weapon was pointing downward.

"I told you to stay away and be prepared to run," Miss Markham said, sounding unsurprised that she hadn't been obeyed.

The girl raised her chin. "And leave you to face danger alone? I must be brave!"

Making a guess, Will asked, "Are you Her Royal Highness Princess Maria Sofia?"

"I am," the girl said grandly. "I did not hear what all the noise is about. It appears that no one is murdering the Olivieras."

"They are celebrating the return of their oldest son, Sergeant Gilberto Oliviera," Will explained. "His arrival was unexpected."

"Gilberto is home? It is right that we celebrate!" The princess set her pistol on the refectory table so quickly that it skidded across the top as she darted inside the Olivieras' apartment. Mercifully, the weapon didn't fire.

Will watched her disappear into the happy turmoil. "I feel very old and very boringly British."

"I know exactly how you feel, Major Masterson." Miss Markham — Lady Athena? — smiled as she lit one of the extra candlesticks on the sideboard. After collecting the princess's pistol, she said, "You need a bed for the night, I assume, and I would love to hear the latest news. Come upstairs to the family floor and I'll find you a room. If you're not too tired, I'll also ply you with wine and cheese as long as you'll tell me what's happening in the outside world."

"I'll happily accept both bed and board," he said as he lifted his saddlebags and carbine. In England, her suggestion would have been considered improper. Here it was recognition that they were both adults, a long way from home, who just happened to be male and female.

So Will told himself as he followed Miss Markham up two flights of stairs to the family quarters. He also told himself that a gentleman wouldn't be so blatantly admiring of the way her strong, supple body moved under her heavy robe, or the way the wavering candlelight caressed hidden curves.

Luckily, she couldn't see how ungentlemanly he was being.

When she reached the correct floor, she led him down a passage to the left. She passed several doors to open the one at the end. As she stepped inside, she said, "The castle has very few servants now because their labor is needed elsewhere, but the room should be clean. There may be a little dust, but this guest room has the best view."

She used her candlestick to light the lamp on the desk. Again, the furniture was sparse with only a shabby canopy bed, a wardrobe, a desk, two wooden chairs, and a washstand, but under their feet was another splendid tile floor.

She checked the pitcher on the washstand to confirm there was water inside. "I hope you'll be comfortable here. San Gabriel may be in a poor way, but the traditions of hospitality are strong."

Will set his saddlebags on the floor. "No need to apologize. This is the best accommodation I've seen in months." He crossed to the window and gazed out at the valley.

He was high enough to be above the mist, which was a pale fluffy coverlet over the valley. Above, a handful of stars and a quarter moon brightened the sky. "I look forward to seeing the valley by daylight."

"When you've had a chance to settle in, wine awaits in the family sitting room, which is the door opposite the stairs. I'll collect some food to go with it."

"And then questions. In both directions." He hung his greatcoat on a wooden peg. "I'll join you soon. May I assume that the Olivieras will find accommodations for my batman, Sergeant Murphy?"

"You may. Though it's an open question whether anyone down there actually gets any sleep tonight." She smiled and pulled the door closed behind her. The light of his candle caught a shimmer of auburn highlights sliding down her braid.

He checked the old wardrobe, which had a sturdy lock and key. That should keep his guns away from any curious children. He set his saddlebags and carbine inside, then locked the door. After washing his face and combing his overlong hair, he considered lying down on the bed for a few minutes, then decided against it because he'd fall dead asleep. Best to find Miss Markham and start that conversation, for he had many questions of his own for his magnificent hostess.

CHAPTER 5

Athena descended to the castle kitchen and collected a basket of bread, cheese, and other foods that required no preparation. As she added olives and almonds to her basket, she heard musical instruments being added to the Olivieras' festivities.

So much happiness was infectious and she smiled as she returned upstairs. The sitting room had been used for small family gatherings for centuries, she suspected, and the wooden furniture had been shaped by the bodies of uncounted Alcantaras and their friends. Unlike the grand public rooms a floor below, it was relaxed and welcoming.

Shaken by her meeting with Major Masterson, she concentrated very hard on slicing cheese and sausage and bread. A simple meal, but the wine needed no apologies.

She had just finished laying out plates and napkins when the major entered the room. He looked so solid and handsome and *En-*

glish that she wanted to hug him.

She hadn't realized how hungry she was for the sight of a countryman. Here on the Peninsula, it had been years since she'd seen such a fine strapping fellow. Even in England, there weren't many men she had to look up to.

Even more compelling than those impressive broad shoulders was the humor and intelligence in his eyes. She hoped he'd stay for at least a few days.

Knowing she shouldn't stare, she lowered her gaze and poured two goblets of red wine. "I imagine you need this even more than food. Unless you're so accustomed to having guns pointed at you that your nerves are untouched."

"Anyone who claims not to be upset after staring down the barrel of a rifle is lying." His brows rose when he took his first sip of the wine. "But Sergeant Oliviera wasn't lying when he said the wine was exceptional."

Not wanting to think about the future of wine production in San Gabriel, Athena set out the platters of food. "I haven't much to offer, but this wine does go well with the local cheeses and sausage."

"Ambrosia." He took a seat and transferred samples of everything to his plate. "I'll try not to act like a starving wolf. It's been a long day."

As the major bit enthusiastically into the bread and cheese, Athena took the opposite chair. "My first and most important question is whether King Carlos and Prince Alexandre are on their way home. Have you heard anything about them?"

Masterson shook his head as he neatly cut a pickled onion into smaller pieces. "There was no word before we left Toulouse. Their fate is a mystery, though the man who sent me here is investigating what became of them. It doesn't look good."

"I was afraid of that," she said, wishing her pessimism had been misplaced. "Most people don't know that San Gabriel exists, so who sent you? And why?"

"I was asked to visit by a British Army intelligence officer who was concerned about conditions here."

"I'm glad to know that someone is concerned for San Gabriel," Athena said tartly. "What does he want you to do?"

"Observe how the country is faring after the ravages of the French," Masterson said succinctly. "And if aid is needed, determine what kind."

She stared at him. Grave gray English eyes, not dark brown. "Someone actually wants to help? The situation is difficult, and we haven't known where to turn."

"San Gabriel contributed a great deal to the fight against Napoleon, particularly given the size of the country," Masterson explained. "War is expensive in all ways. Lives, pain, treasure. Now that Napoleon is gone, it's time to start picking up the pieces. Since there was no fighting on British soil, we're in better shape to help our allies."

"That's a fine and noble sentiment," she said, hopeful but a little wary. "There is no self-interest in this?"

He smiled a little. "There is always at least some self-interest in politics. The man who sent me here fears that if San Gabriel is dangerously weakened, it might become the target of lawless guerilla bands that are at loose ends now that the war is over. Having a valued ally displaced by a bandit kingdom is not a pleasing thought."

Athena bit her lip. "That possibility has occurred to me. Your intelligence officer is right. With the king and the prince imprisoned or quite possibly dead, San Gabriel is vulnerable. Were you threatened by such guerilla bands as you crossed Spain?"

"Only fools would attack a troop so well armed and disciplined, and the guerillas I've known were not fools. But we did hear stories of attacks on remote villages," he said soberly. "We drove one such band away from a village west of Vitoria."

She shuddered as she remembered the assault of the French troops. "I've prayed that the mountains would protect us, but they weren't enough to save us from Baudin."

"That will change when the rest of the Gabrileño troops return in a few weeks," Masterson said reassuringly. "They are well-trained fighters and their commander, Colonel da Silva, seemed very competent. Unless you think he might institute a military coup when he returns, displacing the princess?"

"What an appalling thought!" Athena exclaimed. "I haven't seen Colonel da Silva in some time, but he and his family are famously loyal to crown and country. He would have had to change beyond imagining for that to happen."

"He didn't seem like a man plotting to overthrow his established government," Masterson agreed. "Speaking of his family, I promised to call on his wife when I arrived. He said they live just outside the town?"

Athena nodded. "It's not far. I'll take you over tomorrow morning."

"Thank you. After calling on her, will you have time to take me on a tour of the valley? I want to see for myself what conditions are like."

"I'll be glad to. But before seeing Señora da Silva, you should make a courtesy call on the regent."

"Of course. I would do so now, but I assume he has retired for the day." He hesitated before continuing, "I gather Prince Alfonso is advanced in years and not in the best of health?"

"Tactfully put," she replied. "Yes, he is very old and his wits sometimes wander." Often, in fact. "He mistakes Sofia for her mother. And me for my mother."

"Will Princess Maria Sofia make a good ruler if she ascends the throne?"

The topic was one that Athena and Sofia had discussed often. Obsessed about, in fact. "Sofia is intelligent and a good judge of people, and she has a strong sense of duty. She will not flinch from her responsibilities. But her nature is gentle, and she wasn't raised to rule, since it seemed unlikely that she would inherit the crown. She's working hard to remedy the deficits in her knowledge and she's very popular with the people, but she's not ready to rule. By Gabrileño law, she can't take the throne until she turns twenty-five, a little over a year from now. She will be better prepared by then."

"She is fortunate to have you." Masterson lifted the carafe of wine and topped up both goblets. "The loaded rifle made introductions brief. What should I call you? Miss Markham, Mrs. Markham, or Lady Athena?" He gave her a smile that took her breath away. "Athena, goddess of wisdom and war. Being called Lady Athena suits you."

The warmth in his smile gave her a stab of painful yearning for what could never be. Her voice sharp to put more distance between them, she said, "I'm sometimes called Lady Athena because I tend to give orders. The title would be correct if I were legitimate, but since I'm not, Miss Markham will do."

She expected him to look shocked or disapproving, but he merely put the last piece of sausage on a slice of bread and didn't bat an eyelash. "All babies are legitimate. What their parents did or didn't do is irrelevant to the reality of a live, bouncing infant."

Startled, she said, "There aren't many who would agree with you."

He offered her a half smile. "They're wrong, I'm right. My favorite relative is illegitimate and, to the best of my knowledge,

68

he has neither horns nor hooves."

A defensive knot in her midriff eased. "Your attitude is refreshing, Major Masterson."

"Call me Will." He scooped olives from the platter. "Most people do, unless I'm their commanding officer."

She smiled and surrendered to the ease that wanted to flow between them. "Then you should call me Athena, though I make no claim to special wisdom."

He studied her, his gray eyes thoughtful. "How did you come to be here, Athena? If you've lived in San Gabriel for five years, you must have arrived in 1809, when war was exploding throughout out this part of Europe. Do you have a mad adventurous streak?"

"When I arrived, the situation was much more dangerous than I expected," she admitted. "Do you want the whole dramatic story of my bad judgment and close calls, or will the short version suffice?"

"I most certainly want to hear the long story soon." He covered a yawn. "But for tonight, the short version will do because it would be unpardonably rude if I fell asleep in the middle of the full, dangerous account."

Athena considered where to begin. "The

Alcantara family has always maintained strong ties with Britain. Since my mother had friends here, I visited San Gabriel as a child. Long enough to learn the language and make friends of my own.

"Five years ago, Uncle Carlos — the king — wrote me to say his wife had died and could I come to San Gabriel because he wanted an English companion and teacher for Sofia. Someone who also knew San Gabriel." She smiled a little. "He didn't know anyone else who fit that description, I suspect. The letter arrived in the middle of a cold, wet English winter, so I immediately accepted. The plan was that I'd stay with Sofia for three years, until she turned twenty-one and would be ready for marriage."

"Plans so often change when life intervenes." He sampled the almonds and washed them down with a sip of wine. "Do you think of San Gabriel as your home now?"

She hesitated, recognizing that he asked questions she hadn't had the luxury of considering. "I love this place and these people. Sofia is like the little sister I never had. But San Gabriel is a long way from the sea. I thought I would be home by now."

"And now you're needed too much to

consider leaving?"

"Exactly." Athena was aware of irony. A major reason she'd accepted Carlos's offer was because she wanted to be needed. "But I don't suppose I'll be needed forever."

"The world will stabilize in time," Will agreed, "though I don't suppose that's much comfort when you're anxious to return to your family in England."

She laughed ruefully. "I have no family that will acknowledge a blot on the escutcheon like me, but I have friends I want to see again, and I miss England itself."

"I'll miss the sunshine of the Peninsula, though not the summer heat," he said with a chuckle. "You've had enough adventuring?"

She nodded. "I've seen more of the world than most women. Now it's time to plant a garden of my own and watch it grow. What about you? Will normal life be a flat bore after your years of war?"

" 'To everything there is a season.' " He eyed the last piece of cheese and transferred it to his plate when she gestured that he was welcome to it. "I've had my seasons of war, and since I've rather surprisingly survived, it's now the season to return home and take up the responsibilities I've been ignoring for too many years."

Catching something in his voice, she asked quietly, "Did you want to die?"

There was a long silence while he cut the cheese into very thin slices. "I rather did at first," he said in a low voice when he finally ran out of cheese. "I married young. My wife died in childbirth within a year. I couldn't imagine I'd ever again have anything, or anyone, to make life worth living. So I bought a commission, thinking I might as well at least do something useful."

Her heart ached for him. He wasn't all that old now, somewhere in his early-to-mid thirties, she guessed. "I'm very sorry. I hope you now find life worth living."

He meticulously arranged the thin slices of cheese across a round of bread before glancing up, his voice light again. "There is nothing like having large numbers of strangers shooting at you to make life seem desirable. I've been very lucky, and I intend not to waste my good fortune." His gaze was warm. Admiring, even.

Admiration, and desire. She almost didn't recognize desire because it had been so long since she had seen it. Or perhaps, since she had let herself see it.

Even longer since she had felt desire herself. She felt it now and she imagined those warm, strong arms around her. A kiss, ah, she was sure he could kiss well! Any man who could so enjoy such a simple meal must surely have a sensual nature.

If she was more like her mother, she would rise and give him an alluring smile and invite him to her bedchamber. They could have a passionate affair for a week or two until he left San Gabriel — she was sure he'd be willing.

But she was not her mother. So she rose and said, "I'm glad to hear that, Will. Good night. I hope you'll sleep well."

He rose and gave her a formal bow. "I'm sure I shall. Till tomorrow, Athena."

She lifted her candlestick and left the room, wishing intensely that for the next few days, she could be more like her mother.

CHAPTER 6

The bed was sinfully comfortable, which might be why Will had sinful dreams. When the rising sun woke him, he lay still and savored hazy images of a warm and willing woman in his arms. A long and lovely lady with intelligence and wit, whom one wouldn't break and could match him in strength and passion. . . .

The last shreds of the dream vanished when a crisp knock sounded on his door. Murphy called, "Sir?"

"Come in." With a sigh for vanished dreams, Will rolled from the bed as Murphy entered with a jug of hot water. "How late did the celebration go, Tom?"

Murphy grinned. A young and handsome Irishman, he'd shown a propensity for getting into imaginative trouble before Will had drafted him as batman. The more varied duties of an officer's personal servant had suited Tom very well. "Midnight was naught but a memory, sir. These Gabrileños know how to have a good time."

Will poured hot water into the basin and gave his face a good scrub. "Does that include the particularly lovely young woman who made you look like a stunned ox?"

Murphy blushed, a sight Will had never seen before. "Maria Cristina is Gilberto's sister and a sweeter lass I've never met." His blush deepened. "She gave me a kiss to thank me for bringing her brother home safe."

Will lathered up his soap so he could shave. "Did you tell her that her brother managed to make it home very well on his own and you were merely along for the ride?"

"No, sir. I was too busy being a stunned ox," Murphy said cheerfully. "You're invited down to the Olivieras' for breakfast, and Lady Athena will meet you after to take you to the regent, then on a tour of the valley."

"Have you met Lady Athena?" Will asked. "Because I wasn't up for the enthusiastic Oliviera celebration, she fed me bread and cheese and wine up in the family sitting room. An interesting woman." Which was a major understatement.

"I've not met her yet, but she's very well respected here." Murphy pulled Will's uniform from the wardrobe and started brushing off the travel dust. "She's the right hand of the princess and very important. Since she's also English, someone started calling her Lady Athena."

Feeling a ridiculous desire to talk about her, Will asked, "Do you know how an Englishwoman came to be here?"

"She has family ties to San Gabriel, I think. She came as sort of a governess to the princess, but she's knowledgeable about many things, which has been useful this last year. From the way she's spoken of, I think she may have done some brave deeds during the French invasion." Murphy pulled Will's boots from under the bed and began buffing off the mud. "Will you need me for the ride with Lady Athena?"

Will thought as he regarded the cleanest of his shirts, which wasn't very clean. God willing, he could get his laundry done here. He pulled the shirt on, thinking that Murphy would come with him if required, but he didn't look keen.

Noticing Will's expression, Murphy said, "Señora Oliviera said to bring down your clothes for washing. We're honored guests here. Very fond they are of the British."

Since Will and Lady Athena didn't need a chaperone, Will said, "Spend the day with

76

the Olivieras and listen to what they have to say about conditions here in the valley. Their views will probably differ from those of the royal family."

Murphy smiled with delight. "Cristina said she'd take me on a walking tour of the town. There's a grand old church in the central plaza. She's very devout. She said she's been considering becoming a nun."

Will suppressed a smile. A pretty girl was less likely to make such a choice if there were adoring young men around. "Here's your chance to show her what a good Catholic you are, but be careful. I'm sure the Gabrileño men are as protective of their womenfolk as the Portuguese and the Spanish, and I don't want to find your hide nailed to the nearest barn door."

"I would *never* do anything to offend Maria Cristina!" Murphy said hotly before he realized that Will was joking. He relaxed into a smile. "I'll see what I can learn about how people are managing, sir. Maybe I'll run into some of our cavalrymen. They will surely have opinions on what has changed and what is needed."

"The more we learn, the better, though I'm not sure how much Colonel Duval can do. But learning the situation is the vital first step." He pulled on his coat. He'd sometimes envied the 95th Rifles because their dark green uniforms didn't make as good a target as the red worn by most British troops. But when one wasn't actually being shot at, the scarlet uniform was impressive.

With a wry smile, he tried to remember the last time he'd cared about impressing a woman. Too long.

He tugged the short jacket down. The buff facings and silver lace were intact, but he thought ruefully that the uniform had seen its share of war and had the wounds to prove it. Murphy had become adept at mending slices from French sabers or scorched powder marks when a bullet hadn't quite hit him.

On the plus side, wearing a uniform meant never having to decide what to wear. He'd actually have to think about clothing when he was a civilian again. Smiling a little at the thought, Will headed downstairs to the Olivieras' apartment, with Murphy at his heels. He was greeted warmly by Sergeant Gilberto and his parents.

"Major Masterson." Señor Oliviera bowed deeply. "I thank you for bringing my son home."

"I didn't," Will protested. "Sergeant Oliviera and his men are highly skilled soldiers who had no need of me."

"No doubt," the older man said with a glint of amusement, "but I cannot thank the entire British Army for what it has done for all of us on the Peninsula. So I thank you."

Understanding the need to offer thanks, Will said, "On behalf of the British, I accept your thanks, but truly, our victory came of many allies working together."

That being settled, it was time to address the more serious issue of breakfast. The meal was limited to the adult members of the family, which kept the noise level down.

As Murphy said, the British were honored guests and the meal provided was lavish with sweet pastries, Spanish omelets made with fried potatoes, and ham shaved so thin it was almost transparent. Will hoped that a month's worth of food supplies hadn't been used up for this one breakfast, and honored the hospitality by eating with gusto. It was the best meal he'd had in weeks.

He'd hoped Athena would join them for breakfast, but she didn't appear until the meal was over. He was draining his coffee cup when she swept into the dining room, her vitality bringing the whole room alive. She gave Will a swift smile before greeting the Olivieras. He felt an instant of paralyzed shock and again the word "magnificent" sizzled through his mind.

She was dressed for a day on horseback, but instead of a woman's riding habit, she wore a short brown Spanish jacket embroidered in gold over a crisp masculine white shirt. Her tan divided skirt swirled provocatively above her ankles and in her medium-heeled riding boots, she was almost as tall as Will. *Magnificent* indeed.

As she removed her flat-brimmed hat, she said, "If the time is not inconvenient, I would like to take Major Masterson to meet Prince Alfonso."

Señor Oliviera rose. "I shall escort you and make the introductions, Lady Athena."

Will was impatient for his ride with Athena, but manners must be observed, and that meant meeting the regent. The three of them ascended a floor to the public rooms. As Will's footsteps echoed across vast, richly furnished spaces, he said, "There doesn't seem to have been any looting here in the castle. I assume the French were unable to break in?"

Señor Oliviera looked as if he would have spat if not indoors. "You are correct. We were able to preserve the royal treasures of San Gabriel. More precious are the lives of my countrymen. Many more would have died if not for Lady Athena."

Athena made a deprecatory wave of her hand, but Will decided that was a story he must hear before the day was over. He would have asked immediately, but they had reached a tall doorway and Señor Oliviera ushered them into a small reception room occupied by an elderly man in a thronelike wooden chair. Beside him Princess Maria Sofia was reading aloud. She stopped when the others entered, her gaze on Will. Since they hadn't met properly the night before, she was understandably curious.

Señor Oliviera announced in a sonorous voice, "Your highness, allow me to present Major William Masterson of the British Army."

Prince Alfonso, a thin man with white hair and a vague, happy expression, said, "We thank you for your visit, Major Masterson."

"My greetings, your highness." Will made a courtly bow. "Thank you for granting me an audience."

"I am always pleased to see British subjects," the prince said. "I spent two years in London representing my country, and I enjoyed it greatly. That's where I met my dear Lady Delilah." He nodded toward Athena.

Surprised, Will gave Athena a quick

glance. Her face was unreadable, and he remembered that she'd said the prince mistook her for her mother.

"Britain values her long-standing ties with San Gabriel," Will said. "Your troops fought bravely against the French."

Prince Alfonso scowled. "We do not like the French. Savages! They stole the Queen of Heaven! They must be punished for that. Punished!"

"And they will be," Princess Sofia said smoothly as she laid her hand on her great-uncle's arm. "But now it is time for your morning coffee, eh?"

The regent's face smoothed out. "Coffee, yes. You're a good girl, Isabella." He patted her hand. To Will, he said, "Pray take our greetings to your own prince regent, Lord Masterson. I would like to pay a call on him in person, but I fear . . . I fear that is too much for me."

"I shall do as you ask, your highness." Will bowed again, then withdrew, Athena at his side.

As they left the room, Señor Oliviera said, "I shall fetch your coffee, your highness, and we have honey cakes."

The regent's face brightened like a child's. "Honey cakes are my favorite!"

Will gave a sigh of relief when the door

closed behind him. "I understand why you and Princess Maria Sophia have had to take on the duties of governance."

"Prince Alfonso has better days," Athena said as she led the way through the great hall to the stairs. "Fortunately, he is always sweet tempered, except when the French are mentioned. He dotes on Sofia even if half the time he thinks she's her mother, Queen Isabella. They look much alike."

"As you resemble your mother, Lady Delilah?"

She frowned. "I can't imagine why you have any need to know about her, Major Masterson."

"I don't need to, but everything about you interests me, Athena," he said peaceably. "I'd like to know more of your past. In return, ask me whatever you like, though I warn you, I'm not very interesting."

"Families interest me, since I haven't much of any myself." She glanced back over her shoulder as she reached the ground floor. "What was your family like?"

"My mother died when I was six. She was sweet, but her health was never strong so I didn't see much of her. My father wasn't a monster, but he wasn't particularly interested in his offspring. I was raised mostly by servants. Luckily, they were a decent lot and looked out for me."

"That sounds rather dismal. Who was your favorite relative, the illegitimate one?"

"My half brother, Damian T. Mackenzie," Will replied as they stepped outside and headed toward the stables. " 'Trouble' is his middle name."

Athena laughed, her prickliness gone. "Really? I like him already."

"Mac is very likable." Will smiled as he remembered their first meeting. "He's two years younger than I, and his mother was an actress. After she died, her maid brought Mac to Hayden Hall, the family seat, then disappeared."

"How dreadful for him!" Athena's voice held a vehemence that sounded very personal. "Was he fostered out somewhere distant?"

"When my father returned from London, he wanted to do something like that, but I wouldn't allow it. I liked Mac and had him moved into the nursery with me." It had been wonderful to find he had a brother. He'd never forgotten his first sight of Mac, who was terrified, grief-stricken, and trying gallantly not to show it. "I was a well-behaved, rather boring child. Mac was a wonderful companion. Outgoing and full of fun. So I insisted on keeping him."

"Like a puppy?" Athena asked with amusement.

"Exactly." Will's glance was rueful. "I might have been boring, but I was also rather stubborn. When I refused to let Mac be sent away, my father abandoned plans to have me educated at Eton. Instead, he packed us both off to a small new school for boys of good birth and bad behavior so the illegitimate son wouldn't be obvious."

As they entered the stables, Athena asked, "Did that work out well?"

"Yes, we both got excellent educations and made friends for life." Will glanced around the stables and saw several good horses. "My horse could probably use a rest. Do you have any other mounts that would be up to my weight?"

Athena pointed to a large bay gelding. "Herculano is the strongest horse here and has a placid disposition." She glanced at Will mischievously. "He should suit you well."

He chuckled as he went for his saddle and tack. "Is he also stubborn?"

"When he feels the need." Athena collected her own saddle and entered a stall with a tall, handsome chestnut. "Where is your brother now?"

"Running a very fashionable gaming club

in London. Though he's spending less time at the club since he married last year." Will entered Herculano's stall and started to make the horse's acquaintance. "I look forward to seeing him again. I've been enlisted as godfather for a baby that's on the way."

"That sounds lovely." Deftly Athena saddled the chestnut and led it into the aisle between the rows of stalls. As she added saddlebags, she said, "After we visit Señora da Silva, we'll have a long day's ride ahead if you want to see most of the valley. Earlier I packed food, but it will be another very simple meal. Is that acceptable?"

"That sounds perfect." Will smiled to himself as he saddled his horse. A long day with Athena Markham was just what he wanted.

CHAPTER 7

As Athena expected, Will rode like a man who spent half his days on horseback, which he probably had. The rain and mist of the previous day had burned off, leaving sunshine and an intensely blue sky. San Gabriel was at its best.

She was glad he asked no more personal questions. As they rode through the town, all his attention was on his surroundings as he quietly absorbed every detail. The weathered stone houses topped with red tile were typical of this part of the world, but in places there were bullet scars or the marks of fire.

Will attracted attention for both his size and his uniform. Children stared as if he were a being from another planet. He smiled at them amiably. The smallest shrank back shyly, but one bolder boy said loudly, "Why is *he* here?"

Will replied in Gabrileño, "Visiting your

beautiful country. Why are *you* here?"

The boy's jaw dropped before he rallied and called back, "I was born here!"

"Good reason!" Will waved at the children as Athena guided them around a corner into the next street.

"Within an hour, everyone in town will know that we're being visited by a British officer who speaks the language. Unheard of! You'll be regarded as a lucky bird of spring." When Will gave her an inquiring glance, she explained, "It's a local expression for when the first songbirds return. A lucky, happy time, since winter is over."

"I probably look more like a song bear," he said with amusement. "San Gabriel has had a bad year, so I imagine all signs of good luck are welcome. Even song bears."

"Do you sing?"

He grinned. "In a bearlike way."

Athena would like to hear that.

The central plaza was quiet, since this wasn't a market day. As they rode across, Will studied the church that formed one side of the square. "How old is the church? It's very handsome."

"The oldest part, the crypt, is over a thousand years old. It's called the Church of Mary, Queen of Heaven."

Will gave her a sharp glance. "Does that

have anything to do with Prince Alfonso's comment that the French stole the Queen of Heaven?"

"I'm afraid so. The French stole everything of value, including a beautiful old statue of the Madonna," Athena explained. "The Queen of Heaven was the most sacred object in San Gabriel and everyone was devastated. The priest, Father Anselmo, tried to stop the thieves and was beaten and left for dead, but he survived. It's generally thought that the Blessed Mother herself intervened to preserve him."

The bell tower dominated the town plaza, and as they rode past, the church bells began to ring the hour. Will asked, "Can the bells be heard everywhere in the valley?"

"Yes, and the Church of Santo Espirito in the village at the west end of the valley has a matching set of bells. With a war going on just over the mountains, special warning signals were devised. When the French came, the deacon of Santo Espirito rang the warning that enabled people to escape into the caves."

"Very good planning," Will said approvingly as he guided his horse around a cart that had been left in the middle of the street. "If I'd been here, I'd also drill everyone on where they'd go to hide and what they could realistically take with them."

"That's exactly what was done here," Athena said. "Otherwise there would have been many more casualties during the invasion."

Will gave her a keen glance. "Did you suggest the signals and the drills?"

Surprised by his perception, she said, "It wasn't all me, but I was part of the war council the king called to discuss preparations for what might happen, and several of my suggestions were adopted." Carlos had said she was the most valuable member of his council, and privately she knew that he was right. All her years of reading had given her good ideas.

After they left the town behind them, it was only a short ride to the da Silva estate. The sprawling stone residence and outbuildings were surrounded by high walls and wide gardens. The elderly gatekeeper, who admitted them through the cast-iron gates, greeted Athena with a smile.

After returning the greeting, she started up the long drive, saying, "The da Silvas are the second largest landowners after the Alcantaras. Their fields suffered a great deal of damage from the French."

"What is Señora da Silva like?"

"A lovely woman from a Portuguese family. Her youngest daughter is a close friend of Sofia's. They went to school together in Porto. The youngest of the sons is at school in Spain and the oldest is a captain serving under his father. Did you meet him?"

"No, everything happened so quickly." Will slanted her a glance as they reached the stables and dismounted. "There is a middle son?"

Athena sighed. "Was. Alberto was killed fighting under his father."

"Too many young men have died," Will said softly. "At least that is over for now."

Athena's mouth twisted as she led the way to the house. "I wonder if mankind will ever outgrow the desire for war. Womankind already has."

"I've met some female guerillas as fierce as any man, but, in general, you're right. Perhaps the world needs more queens and fewer kings."

Athena pulled the bell rope by the front door. "What do you think of war, Will?"

"Sometimes it's necessary. Always it is hideously destructive." Will smiled wryly. "And too often it's dangerously addictive. Some men thrive on danger and uncertainty and will never be content with peace."

"Then they should all be put into an arena

with weapons so they can fight it out," Athena said tartly.

"Was that one of the suggestions you made in the Gabrileño war council?" he asked with interest.

"No," she said. "But it should have been!"

A tiny old maid ushered Will and Athena into a reception room handsome with carved furniture and fine, slightly worn carpets on the polished tile floor. Apparently, the da Silva walls had protected the house from casual looting.

Will barely had time to survey his surroundings when the lady of the house entered the room with swift, anxious steps. Señora da Silva was an attractive woman of middle years dressed in mourning black and with a dramatic streak of silver waving through her dark hair.

She appeared on the verge of fainting. With her gaze fixed on Will, she asked tensely, "My husband? My son?"

"Both are well," he said immediately. "I am here not to deliver bad news, but because Colonel da Silva asked me to accompany a unit of Gabrileño cavalry home. Though he and your son suffered some injury in the battle for Toulouse, both are recovering without problems. The colonel and the rest of his troops will be home in a few weeks."

Her eyes closed and she gave a shudder of relief. Athena stepped to the older woman's side and guided her to a chair. "Good news can be as jarring as bad news," she said soothingly. "Would you like something? Brandy? Coffee?"

"No, thank you, my dear." Señora da Silva opened her eyes and patted Athena's arm. "When I saw a British officer, for a moment I feared the worst. But now I can breathe again."

"I'm glad to have brought you good news, Señora. But your husband also entrusted me with more sobering information." Will reached inside his coat and removed several folded sheets of paper that had been sealed with red wax. He handed them to the colonel's wife. "Here is a list of casualties among your troops. He said that some of the families already know because of earlier letters, but there were more casualties at Toulouse."

Señora da Silva gazed down at the pages, her expression sad. "I shall call on all these families. Lady Athena, do you think the princess will accompany me? Her presence will mean . . . much."

"I know she will want to go with you,"

Athena said softly.

"Then I will send a message to Sofia now." Señora da Silva rose, her expression determined. "The sooner this task is done, the better."

"Your husband sent one other thing," Will said as he pulled a small velvet pouch from his inside pocket. "A gift for you."

Curiously the older woman opened the pouch. The object inside was wrapped in soft cotton. She unwrapped the fabric, and a blaze of crimson jewels spilled across her hand. "A ruby necklace!" she said, startled. "He knows that I have always loved rubies. Dare I wonder where this came from?"

"If you fear that he tore these from the throat of a screaming Frenchwoman, the answer is no," Will said firmly. "There is often looting after battles, and it's not uncommon for a soldier to take what he can find, then later sell it to an officer for enough money to become drunk. That's my guess as to how Colonel da Silva acquired this. You can ask him when he comes home."

"When he comes home," she repeated, her face shining. "I would offer you hospitality, but I must begin the tasks I have been given."

"And we must tour the valley," Athena said with a glance at Will. "Are you ready to learn the worst?"

"That's what I'm here for," he said promptly. Meeting Athena Markham was just a lucky bonus.

CHAPTER 8

When Will and Athena left the da Silva residence, they rode through a grove of trees. Some looked fairly intact, others had been partially destroyed, and too many were charred skeletons. "Olive trees," Athena said. "Though the cork trees survive fire reasonably well, the olive and almond groves were badly damaged."

Will's mouth tightened as he surveyed the damage. "This kind of gratuitous destruction is vile. What did it profit them to destroy sources of food?"

"General Baudin seemed very fond of gratuitous destruction," Athena said, her voice flat. "He and his men were like a swarm of locusts, destroying everything they passed over. The vineyards suffered even more."

They emerged from the damaged grove and Will saw great stretches of terraced vineyards stepping their way down the south-facing hills to the river that ran through the heart of the valley. His mouth tightened when he saw that most of the vines had been burned. A few had survived and were now leafing, but the vast majority had been destroyed, leaving the desolate terraces marred by lifeless blackened vines.

"I'm told that grapes have been grown on these hills since before the time of the Romans," Athena said. "Now look at them! Baudin and his men were furious at how the Gabrileños fled and concealed so much of value. Before they set the fires, they packed straw around the bases of the vines so the heat would destroy the roots. As you see, very few vines survived."

"It will take several years to develop new vines, won't it?"

She nodded. "Yes, even if there were good cuttings available, it would take years. And we have very few good cuttings."

As they turned right to follow a narrow road that ran between two sets of terraces, Will asked, "Where did people take refuge?"

"The valley has many caves, some very deep. Large enough to shelter everyone in San Gabriel along with a few of their most valuable possessions. Not everyone got to safety, but most did," Athena explained. "Part of our preparations was to disguise the cave entrances so they were difficult for strangers to find."

"But the fields couldn't be hidden. I see wheat sprouting ahead of us." He calculated the ripeness of the crops when the French had come through the year before. "The invasion was before the harvest, wasn't it? Did they torch the fields?"

"Yes, and for an encore, they tore apart the valley gristmills. We'll ride by the largest mill later so you can see the damage. The mills are repairable, but we haven't been able to spare the labor to raise waterwheels and millstones. Not when there's no grain to grind and there are so many other urgent tasks."

Colonel Duval had been right to worry about this little country. "It must have been a hungry winter. Did the French take most of the livestock?"

"Yes, only a few of the best beasts could be hidden in the caves. They also carried off any other food they could find. Baudin's army probably didn't have to forage again until they were halfway across Spain."

Will studied Athena's elegant, determined profile, thinking he'd never met a woman like her. "How did people survive through the winter?"

Athena shrugged. "I used my savings and

persuaded my trustee to advance me this year's income. I suspect that he actually loaned me the money out of his own pocket. For which I'm grateful, because otherwise there would have been people dying of starvation. I was able to supplement the available food with staples like flour, beans, potatoes, and dried cod. I used the last of my funds to buy seed stock, but I couldn't get as much as was needed."

Though starvation was a familiar legacy of war, Will hated to think of the inhabitants of this pleasant valley in such desperate straits. "The Gabrileños are lucky you're here. Feeding a whole country, even a small one, is an expensive proposition."

"I'm not much of an heiress, if that's what you're wondering," Athena said. "But I inherited a bit of money from my mother, and my father pays a very small quarterly allowance with the understanding that I never, ever mention that I'm related to him."

Will's mouth tightened. "You'd best not tell me the family name or I'll be tempted to hunt your father down and hurt him when I return to England."

"You needn't look so murderous," Athena said. "I'm a serious embarrassment. I've always suspected that my mother might have seduced my father just to humiliate him. At least he felt some sense of responsibility. He didn't have to give me anything."

"You're very forgiving."

"Merely pragmatic. There is no point in wasting resentment on a man I only met once in my life. He acted as if I was something one of the dogs dragged in. But he didn't have me sent to the workhouse, for which I'm grateful."

Dismissing the subject, she pointed ahead to where their current road met the river. "You can see the remains of the bridge there. It was the only bridge in the central valley, so losing it causes a good deal of inconvenience. There's another bridge higher up the river, but using it makes journeys across the valley much longer."

"I was sometimes seconded to help the engineers, and bridges were a specialty." He studied the width of the river, the rushing force of the water, and the stone piers that were all that remained of the old bridge. "If timber is available and we can draft enough workers, it won't be hard to build a new one."

"Both wood and labor are in short supply," she said. "Do you think the soldiers who returned with you would be willing to help rebuild?"

"Most have family obligations to attend

to, but they'll surely contribute some time to such an important project. Which leaves the problem of timber." Will gestured toward the sunny expanses of the valley. "This part of the world doesn't have a lot of trees."

"We'll find something," Athena promised. "Shall we continue on? A dam was destroyed on one of the creeks that leads into the river and it is also much missed."

Will grinned. "Bridges and dams are an engineer's notion of amusement. Lead on, Lady Athena."

She laughed. "I'm very glad you were Colonel da Silva's choice to come here!"

As he watched her face light up with laughter, Will was equally glad.

By the time Athena had shown Will the worst problems in the valley, it was time for lunch. She led the way to a favorite spot of hers when she was in the area. Long ago, someone had built a wooden bench inside a shallow cave that wasn't much more than a stone overhang. In front was a patch of soft grass and a dozen feet away, a spring emerged from the hill and pooled in a small stone basin perfect for horses or humans to drink from. The overhang was about halfway up the valley wall and gave a sweeping view of the river, farms, and vineyards.

While Will tethered the horses in a spot where they could enjoy water and grass, Athena unpacked her saddlebag and spread a cloth in the middle of the weathered bench. "Sorry that lunch is another really simple meal," she said as she set out packets of bread, cheese, and olives. Last to emerge was a jug of wine, a knife, and two sturdy glass tumblers.

"No apologies needed," Will said as he settled down on the other end of the bench. "Good food, good wine, a wonderful view, and most excellent company." His gaze was warm.

Even without looking, she was very aware of Will's strength and presence. It was difficult not to stare at him. She'd given up trying to persuade herself that her attraction was merely because they were both English. She was attracted because he was unnervingly appealing. Intelligent, kind, quietly charming, and rather beautifully strong and handsome. Of course she noticed. She was human and female.

So be it. They could be friendly and speak English for a week or two, and then he'd leave and she'd never see him again. Not ever. So enjoy his company, and give thanks for his presence.

With an internal sigh at her foolishness,

she poured wine. When she handed him a glass, he clinked it against hers. "To San Gabriel!"

"To San Gabriel, and someday England!" Though heaven only knew if she'd ever make it back there. She sipped appreciatively as she gazed at the fields and terraces and the distant glint of the river. "It's a luxury to relax and enjoy a beautiful day. Most of my time recently has been spent jumping from one crisis to another. Dealing with trees and missing the forest."

"Metaphorically speaking," he said with a wave at the mostly treeless valley.

"Metaphorical trees," she agreed. "But touring the valley has reminded me of just how much needs to be done. We barely made it through last winter. If more fields aren't planted soon, next winter might be even worse."

Will cut a slice of cheese and laid it on a piece of bread. After swallowing a bite, he asked, "If you could wave a magic wand, what would you ask for?"

"Money and men," she said promptly. "Money for seed and equipment and to pay laborers hired to do the work." She frowned as she considered other needs. "I'd also wish for really good vine stock to replant the vineyards. There will be few grapes harvested this year, and if we don't start planting, the future will be no better."

"I assume the French drank or carried off most of the wine," Will said. "How much is left for the Gabrileños? Clearly, it's vital for morale."

"Actually, the French didn't get much of our wine, but most of what's left isn't accessible," Athena said. "The local vintners have always stored wine in the caves because the temperatures are so steady. A troop of French cavalry was on the verge of capturing the two main storage caves when an avalanche sealed them off."

Will's eyes widened. "I'm guessing that wasn't an accident. Or else the patron saint of your valley is very, *very* good at his job!"

Athena chuckled. "You're right, it was no accident. Sofia and I were visiting the Benedictine convent when we heard the warning bells from Santo Espirito. I had a spyglass with me and I could see the French pouring into the valley from the west. They moved at amazing speed. They'd obviously planned the invasion and sent in spies to learn the lay of the land because the cavalry troop was heading right for the storage caves. The convent wasn't far off, so Sofia and I were able to get there first."

Will stared at her, appalled. "The two of

you thought you could take on a troop of French cavalry?"

"Not directly, of course. But a violent storm earlier in the summer had washed away the soil around a group of boulders above the storage caves. The vintners had been arguing about whether the hillside could be stabilized, or if it would be necessary to move the wine barrels into new caves, which would be a huge job. I'd inspected the damaged area a fortnight or so earlier and I knew it was unstable." Athena smiled wickedly. "So with the help of the horses, some levers, and the basic laws of physics, Sofia and I triggered a landslide."

"You're an intrepid pair," he said admiringly. "Then what? I assume you raced off at top speed."

"Exactly. We took shelter in a small cave higher up and hid for several days. That's why Sofia wasn't taken by Baudin as her father and brother were." Athena made a face. "Baudin was enraged that she escaped, but he couldn't take the time to search for her because he was retreating from Wellington's army."

"I suppose he declared Prince Alfonso to be regent because he wanted to leave the country weakened," Will commented.

"Perhaps. No one disputed the appointment since there was no other senior member of royal family available and Sofia is too young to rule," Athena shook her head. "We were all too busy recovering from the damage Baudin caused to think about his motives. At least we could take pleasure in depriving the French of their loot, but, of course, the caves are sealed off from us, too. I'm sure they can be dug open, and I think that most of the wine barrels will have survived, but it will be a huge job. Once again, we need laborers and the ability to pay them."

"If people run out of wine, I'm sure you'd get many volunteers to clear the debris, but there are other priorities," he agreed. "What is most important?"

Between them, they'd polished off all the food and half the bottle of wine. Athena shook out the cloths, wiped the knife blade clean, and returned everything but the wine and wineglasses to her saddlebag.

"The answer to that depends on what kind of help is available," she replied. "Now that you've surveyed the valley, what do you think is doable? Despite your Colonel Duval, I have trouble believing that the British government that never gave Lord Wellington sufficient resources to fight a war will contribute anything to help a tiny country most Britons have never heard of." Her mouth twisted. "Even if they want to help, heaven only knows how long it would take for effective aid to arrive."

"I have some ideas," Will said, unperturbed by her pessimism. "An old school friend of mine, Justin Ballard, lives in Porto. He runs his family's wine-shipping business and I think he'd be willing to help you out."

"Ballard Port, the Scottish company?" she asked, surprised. "Everyone has heard of them."

"His family has been in the business for several generations," Will said. "The port business has been badly disrupted by so much war in the region, and it's been frustrating for Ballard because he hasn't enough to do. I'm sure he'd be happy to send grape vine cuttings and the men to plant them, and he could do it quickly."

"That would be wonderful!" she exclaimed. "I'm sure it would even be the right varieties of grapes. But who would pay for it?"

"I will," he said calmly.

She gasped. "As you observed earlier, supporting a whole country is a very expensive proposition."

He shrugged. "I'm comfortably off and I

haven't had much chance to spend money while in the army. I can afford to pay for some practical help for San Gabriel."

He was completely serious, she saw. "I don't know when, if ever, the royal treasury will be able to repay you," she said uncertainly.

"I'm too cautious to lend anything I can't afford to lose, so I don't. This is a gift to a gallant country." Seeing her doubtful expression, he grinned. "Christian charity?"

She took a deep breath. "I have no official authority here, but nonetheless, on behalf of San Gabriel, I accept! How long do you think it will take to contact Mr. Ballard and get a response?"

"Perhaps a week? Porto is much closer than Toulouse and I suspect there are many men in the city who are eager for work. Plus, Justin is very efficient." Will's brow furrowed. "I just had another thought. Does your river run down into the Douro? I'm no expert, but to me the wine tastes very like the expensive wines from the upper Douro."

"Yes, the San Gabriel River is a tributary of the Douro and the soil and climate here are much the same."

"Have the local wines ever been sent down to Porto for export? When the vineyards are restored, that could be profitable if transportation is practical."

"The river isn't navigable and the land route over the mountains into Portugal is too difficult for large-scale shipping. Gabrileño wine is consumed locally or sent east into Spain." She split the last of the wine between them, corked the bottle, and stashed it in her saddlebag. "It's a pity there's no reasonable transportation. Our wines keep well so they'd be ideal for export. On good years, there are sizable surpluses so the vintners add brandy to the excess and it keeps even longer."

"Could the river channel be improved to become navigable?" Will asked. "It used to be impossible to sail up the Douro farther than the Cachão da Valeira Gorge, but the waterfall and overhangs were blasted open twenty years ago so boats could continue up the river. Now there are vineyards almost all the way to Spain and wine production has increased dramatically. Perhaps the same could be done for San Gabriel River."

"Uncle Carlos may have considered improving the river, though if he did, I heard nothing about it," Athena said thoughtfully. "San Gabriel has been a sleepy, isolated, and content little country for a very long time. But Uncle Carlos realized that the world is changing, and his country must also. That's a major reason he sent troops to fight Bonaparte. The young men who return will have new ideas and know a broader world." Her voice broke for a moment. "Now he'll never see that."

"It's too soon to assume that he and his son are dead," Will said quietly. "But if they are, San Gabriel will go on, so the future must be considered."

"You're right, of course. Will you have time to survey the river to see if improvements can be made without it being prohibitively expensive? If work could be started soon, perhaps the river could be sailed about the time the vineyards are reestablished."

"I'll ask Ballard if he has time to come up here himself," Will replied. "He can take a look at the river channel. His family was involved in improving the Douro so he would know something about what is involved." Will lifted his glass in an informal toast. "Plus, I'm sure he'd be interested in your wines. If the storage caves can be opened up and the wine is still good, you might be able to sell some sooner rather than later if the shipping problems can be solved."

"What a wonderful possibility! Bless you,

Will." With the first optimism she'd felt in months, Athena leaned over to brush a light kiss on his cheek, but he turned his head and her lips landed on his. He tasted of wine and sunshine, warmth and kindness — and something much deeper and more dangerous.

The kiss deepened, and her world turned upside down.

CHAPTER 9

Athena's wineglass tumbled to the grass as shock and desire flooded her senses. She felt Will's large hand behind her head, cradling her neck and drawing her closer. She surrendered to the moment, hungry for his warmth and tenderness. As the kiss deepened, his arms came around her in an embrace that fitted her against his broad chest. It would be easy, so easy, to fall into this man and lose herself and her fears and worries. . . .

Will shifted, murmuring, "You are so lovely. . . ."

His words broke the spell and Athena pulled away, angry with herself and her lack of control. "I won't be your mistress," she said tightly. "Or is that the price of the aid you've offered?"

He looked as startled as if she'd slapped him. Then he began to laugh. "And here I was trying so hard to behave like a gentleman. I suppose it wasn't very gentlemanly to kiss you, though you started it, you know."

"So I did." She wiped damp palms on her riding skirt. "I'm sorry, I shouldn't have said what I did. Unless you actually do want me to lie with you in return for your aid to San Gabriel?"

"What would you say if the two things were linked?" he asked with interest. He turned toward her, his chest looking impossibly broad in his scarlet army coat. A wave of brown hair fell over his forehead and one arm stretched along the back of the bench. Even though he wasn't touching her, she was acutely aware of his physical presence and nearness. Mere inches away. . . .

She edged back as far away as the bench would permit, which wasn't very far. Though smoky desire had dissipated, a sense of connection remained. Which was absurd, since twenty-four hours earlier, they hadn't even met.

Wanting to put more emotional distance between them, she said ironically, "An intriguing question, Major Masterson. Would I sacrifice my honor to help my adopted country? But since I was born in dishonor, it might not be a fair question."

His dark brows arched. "Nonsense. You

know my views on what is considered legitimacy. Let me add that I have no desire to acquire an unwilling mistress."

"A surprising number of men lack your scruples," she said dryly. "But it's clear I overreacted. All you wanted was a kiss, not a mistress."

"Did I say that?" he said with a slow smile that lit his whole face. "I'm neither blind nor stupid, so of course I would love to lie with you. I've wanted to kiss you since the moment we met. But anything that might be between us is separate from what must be done in San Gabriel."

Her return smile was sad. "How can there be anything between us when you'll be gone so soon? You're anxious to return home, while I am committed to staying here indefinitely. I'm no innocent just emerged from the schoolroom, but I'm nowhere near reckless and worldly enough to lie with a virtual stranger. We haven't the time for more than the first levels of friendship."

"That is . . . not necessarily true." His gaze held hers, his gray eyes turning serious. "Though I yearn for my home, some things are more important. Becoming better acquainted with you is one such thing."

She stared at him. "You're a most unusual man, Major Masterson."

"I've been told that before," he said sadly. "It's never a compliment."

She had to smile. "Now I know you're teasing."

"Possibly," he agreed, his expression sober, but his eyes amused. "If I'm forgiven for the kiss, will you call me Will again? I prefer to be on first name terms with you."

"Very well, Will." She preferred that as well. "For whatever time you're here, we can be friends. After you leave . . ." She shrugged. "In my experience, men are not such good letter writers as women, and it's a long way from San Gabriel to Oxfordshire."

"I'm a rather decent letter writer, actually." His gaze intensified. "Friends. And who knows? Perhaps we can become more than friends."

She felt as if the breath had been knocked out of her. He could not possibly mean what he seemed to be implying. Returning to irony, she said, "What are the relationship possibilities?" She held up her left hand and ticked off one finger. "Friendship is the broadest category and can range from mild acquaintance to deep, enduring loyalty. I think we are already mild friends?"

"If we weren't more than mild friends already, we wouldn't be having this extremely interesting discussion," he agreed.

She ticked off another finger. "We could become enemies."

"I will *not* allow that," he said firmly. "I have had enough of enemies."

"One does not always have a choice." She tapped her middle finger. "The opposite of love or hate, which is indifference."

"It is much too late for indifference," Will said seriously. "I believe I mentioned my immediate interest in kissing you."

"Do you always want to kiss women who aim rifles at you?" she asked curiously.

"No, you're the only one," he said. "Though if the truth be known, women seldom greet me with weaponry."

"I'm glad to hear that." She studied her hand. "Two fingers left for listing relationships, and those remaining are deeply implausible."

"But these are the most interesting possibilities!" he exclaimed.

" 'Interesting' doesn't mean *good.*" She ticked her ring finger. "We could have an affair. That will not happen for any number of reasons, most of which you can imagine."

"Which leaves another possibility," he said, his voice soft.

She closed her hand into a fist. "You can't possibly be interested in marriage! You scarcely know me."

"That's true, as is the reverse. If we get to know each other better, one or both of us might decide we'd never suit."

She stared at him, feeling as if time had stopped. She was sharply aware of the sweeping valley and mild breeze, the sunshine warming them both, his tanned complexion.

The bleak impossibility of what he was saying. "Forgive me if I'm misunderstanding, but are you actually proposing courtship?"

"Indeed I am. A courtship of two wary but wise adults." He hesitated before continuing, "It's possible I am too old and jaded to ever be fit for marriage again."

"You're not that old," she said firmly.

He smiled a little. "Perhaps not. But I have seen too much of the world and made too many mistakes."

"I often feel the same," she said. "Perhaps that is why I interest you?"

"Very likely. I have trouble imagining myself making conversation with the typical well-bred young lady back in England."

"No more than I could converse with an English country gentleman, the sort who cherishes delicate females," she said wryly. "Which is one of several reasons I've sworn never to marry."

" 'Never' is a very long time. We change with age. Things that seemed implausible can come to seem desirable."

"True in theory, but I'm settling happily into eccentric spinsterhood," she retorted. "I doubt I'd change my mind."

"But you do concede the possibility of changing your mind." He smiled. "I can work with that."

She couldn't resist smiling back. "You're very persistent, Will. But you haven't much time to change my mind."

"True," he said thoughtfully. "Are you willing to experiment? My brother's wife is full of interesting thoughts and theories. She said that courting couples meet under such artificial circumstances and see so little of each other that it's far too easy to choose one's life partner very badly."

"Was she mistaken in your brother?" Athena asked, surprised.

"No, but they didn't meet under artificial social conditions," Will explained. "Kiri met Mac after she'd narrowly escaped engaging herself to a man she met conventionally. It would have been a very bad match for her, so she now advocates avoiding conventional courtships."

"In what unconventional way did she meet

your brother?" Athena asked curiously.

"He rescued her after she'd been kid-napped by smugglers." Will grinned. "So they skipped superficial chat and went straight to deeper issues."

"Kidnapped by smugglers. Of *course*! I should have remembered that's the very best way to meet a husband," Athena said with mock seriousness. "She sounds like an interesting woman."

"You'll like her," Will promised as if a future meeting was inevitable. "But the two relationships, the wrong one and then the right one, inspired Kiri's theory of how to quickly learn a great deal about a potential partner."

"What is her suggested method?" Athena asked, reluctantly interested.

"To ask each other difficult questions, the kind that makes one reveal oneself," he explained. "It isn't easy, but the process is far more useful than exchanging pleasantries over tea and cakes or trying to converse in a noisy ballroom."

She frowned. "That sounds deucedly uncomfortable. What if one party flatly refuses to participate?"

"Doesn't that tell you something impor-tant right there?"

"It says that the prospective mate is

uncomfortable with emotion and intimacy," Athena said thoughtfully. "Most people are uncomfortable with revealing too much, of course, but one would hope for more from a possible mate."

"Are you game for a few questions now?" he asked, his gaze intent. "If we don't immediately alienate each other, we can continue to ask a question or two a day."

She studied Will's strong, honest face. She'd long since given up the idea that she'd ever marry and she doubted she'd change her mind, no matter how persuasive he might be. Even though he was the most appealing man she'd met in years. "I don't think you'll change my mind, Will. Is it worth the effort when I'm such a recalcitrant female?"

"I won't regret the effort if you're willing to try," he said seriously. "I *will* regret it if you flatly refuse to make the attempt."

When she hesitated, he continued, "It's also a good way to build a deeper friendship, and we're already on our way to achieving that."

"What if a question is something one of us can't bear to discuss?"

"Then it doesn't get answered," he said promptly. "This is all voluntary. A tool to improve our acquaintance, not a bludgeon."

"Very well, I'll try." She smiled ruefully. "I've always had far too much curiosity. I'll ask the first question so you can be the one alarmed and discomforted."

"That's only fair. Ask away!" he replied. "I suspect that any one question will probably lead into related questions. We'll see."

Where to start? Not with anything too difficult, she decided. "You identified yourself as from Oxfordshire as soon as we met, so your home is important to you. Tell me about it, not just what your home looks like, but how you feel about it."

"Describing the house is easy. The oldest section of Hayden Hall goes back to Tudor times and bits and pieces have been added ever since. An architectural purist would shudder, but I find it — welcoming. As eccentric and charming as a favorite aunt." He smiled with fond reminiscence. "Oxfordshire is lovely, with rolling hills and streams and fertile fields. It's not far to Oxford, one of the most beautiful little cities in Europe. And London is also convenient when one is in the mood for city life."

"You were a farmer, a landed gentleman, before you entered the army?"

He nodded. "I'll have much to learn when I return, but I have a good and patient steward to teach me. I look forward to it.

There is something very sane about growing crops and raising livestock."

Beginning to understand the value of this exercise, she asked, "Why did you leave a comfortable life in a home you love? Was it youthful restlessness?"

A shadow crossed his face and he looked away from her. "I couldn't bear to stay there after Lily died," he said haltingly. "Whenever I entered a room, I felt as if she'd just stepped out, and if I looked hard enough, I'd find her. It was madness. I . . . I felt that if I stayed, I'd end up shooting myself."

Yes, this kind of questioning was not easy. "So you chose to let the French do the shooting," she said quietly.

"I thought at least I'd die doing something worthwhile." He grimaced. "I didn't realize that soldiers are more likely to die of fevers than bullets."

"Will you still be haunted by Lily when you return home?" she asked, knowing this was one of those uncomfortable questions.

His brow furrowed as he thought about it. "I don't think so. The memories of her are happy and . . . distant."

"Do you love her still?" Athena asked softly.

Will sighed. "The young man I was then loved her deeply, but he didn't survive all those muddy fields on the Peninsula. I'm not that young man anymore." He raised his eyes and studied her face. "Now it's time for me to ask a question and make you uncomfortable."

"That's only fair," she said without enthusiasm. "Ask away."

"Tell me about Lady Delilah."

She caught her breath, realizing that such a question was inevitable. Her mother had been such an important part of Athena's life that she must be discussed.

But dear Lord, how could she possibly explain her mother?

CHAPTER 10

After Will asked his question, Athena stared at her interlocked fingers, her face frozen. Quietly he asked, "Should I start with something simpler?"

Athena rose from the bench in one swift movement and began prowling around beneath the overhang. "No, if we are going to be digging into each other's souls, I must speak of her. But Delilah is . . . hard to explain."

Guessing she didn't know where to start, Will asked, "Was her name really Delilah?"

"She was christened Cordelia and called Delia when she was a child." Athena crossed her arms across her waist and continued to pace. "When she left the schoolroom at sixteen and realized that she could persuade any man to do anything, she announced that she wished to be called Delilah. It was such a suitable name that soon everyone called her that."

"Even her parents?" Will asked, surprised.

"I don't suppose they did, but her father threw her out of the house when she was seventeen so the issue was moot."

"A well-born girl that young was disowned?" Will tried to imagine doing such a thing to a child of his, and couldn't. "That's appalling!"

"She was in no danger of starving," Athena said dryly. "She moved into the home of an Austrian diplomat three times her age and became his mistress. She was pampered outrageously until she decided that she was bored and left him for another man."

"So she was beautiful, like you."

Athena gave him an incredulous glance. "You're joking again. I was never more than average-looking, even as a child. One could easily see that we were related, but Delilah was stunning. Tall — but not too tall, as I am. Dazzling dark red hair, not brown like mine. Charming and outgoing — not practical and reserved, as I am."

"Except when you have a rifle in hand?"

She smiled a little. "That was practicality, not an outgoing personality."

She resumed her pacing, the divided skirt swinging provocatively around her shapely ankles. "But more than her physical beauty, she had . . . sensual allure. Even the most happily married men would stare and wonder what it would be like to bed her. You could see it in their eyes."

"She sounds like a . . . challenging parent," Will said carefully.

Athena stopped pacing and stared at the stony wall of the overhang. "I loved her more than anyone else in my life."

"I hope she loved you as much in return," Will said before he realized that might be a painful comment if her mother hadn't been a loving person.

"She did." Athena turned to face him, her arms still crossed at her waist as if her stomach hurt. "I was not an accident, but a pampered pet and companion. She told me often that more than anything in the world, she'd wanted a daughter to love. I gather her parents were cold and disapproving, so she did her best to give them much to disapprove of. That included having a bastard child."

It sounded monstrously selfish to Will, but he couldn't wish Athena had been unborn. Perhaps she had been an accident and her mother told her otherwise to make her feel wanted. "Being her pet and companion sounds both wonderful and terrible."

Athena smiled humorlessly. "It was both."

"Was Athena a family name?"

"She said that when I was born, I looked like a serious little owl. Since the owl is the symbol of Athena, the name suited me. Also, of course, Athena was the goddess of wisdom and she wanted me to be well educated and well traveled and wise." Athena's smile became real. "The first two are true. 'Wise' is debatable."

Will laughed. "What would she have done if you'd been a boy?"

"I'm not sure. She would have loved a son because she had a great capacity for loving. But the relationship would have been very different from what she and I had. I think it was better for all concerned that she had a daughter."

Certainly it was better for Will. "From what you've said, it sounds as if Delilah spent much of her time having passionate affairs. What was she like as a mother?"

"She was a wonderful companion, always interested in new things and taking me to new places. Even when she was in the early throes of an affair, she would take time to be with me, and she would instantly break with any lover who was rude to me."

"Did that happen often?"

"No, she always made clear to her lovers that if they wanted to be with her, they must

127

treat me with courtesy and respect. Some of them gave me splendid gifts to curry favor with Delilah." Athena smiled reminiscently. "The best was a beautiful little pony when I was six. I hated saying good-bye to that pony, but we traveled a great deal and seldom stayed anywhere longer than a few months. Delilah always engaged excellent tutors wherever we were, so I learned all kinds of interesting things. How to use firearms because she said a woman must know how to defend herself. She often moved in diplomatic and government circles, so she discussed politics and statecraft with me. If we stayed on someone's estate, she would ask the land steward to explain planting and animal husbandry. It was . . . an unusual way to grow up, but wonderful and exciting." Athena's eyes closed and her voice cracked. "She was everything to me."

Tired of looking up at his companion, Will rose from the bench and took a relaxed position against the stone wall opposite where Athena was standing. "The drawback, surely, was that when you lost her, you had no one else."

Athena opened her eyes and smiled with brittle humor. "You are much cleverer than you look, Will."

He thought a moment. "Should I be insulted?"

Her tension eased into a genuine smile. "I hope you aren't. What I meant was that you look like a solid, unimaginative officer, vastly competent but not . . . not . . ."

"Not very intelligent?" he suggested.

Athena bit her lip as if suppressing laughter. "I would rather end my sentence by saying you don't look particularly imaginative. Or insightful. But you are both."

"Being imaginative, I'm now wondering if one of your mother's wandering amorous adventures brought you to San Gabriel."

"*Much* cleverer than you look! My mother met Prince Alfonso when he was in London and followed him back here. She was a great favorite with the whole royal family, so we were welcome to stay even when the affair burned out. We lived here long enough for me to learn the language and make friends, and visited again later. I was told to call the king and queen Uncle Carlos and Aunt Isabella. She and the king had lively discussion about how to run a small country, and she let me sit in when they did. That proved really useful when I ended up being an advisor to Sofia."

"Which is why Prince Alfonso confuses you with Lady Delilah. Is San Gabriel as much of a home as you've ever had?"

Athena's brow furrowed. "I suppose it is. The longest I've ever spent anywhere else was in school, and I hated the place."

Since it didn't sound as if Delilah would have put her in a hateful school, Will asked, "Were you sent there after your mother died?"

Athena nodded and began pacing again. "I was fourteen. Delilah was very ill and she explained to me that she was dying, so she must put me under my father's protection. I was devastated, of course." Her paces tightened to swift, tense steps. "She took me to my father's family seat and marched in with me beside her. He was furious and horrified, yet I could see that he also still desired her."

Will frowned, imagining what such a meeting must have been like for Athena. "It doesn't sound like a scene that any fourteen-year-old should have to witness."

Athena sighed. "I needed to be there, if only to meet my father for the first and last time. Delilah told him that I was a good, intelligent, obedient girl who would be a credit to him."

"Were you obedient?" Will asked with mild surprise.

She shrugged. "When I wanted to be. Not that it mattered what she said about me.

My father was revolted by my existence, but apparently the resemblance to his legitimate children was strong enough that he couldn't deny fathering me, particularly since he'd known of my existence since Delilah first found herself increasing. He snarled that I would be cared for and slammed out of the room."

"My father was not an easy man, but he was a saint by comparison," Will said sympathetically. "Your father sounds appalling."

"Based on our very brief acquaintance, that's an accurate description. But he did fulfill his word to see that I was cared for."

"And your mother trusted him enough to know that he would. That's an interesting point."

"Yes, it is." Athena looked thoughtful. "He's an English gentleman who prides himself on behaving honorably, though I doubt if you'd agree with his definition of 'honorable.' He was so rich that supporting one schoolgirl was nothing to him, but he could have sent me to a workhouse rather than fulfilling his responsibilities. So he could have been worse."

"Yet he did send you to a school you hated."

She grimaced. "It was a grim girls' school in a ramshackle manor house by the Irish

Sea. The icy winter drafts would blow papers off a desk. The headmistress followed that fine Christian dictum that sparing the rod would spoil the child. All the students hated the place, so I became a convenient target for malice because of being a bastard. Too tall, too different, and far too illegitimate. I developed a truly intimidating glare when other girls went too far, and I studied a lot, which kept me busy and improved my mind."

Will winced as he imagined years of living in such a place. "Was your father deliberately trying to punish you for existing?"

"I don't know. Probably he didn't care where I went as long as it was out of his sight. He might have specified a very strict school to counter the wild tendencies I must have inherited from Delilah."

Even at fourteen, she would have been independent and ingenious. Will asked, "Did you ever try to escape from the school?"

"I thought about it." A faint smile flickered over her lips. "I *really* thought about it. But I had no place to go in England, and no money. I couldn't possibly have made it here to San Gabriel, the only place likely to welcome me. So I endured."

"Were you ever told what your future held?"

"The solicitor who took me to the school said I would be there until I was eighteen, at which point I could leave and I would be granted a modest but adequate quarterly allowance on the condition that I never tell anyone I was related to my father's family. Delilah and I had used the name Markham, which was in her family several generations back. There was no obvious connection to my father's family, so I was able to continue using the name. Generous of him, wasn't it?"

Will suppressed a strong urge to find out who her father was so the man could be throttled. "Your father should have been *whipped*!"

"Members of the House of Lords wield the whips," she said dryly. "They don't suffer under them. You can see why I am not fond of peers of the realm. Both my grandfathers were lords. The one on my mother's side I never met at all."

As a member of the House of Lords himself, Will said, "Not all lords are so dreadful. I went to school with some who are very good fellows."

"Then I hope they treat their bastard descendants better than my grandfathers

133

did. Your own brother would not have fared well if not for you. But enough of that." Athena made a dismissive gesture. "It's time for you to bare your soul and do some more suffering. What are the three worst things that have happened to you? The loss of your wife is surely on the list. What about the loss of your mother? Your father?"

She was right. The knife cut both ways, and it was time for him to speak of things he had long buried. "The siege of Badajoz would make the list of most dreadful things for anyone who was there, but that's a broadly shared horror. Perhaps we need a separate category for such terrors? Having lived here for the war years, surely you have similar memories."

She made a face. "None so bad as Badajoz, but bad enough. Another day, perhaps. I'm more interested in what personal trials have tempered you."

"I dislike ranking tragedies," he said slowly. "Losing Lily and our son was certainly the first great tragedy of my life, and the event that most changed my life, because if she hadn't died, I never would have joined the army."

"Living in England and raising a family would have been such a very different path from the one you're on," she mused, her gaze assessing. "I've heard the tales of mud and slaughter and horror. The Peninsular Wars have been brutal. Do you regret walking this path?"

He'd not really thought of his life in terms of the path taken versus the one ended by tragedy. "I do not regret the army," he said, his brow furrowed. "I feel as if I've contributed to a worthy goal, and I have made strong friendships. But I'm ready for a change. The peacetime army would be deucedly boring."

"Then it's good you're on your way home." She cocked her head to one side. "What is another of your worst experiences?"

"When I read the news that my brother, Mac, had died in London." Will halted, remembering the numbness that dissolved into a tidal wave of pain when he'd read the fatal words. "I was visiting my friend Ballard in Porto on the way home to England when I saw the notice of Mac's death in a London newspaper that had just arrived."

"I'm so sorry!" she said, her golden hazel eyes warm with compassion. Then her brow furrowed. "From the way you spoke of him, I thought he was still alive?"

"He is. His death was misreported, and finding him alive when I returned to England was the greatest happiness of my life," Will said simply. "That didn't mean my grief hadn't happened, but at least it ended quickly."

"Tragedies with happy endings are the best kind, but sadly rare." Athena looked a little wistful before continuing. "What else would you put on your painful experiences list? The deaths of your parents?"

He sighed. "Neither of their deaths caused me more than a brief, dutiful twinge of regret. I didn't really miss them when they were gone because I didn't see a great deal of either. My mother was frail and my father was busy with his own interests. He had a reliable heir, but he wasn't much interested in me as an individual."

"That is a tragedy of another sort, but I do understand. If I someday hear that my father has died, I would feel nothing because I didn't know him." Her voice turned dry. "At least I knew nothing good of him. It's possible his legitimate children adore him."

"Equally possible they don't, since he sounds like an unpleasant fellow." A thought struck Will. "Would you like to meet other members of your parents' families? Surely, they aren't all bigots. Your half brothers and sisters must be around your age, and perhaps you have cousins on your mother's side. They might like to know you."

"No!" Athena said sharply. "I don't need more people who wish I had never been born." She reached for her hat, which she'd hung on one end of the bench. "I think we've had quite enough harrowing questioning for one day. Do you really think there is value to this mutual baring of souls?"

He studied her face, seeing a strong, capable woman who had learned to play the difficult cards life had dealt her. But in her eyes were shadows of the injured child she had been, and that vulnerability called to him powerfully. "Yes, there is value. I feel I know you much better than I did when we stopped here to eat, and I'm glad for that. But I realize you might not feel the same." He smiled ruefully. "I'm rather afraid to ask."

She bit her lip as she stared back. "I do know you better, and . . . I think I'm glad of that even if we can never be more than friends."

He thought of saying that whether they might be more than friends remained to be seen, but he didn't want her to retreat. Instead, he said, "Surely, friends can hug each other." He stepped forward and drew here into a gentle embrace.

She stiffened for a moment, then exhaled

and relaxed into his arms. She was lean strength and soft, feminine curves, and she fit against him perfectly. "A hug is a very fine thing," she murmured. "You're a very good size for hugging."

"My thoughts exactly. If I were to kiss you, I don't think I'd have to bend over much at all." He demonstrated, and her lips were soft and willing under his.

He was not surprised when passion stirred, and he was prepared to tamp it down. Only a fool wouldn't recognize that Athena would need a gentle wooing. She was rare and special, unlike any woman he'd ever met, and the real surprise was the sense of peace he felt in her arms, as powerful as passion.

Already he was thinking of that forbidden fifth category of marriage. And if it took time to bring her around to his way of thinking — well, he was a patient man. For now it was enough to be holding her.

Eventually she sighed and stepped away. Gently, to indicate that she was not regretting that quiet kiss. "Now what, Major Masterson?"

She used his rank to distance herself, but her hazel eyes were molten gold when Will smiled down into them. "We finish our tour of San Gabriel and return to Castelo

Blanco, where we will discuss my suggestions with Princess Sofia. If she agrees . . ."

"She will," Athena assured him. "She will probably fall on her knees and offer up prayers of thanks."

"That will *not* be necessary," he said firmly. "Assuming she agrees, I will write a letter this evening to Justin Ballard in Porto and tell him what we need — and the sooner, the better." Will laughed, happy with the world and the future. "And then, my dear girl, I will build you a bridge."

CHAPTER 11

As Athena and Will rode toward the site of the blocked wine storage caves, her tension gradually eased. Their unnervingly intimate discussion made her worried about what he'd ask next. But he'd reverted to his usual calm as he continued his evaluation of what needed to be done.

For a man who was so direct, the major was something of an enigma. Or possibly he was a puzzle that she was reluctantly drawn to solve. His interest in her was flattering, though she still couldn't imagine a future beyond friendship with him. She might fit with Will, but she doubted his neighbors would take to a wife as odd as she was.

And yet . . . the physical attraction was undeniable. She loved being held by him, loved his kisses, and couldn't deny that those searching questions had created a sense of closeness. What to do about the attraction and that alarming closeness were the difficult questions.

The road that led to the wine storage caverns ended in a mound of dirt and stone from the landslide Athena and Sofia had created to prevent the French from pillaging the wine vaults. As they reined in their horses, Athena said, "Here we are at the scene of the crime. I'm not sure how much will have to be excavated. Between thirty and forty feet, perhaps? I don't think it's an impossible task, but the French didn't have the time to do it, and after they left, we didn't have the labor."

Will studied the sloping mass of rubble. "Does this road run right to the entrance of one of the caverns, so we'll know where to dig?"

"As I recall, the road goes to the mouth of the smaller cave, then turns to the right and runs along the hill to the larger one, which is about a hundred feet to the right. One of the vintners can confirm that. The vaults are right next to each because the hillside was particularly suitable here, I'm told."

"This will have to be excavated like a mine shaft." He frowned. "Getting enough wood to shore the tunnel up will be a challenge. A pity I can't just blast all this away, but that would cause an even worse landslide."

"Not to mention the likelihood of destroying the wine." Athena thought for a moment. "You might be able to find some usable wood higher up in the streams that flow into the river. Branches and sometimes even trees get tangled up there in the winter rains. People collect the usable pieces in the spring, but I don't think much of that was done this year, so there might be some good wood."

"Worth investigating. There probably wouldn't be many long tree trunks that would work for the bridge, but shorter pieces will do for shoring up a tunnel."

Athena glanced at the sun's position. "It's time to head back to the castle."

Will gathered his reins, but his frowning gaze remained on the landslide. Under his breath, he murmured, " 'By the pricking of my thumbs, something wicked this way comes.' "

The quote from Macbeth made Athena feel as if chilled fingers had touched her nape. "Would you care to expand on that comment, Major?"

He turned to her, his expression sober. "Soldiers who survive long in the field develop a kind of sixth sense about possible danger. Last night we discussed the fact that San Gabriel could be very vulnerable to attack by bands of dispossessed soldiers or guerillas. As we've traveled through the valley, that itchy feeling of possible danger has been getting stronger."

Athena bit her lip, wishing she could believe he was just overcautious, but she couldn't. Her own instincts had also been twitching. "What do you propose we do?"

"I have some ideas." He turned his horse and started down the road. "This evening I'd like to have a meeting with you, Princess Maria Sofia, the senior Olivieras plus Gilberto, and my batman, Tom Murphy, to discuss my concerns and see what they have to say. Will that be possible?"

She nodded. "Everyone will be eager to come, particularly Sofia. We all know our situation is difficult. The ideas and help you're offering are a blessing."

"Good. It's Sofia's country, after all. I'm just passing through with no authority here," Will said. "Even though she's too young to take the throne, from what you say, the Gabrileños will listen to her?"

"They will," Athena assured him. It felt good to be making plans instead of just barely managing to hold the situation together. And Major William Masterson seemed like a man who could get things done.

■ ■ ■ ■

Athena set the meeting time for after dinner, and everyone gathered in the family sitting room of the castle. Athena started by saying simply, "Major Masterson has spent the day touring the valley and he has some thoughts about how we might proceed."

Petite, dark-haired Sofia looked regal as she said, "I'm very anxious to hear any ideas you might have, Major."

"For the short period of time the French were here, they did a lot of damage," Will said. "Basic repairs like the main bridge over the river and the gristmills aren't too complicated if there are the right materials and enough labor. I can order nails and other hardware from Porto.

"Also, Lady Athena says you need vine cuttings and seeds for planting. Those can be ordered, along with some basic food supplies like beans and dried cod to get people through the summer." He glanced at Señora Oliviera. "I suspect you have the best idea of what is needed in the way of foodstuffs?"

Expression relieved, the older woman said, "I shall write down what is needed. Supplies have, indeed, been scarce."

"I'd also like to hire several dozen laborers to work at whatever needs doing," Will said. "Not only for rebuilding but the farm work as well. My friend Justin Ballard in Porto will be able to purchase what is required and hire good men and send them all up here."

"Of the port shipping family?" Sofia asked. When Will nodded, she said bluntly, "The House of Ballard has a good reputation and we need men and materials, but we have no way to pay for them."

Will smiled. "I'll cover the initial costs, then make the British government reimburse me. The government does want to help San Gabriel, and this will be much faster than requisitioning materials through channels."

Sofia glanced at Athena, who guessed that the princess had made the same deduction Athena had: Will would find it difficult and perhaps impossible to be reimbursed by the British. If the issue was personal, Sofia would have rejected charity, but as a young ruler, she was learning pragmatism. "We would appreciate that very much, Major."

"Then I'll draw up a list of what is needed. Sergeant Murphy, you'll leave for Porto in the morning to deliver the message to Ballard. Then you can stay and escort everything and everyone back."

"Yes, sir. I'll be back here sooner than you think possible," Murphy said.

"Let us move on to the ever-popular subject of wine," Will said. "And other matters agricultural."

That produced smiles, and a discussion of his proposals to import vine cuttings, reopen the wine caverns, and possibly survey whether the San Gabriel River could be made navigable. Señor Oliviera had vast knowledge of every aspect of San Gabriel, and he participated enthusiastically.

Athena admired how Will ran the meeting, encouraging suggestions, proposing compromises, and quietly building a sense of excitement and possibilities.

After general plans had been agreed upon, Will said gravely, "I have another topic, and this one is military. The valley is vulnerable to roving groups of bandits even more undisciplined than Baudin's forces were. The situation will be much better when Colonel da Silva returns with the rest of the Gabrileño troops, but I think it would be wise if plans are put into place now to protect people and property and to resist marauders."

Gilberto frowned. "I talked with several of my men today. Growing up, we all believed San Gabriel to be safe from war in our mountains. Now we know better. If that French pig of a general could attack, so can others. We talked of organizing many small militias, perhaps a dozen or so men who live close to each other. And we could do more with the warning system of the bells."

"We need to practice our emergency drills," Sofia said firmly. "The ones that we had helped to save many Gabrileños when Baudin invaded, but more sanctuaries are needed, for not everyone is close to a cave. There are many large-walled homes scattered across the country. They can become refuges in emergencies."

Señor Oliviera nodded. "We will organize small defense precincts and talk to your caballeros, Gilberto. Drills and plans stave off panic when disaster strikes."

"How many weapons are available?" Will asked. "The cavalrymen are armed, but more ammunition will be needed."

"There are blacksmiths in both the town and Santo Espirito who can make musket balls," Señor Oliviera said. "I shall find how much lead they have."

After a few more minutes of discussion, Sofia rose to signal the end of the meeting. "You give me great hope, Major Masterson. My thanks for offering us the benefit of your experience." She inclined her head to Murphy. "Travel safely, Sergeant Murphy, and go with our thanks." Then she daintily covered a yawn. "And now to bed, where tonight I will have good dreams!"

Most of the group left, talking animatedly. Athena smiled fondly after Sofia. Her little sister of the heart was becoming a queen.

CHAPTER 12

Only Athena and Will remained in the family sitting room. "That went well," she said. "Most Gabrileños have been numb since the French invasion. All their energy went into surviving and there wasn't much left for looking ahead. Your offer to bring in workmen and materials has changed that."

He shrugged. "That helps, but I think much of the energy comes from the young men like Gilberto Oliviera returning home. A few now, many more soon. They are the leaders of the future."

"There will be marriages and festivals and new babies." Athena moved to the drinks cabinet and took out a corked bottle and two tumblers. "But for now, would you like some of our brandy-fortified wine?"

"A good way to end a long day." He accepted the drink and took a sip. "Very nice! San Gabriel wines can hold their own with those of the lower Douro Valley."

Not ready to go to bed, Athena said, "It's a clear night. Would you like to go up to the roof and see the stars?"

He gave her a warm smile. "That's even better than brandy. I'll take the bottle, since I enjoy looking at the sky."

Athena collected a shawl that always hung in the family room and a candlestick and led the way to the stairwell that ran up the tallest tower. Several flights of steps up brought them onto the tower's flat roof. She inhaled deeply, enjoying the crisp, cool air. The moon was only a sliver, so the stars were brilliant in the night sky.

Athena crossed to the gazebo, which by day commanded sweeping views of the mountains and the valley. As she settled on the inside bench, she explained, "The tower is a popular place to enjoy the breeze and the view, so Uncle Carlos built the gazebo. In better days, there were great tubs of flowers here, but this year it didn't seem like a good use of time and effort."

"Next summer there will be flowers here again." Will sat beside her, the bench creaking a little under his weight. "On a clear day, you can probably see almost to Porto."

"Not that far, but it's possible to see almost all of San Gabriel. That cluster of lights to the north is Santo Espirito."

"So peaceful up here." He glanced at her, his face a pale oval in the night. "Here's a question for you. You want to return to England, but you seem to feel you won't fit in well there. How do you envision your ideal living situation?"

"More questions, Will?" she said with amusement. "At least this one is fairly painless. I'd like to live in a London neighborhood inhabited by mad poets and artists and musicians. That way I won't stand out, except for my height. What about you? Will you be content to rusticate on your Oxfordshire estate? Or will you become a Member of Parliament so you can live part of the year in London?"

He laughed. "I'll never be an MP, but I will spend some of the year in London. Spring is a good time to catch my friends there. They're an intelligent lot, so talking with them will prevent me from becoming completely countrified."

"School friends? Army friends?"

"Both. Plus, my brother spends a good part of his time in London. I look forward to seeing him face-to-face regularly. Letters are not the same."

"Perhaps I'll find such friends among the mad poets and artists," she mused. "And if I meet any of the dreadful girls I went to

151

school with, I'll give them the cut direct."

"Or you can say casually that you've just returned to England after a lengthy stay with your friend the Princess Maria Sofia del Rosario Alcantara."

Athena laughed. "I like that idea." The breeze was cool, so she wrapped her shawl more closely. "I hope Mr. Ballard is swift at collecting the men and materials you requested."

"He's very efficient and, from his letters, a little restless, so I'm sure he'll do well by us," Will said. "It's been a couple of years since I've been able to visit Justin in Porto. I'm looking forward to seeing him again."

Athena frowned. "It's been five years since I've been in Porto. Have they repaired the damage from when the French captured the city?"

"They were working on it, but there was still much to be done. I'm sure you heard about the collapse of the bridge of boats that caused the drowning of huge numbers of fugitives from French troops?"

Her mouth twisted. "If I answer this, I must be allowed to use it for a future 'worst experiences' question. I didn't just hear about that day of horrors. I was there."

"Good God, how did you come to be caught up in that?" Will exclaimed as he turned on the bench to stare at her, his shock visible even in the starlit darkness.

"After Sofia's mother died, she was sent to a convent school in Porto. She was miserable and begged to be allowed to come home," Athena explained. "Because Uncle Carlos was worried about her and also about the threat from the French, he wrote and asked me to collect Sofia in Porto and bring her home, then stay on as her tutor and companion until she was of age."

"I gather you arrived in Porto shortly before the French attack?"

Athena swallowed hard. "My timing was atrocious. When I arrived at the convent, I was invited to stay a few days to tell the students about my travels. Two days after I arrived, the French attacked. One of the devils broke into the convent, which had only a low wall around it. He was drunk and violent and he began shouting for the prettiest nun in the house, since he'd always wanted to have a nun. I . . . I got his rifle away from him and . . . shot him." She swallowed hard.

"It's not easy to kill a man." Will's warm, strong hand closed over hers comfortingly. "Even if it's necessary. The sisters were fortunate that you were there."

"They were gentle souls, so you're right. I

doubt any of them had ever shot a gun, much less a man." She shivered at the memory. "The sounds of battle were drawing nearer and the house wasn't secure, so the mother superior decided to evacuate to a sister convent across the river. It was larger and had high walls and would be much safer."

"Then you reached the bridge over the Douro and found that the Portuguese defenders had destroyed it, and desperate refugees had built a temporary bridge of boats across the river," Will said soberly.

"There was a huge crowd of people shoving to get onto the bridge. We circled around the girls and the nuns' habits provided the group some consideration. When our turn came, we made our way very carefully onto the bridge. It was frightening to attempt, swaying and shaking from the river current and so many people trying to cross over. Three times I had to drag someone from the water. The advantage of long arms." She drew a shuddering breath. "We had almost reached the southern bank when the boats began breaking apart underneath our feet."

She burrowed under Will's arm, getting as close as she could. "It was *horrible*. I almost lost the littlest girl, Mariana. When I managed to grab her arm, I almost drowned myself because my soaked clothing was so heavy. Then a Portuguese man grabbed my hand and pulled us both ashore."

"You were dressed as a nun," Will said softly. "And by heroic efforts were able to save most or all of those under your protection."

"All of us survived. I had a great deal of aid from the local men who helped haul us to shore." She frowned as she realized what he'd said. "How did you know I was dressed as a nun?"

"Because I was there," Will said grimly. "I'm a good swimmer, so I dived into the river and started pulling people to safety, including you. It was bloody bedamned chaos, with screaming and gunshots from some French soldiers while other Frenchmen joined the rescue efforts." He drew a deep breath. "I have a vague memory of helping a remarkably tall nun with a rifle out of the water. Then she gathered her charges and disappeared."

"You were *there*?" she gasped. She'd tried to forget that horrible day, but she remembered some of the men who had helped the girls and the nuns. "You were the one who rescued me and Mariana? I only got a glimpse of your face and you were badly in need of a shave — I never would have recognized you."

Though now that he'd said he was the man who'd saved her, she recognized that his broad shoulders and powerful build matched those of her rescuer. "I was so frantic to get us all away. I never even said a thank-you." Her voice was shaking.

"You looked half mad, so I didn't expect thanks. You immediately started rounding up your girls. I wondered later if you were able to get everyone to safety."

She closed her eyes and calmed herself as she absorbed the amazing fact that Will had rescued her on the worst day of her life. "We did. When you helped me ashore with Mariana, another couple of men were collecting all the students around the sisters. One yelled for us to get away as quickly as we could. A group of French soldiers were charging toward us." She winced, remembering. "One was bellowing out vile obscenities about what he liked to do to little girls."

"I heard," Will said tersely. "Until someone shot him. I wasted no tears."

She nodded, swallowing hard so that she could continue speaking. "That's when you and several other men moved between us and the French. Later I was surprised because none of your group were in uni-

156

form, but you acted like soldiers."

"As it turns out, at least two of us were soldiers, but more about that later. How did you manage to escape safely? I wondered if you'd succeeded, but there was no way to know." His voice caught. "There were so many horrors that day."

She was remembering too many of those horrors, yet talking to Will, who had been there, was strangely healing. "We ran as fast as we could away from the river. I was holding Mariana because she was too small to get far on her own, and she was shrieking in my ear and almost strangling me."

"How far did you have to travel before you were safe?"

"We didn't get far. Little girls and elderly nuns are not swift of foot, and there were only a handful of young nuns and me to help the others." She shuddered again. "A French officer appeared in front of us and I thought we were doomed, but he shouted in bad Spanish that we should come to the church just down the street. He had several men with him and they escorted us through the mob to the church. In English, the name would be Our Lady of Perpetual Salvation."

Will laughed, his voice a deep rumble in his chest. "How very appropriate."

Athena smiled a little. "When we were

inside, the mother superior and several of the other nuns dropped to their knees in front of a statue of the Blessed Mother and prayed their thanks. The French officer was collecting other women and children in the church, and he had some of his men outside as guards. We spent the night there. In the morning when it was quiet, he detailed several men to escort us to the convent we'd been heading for the previous day. It was a long walk, but his men helped carry the littlest girls."

"A reminder that there are good men everywhere," Will said. "I've met Frenchmen I'd trust much further than some of the Englishmen I know."

She nodded agreement. "After a couple of days at the convent while we recovered, the mother superior found several reliable men who were willing to take me, Sofia, and Maria Mercedes da Silva to San Gabriel without being paid until we reached here safely."

"Good of them to do it without money in advance."

At that, Athena actually laughed. "Sofia showed them her mother's cross, which she was wearing under her school uniform. It's gold and set with jewels, very impressive. She said that was proof of her good faith, but if they tried to take it from her by force before we were safe in the Castelo Blanco, her dead mother would curse them all to hell. Our escorts treated us very, very well. Though to be fair, they might have done so even without the threat."

Will chuckled. "Your princess is a very resourceful young lady."

"She is a true royal Alcantara." Athena exhaled roughly. "It was such a relief to reach here safely. I haven't set foot outside of San Gabriel since." She bent for the bottle of wine and silently offered to refresh Will's drink.

He accepted and clinked his tumbler against hers. "To survival against the odds!"

"Amen." She took a swallow rather than a sip, grateful for the burn of the brandy that fortified the wine. "What about you? How did you manage to escape?"

"I didn't manage that," he said dryly. "There was a hand-to-hand battle after you left. Fugitives, French troops, Portuguese soldiers, civilians who were trying to help. Luckily, not a lot of bullets and casualties, but I got bashed on the head and woke up that night locked in a cellar with a firing squad scheduled for dawn."

Athena's heart clutched, even though he'd obviously survived. "How did you escape execution?"

"I was locked in with four other men who'd been part of the attempts to block the French advance. A French colonel decided all five of us were English spies, so he imprisoned us in the cellar of the house he'd commandeered as his headquarters and ordered us shot. A nice, simple solution from his point of view."

"Were you a spy?" she asked. "You were wearing Portuguese dress."

" 'Spy' is such a strong word," Will said mildly. "I considered myself an observer. Since I spoke Portuguese and had visited my friend Ballard in Porto, my commanding officer asked me to go into the city and find out what the situation was. Like you, I had atrocious timing."

"What about the others? Were they English spies?"

"I have no idea," Will said reflectively. "Four of us admitted to being British. One was a fellow I'd known at school. The fifth, Duval, said he was a French royalist, but it turns out he's half English and half French, and he's the British colonel who sent me to San Gabriel. He was surely spying, but I don't know what the others were doing in Porto."

Athena hesitated before succumbing to curiosity. "What does it feel like to know that you'll be shot in a few hours?"

"That's an interesting question." Will frowned. "Going into battle or riding in ambush country, you know you might die in an instant, or perhaps be mortally wounded and die in agony. Fear is a constant, quiet drumbeat in the back of one's head. But there is something much uglier about the cold-blooded deliberation of an execution. Feeling the clock ticking, wondering how well one will face the end, how long it will take to die . . ." He shook his head. "An interesting experience, but not one I want to repeat."

She slipped her free arm around his waist. "It must have been a long night."

"It was. We shared what alcohol was in the cellar and talked fancifully about how we would redeem past sins if we survived, which none of us expected to do."

"Are your sins that great?" she asked, surprised.

"Not compared to some, I suppose," he said slowly. "But there were enough failures of duty, things I should have done, people I should have treated better, to weigh on my soul."

She understood such small but never forgotten past sins. "A strange night indeed. How did you escape the firing squad? Did the French colonel change his mind?"

"I noticed a Masonic symbol carved into a stone behind a set of shelves. It's not unknown for Masons to build escape tunnels from their homes, so we investigated and found that behind the stone was a shaft angling up and out. It was a tight fit, but we all managed to get out before dawn."

"And went your separate ways after sharing a shattering experience. Were you glad to see each other's backs?"

"Oddly enough, no," Will replied. "The wicked little secret of soldiering is that it creates intense bonds among those who share the experiences. Facing danger together, us against the enemy, brings a powerful closeness. We stole horses and rode east away from Porto and Gaia, but when the time came to split up, we found ourselves reluctant to say good-bye." He shook his head. "It was one of the stranger episodes in my life, but not one I want to forget. The others felt the same."

"At least you met Duval, even if you never see any of the others again."

"Perhaps now that the war is over, we'll have a Rogues Reunion and see if we've been living up to our vows to redeem ourselves," Will said with a laugh. "We agreed to use Hatchard's bookstore in

London as a postbox. The manager keeps letters for us. When I was in London because of my brother's alleged death, I stopped by and found letters from two of the other men. They were rather cagey about what they're doing now, but at least they were still alive in the not-too-distant past."

"Did you add a letter?"

"I did. I suspect I was the least devious of the group, so there was no reason not to mention that I was an officer in the Fifty-second. Perhaps that's how Duval found me."

"Returning to normal life after sharing such danger and closeness will be difficult," Athena observed. "Is that why you want to develop greater closeness with me, a chance-met female whose principal recommendation is to be tall enough for you?"

"You may very well be right about the closeness," he said thoughtfully. "But your height is far from your only appealing quality." He brushed a kiss on her temple and murmured mischievously, "It's more in the nature of a delightful bonus."

CHAPTER 13

In keeping with his resolve to move slowly, Will made sure that his kiss was light and undemanding. He wasn't prepared for Athena to turn her face up so that their lips met. The kiss began as friendly recognition of all they had shared that night, but the sweet intimacy of her soft mouth jolted fire through his veins.

The possessive male part of him wanted to claim her as his mate, for surely they were meant to be together. They had first met under savage circumstances, a bond that had gone unrecognized till tonight, but which could not now be ignored.

The saner part of him realized that a strong, independent woman needed to be wooed and won, not claimed like a conquered city. Yet it was impossible to be sane when she slid her arms around him and responded with the buried passion he'd sensed was a vital part of her.

He loved the way she filled his embrace, woman-soft, woman-strong, and woman-scented. When she opened her lips, their tongues touched, a feather-light caress that turned mind-meltingly erotic. Illicit fire in a cool, sweet night. She tasted like fine wine and brandy and tantalizing sensuality.

A joyous madness bubbled through his veins and his breath quickened as he whispered, "Athena, goddess . . ." Unable to resist the rose petal softness of her fair skin, his lips moved hungrily across her cheek to the delicious whorls of her ear.

She gasped, her fingertips digging into his back before she reclaimed his mouth with feverish urgency. He wasn't sure she even realized when she swung a leg over his legs and slid onto his lap, her legs bracketing his.

Dizzily he rocked against her as their lips and loins pressed together, heat to heat. His hands under the shawl roamed over the supple curves of her back and hips. In a remote corner of his mind, he realized that he should stop this *now,* but his better judgment had fled, leaving only hot, mad craving.

His right hand slid down the back of her thigh into the skirts tangled around her knee. When he pushed the folds of fabric away, his palm found the smooth flesh on the back of her knee. His hand began caressing higher. . . .

No! He froze, realizing how close he was to losing control entirely. "This is *not* a good idea," he said in a choked voice.

Needing to get away from her intoxicating self, he caught Athena's waist with both hands and swung her onto the bench. Then he lurched to his feet and escaped from the gazebo. A breeze in his face cleared his wits as he stalked across the flat roof of the tower. He was here to help San Gabriel and that meant working with Athena. But how the devil would they face each other in the morning after such reckless intimacy?

Knowing there was no other choice, he swung around to face her. She stood in the doorway of the gazebo, her shawl gripped tightly around her and hair tumbling loose over her shoulders.

"I'm sorry," he said raggedly. "I didn't mean that to happen. We're still working on friendship, and I know you don't want to go further."

Though her tall figure was taut and her eyes were great dark pools of shadow, her voice was wryly amused when she said, "I must admit that for a few minutes there, I did want to go further. You're rather dangerously attractive, you know."

He blinked. "That is *not* a comment I've ever heard before."

"Then you've spent too many years in the masculine environs of the army. If you moved in more normal society, you would find yourself being hunted."

"I'm quite sure you're the only woman in the world who would think that, but I'm flattered." His smile faded. "Delightful as it is to kiss you, I know that premature passion might lead to disaster. I don't want to risk driving you away and destroying the friendship we're developing."

Arms still crossed under her shawl, she leaned against one of the narrow pillars that framed the entrance to the gazebo and regarded him thoughtfully. "I've never met a man who values friendship with women as much as you do." Her voice turned dry. "Most males seem far more interested in bedding than in being friends."

Her perception was part of what drew him to her, even when it was uncomfortable. He began pacing across the roof with tight steps as he chose his words. "I do value friendship greatly. I was a very lonely child until my brother, Damian, came to Hayden Hall. My father didn't understand how much I needed a companion, which was why I would not allow my brother to be sent away."

"Did your father ever take the time to know your brother?"

Will's lips tightened. "No. He accepted that he was responsible for Mac and paid school fees and living expenses, and later he bought Mac a commission. But he could barely stand to be in the same room with him. Mac's existence was a reminder of my father's less-than-respectable behavior."

"It sounds as if your father was something of a hypocrite," she observed.

"He was," Will agreed. "Apart from Mac, my family wasn't terribly satisfactory, which is why friendships have been so important to me. The friendships formed at my school have become so deep and lasting because we were all misfits of one sort or another. But we learned we could trust each other. That created lasting bonds."

"Like your battlefield friendships?"

Will thought of the night Lily had died, when his frantic message had brought one of his oldest school friends, Ashton, to his side through a near-lethal blizzard. If the circumstances had been reversed, Will would have done the same for Ashton. The mutual loyalty and trust were beyond question. "Very like."

"You said Justin Ballard was a school friend, so I assume he's one of that school brotherhood?"

"Yes, which is why I know he'll send the aid I requested. I would do no less for him. Friendships make life worth living." He hesitated, then continued. "Honesty compels me to admit that friendships between men and women can be difficult because there is always that underlying awareness of difference."

" *'Vive la différence,'* " Athena murmured in French. In her normal voice, she asked, "Do you have many female friends?"

"Not as many as I would like. As you point out, I've been living mostly among men for years. But Lady Agnes Westerfield, founder of the school where Mac and I were sent, is an extraordinary woman. She has a gift for educating boys and I treasure her friendship. Several of my school friends are married, and the wives I've met are remarkable women. We're friendly now, and I hope that when I'm back in England, we'll develop deeper friendships. My brother's wife, Kiri, is amazing. You'd like her, I think. You have much in common."

"That could mean instant antagonism instead!" Her eyes narrowed thoughtfully. "Your proposal that we ask each other personal questions leads into interesting and impertinent subjects. Is there one of your friends' wives whom you wish were yours?"

Will shook his head decisively. "They're all intelligent, attractive women, but I've never once thought of any of them like that. Wives of friends are untouchable."

"An admirable sentiment," she said with approval.

He studied the subtle play of starlight that defined Athena's tall, graceful figure, and thought of how they'd met thrashing in the crowded waters of the Douro. She'd been on the verge of drowning from the weight of her saturated nun's robes, but she'd struggled on to save herself and the child locked under her arm. "Even if the ladies my friends married were free, none would be quite right for me. Or me for one of them."

"That will make it possible to develop deeper friendships with them." Athena straightened and stepped down to the level roof, her lips curving in a slight smile. "Very well, we shall continue to develop our friendship. But perhaps it's better if we stay out of touching distance."

There was nothing he would like better than to close the distance between them and wrap his arms around he again, but only a fool would ignore what she was saying. Glad she wasn't ending their tentative relationship, he said, "Luckily, there is so much to be done in San Gabriel that we should be able to behave with decorum."

For now, at least . . .

Athena was grateful for the shadows as she led the way down the stairwell, because the erratic light concealed her trembling. She'd found Will Masterson attractive from the beginning, but she hadn't expected that serious kissing would swiftly dissolve all her good sense. She'd been close to tumbling into category four, an affair, without any conscious thought. Thank God that Will had more self-control than she did!

As she reached the family floor and stepped into the corridor, then turned back so the light of her candlestick illuminated the last steps for her companion, she thought about what a truly decent man Will Masterson was. Kind, considerate, and honorable to a fault, not to mention powerfully attractive. If she wanted to have an affair, she could hardly choose better for a lover.

But the fiercely independent part of her nature that had enabled her to survive and build an unconventional but satisfying life drew back from the thought. Passion was a kind of madness that destroyed good judgment, as this evening had demonstrated. She would be no man's mistress because no matter how careful lovers might be, there was always the risk of pregnancy. As a bastard herself, she'd sworn never to inflict the state on a child of her own.

And category five was impossible. Now that the long wars were over and Will was returning home, it was natural for him to want to find a wife and settle down. But he should wait until he was in England, where there would be many choices of a bride.

She and he did like each other and there was some attraction — actually, quite a lot of attraction — but she was just a chance-met female who happened to be a fellow Briton in an unexpected location. That wasn't enough to build a marriage.

No matter how hard she tried, she could not imagine fitting into the comfortable life of a country gentleman, even with a man as lovely as Will. Growing up, she'd had enough of cuts direct and whispers behind her back. Being the honorable sort, he would feel that he must defend his wife, but that would put him at odds with some of his friends, which wasn't fair to him.

If she was going to be an outsider, she

would be one on her own terms.

Will was glad he'd had the discipline to escort Athena to her rooms, bow politely, and head off to his own bed without touching her. But he paid for his restraint by sleeping badly. Romance and passion had had little place in his life for years. Now that he'd met Athena Markham, they'd come roaring back with a vengeance.

He was painfully aware that she was perhaps a hundred paces away at the opposite end of this long corridor. If he broke down and went to her door, would she open it? Probably not. But if she did, what then? They might share a night of glorious fulfillment — and in the morning she'd never want to see him again.

Patience, William. Patience. More and more, he believed he wanted her for category five, marriage. But that wouldn't come without a great deal more wooing and winning. And if he was to keep from destroying all chance of success, he'd damned well better get out of touching distance for a while.

He could do that. With a plan in mind, he finally drifted into sleep.

Athena slept badly as the merits of an affair were debated between her sensible, rational mind, which had always served her well, and her blazing physical desire, which had *never* served her well.

Perhaps she should have included a sixth category on her list? Flirtation, in which two people enjoyed one another's company in a romantic way, but without the intention of going further. She'd tell Will about it in the morning. . . .

She awoke with reason firmly in charge. That lasted until she went downstairs to breakfast with the Olivieras, who were their usual cheerful selves. She was halfway through eggs scrambled with onions and peppers when Will entered the dining room, and her reason collapsed. Why did that scarlet uniform have to be so damnably attractive?

His smile briefly touched her, but it was for everyone in the room. He looked as if he'd slept better than she had.

Señor Oliviera said, "Major Masterson, we worked well last night. Our plans are good."

"Yes, and today we start to put them into effect." He pulled up an empty chair at the far end of the table from Athena and seated himself. "After breakfast, I thought you and Sergeant Oliviera and I could sit down with a map of San Gabriel and tentatively lay out the defense districts."

Señor Oliviera blinked. "You move quickly."

"It's a British trait," his son Gilberto explained. "Very exhausting for those of us accustomed to savoring life at a slower pace, but sometimes useful. Once we have an idea of the districts, we can ride through the valley to discuss and organize."

Will nodded as a well-piled plate was set in front of him by a young Oliviera daughter. He thanked her, then said, "By this afternoon, we should be ready to ride out. I thought you, Señor, and the sergeant? You for persuasion, Gilberto to speak to his fellow soldiers and to start to organize the defense units."

Athena couldn't resist asking, "And you to lend the power and majesty of Britain to the quest?"

Will grinned at her. "Me to take notes about food and water supplies and available weapons and defensible position. The boring but necessary details."

"It will take a week or so of travel over the whole country," Señor Oliviera said. "Perhaps we should do several short trips instead."

"I think this work should be done as soon as possible." Will's gaze met Gilberto's for a moment of silent communication before the younger man nodded. Athena guessed they shared the soldier's sixth sense of impending danger.

The oldest Oliviera daughter, Beatrix, said teasingly, "My brother wants to go to Santo Espirito to see if a certain young lady has been waiting for him."

Gilberto said cheerfully, "If she has forgotten me, no matter. She has younger sisters. One of them might do."

Beatrix snapped a kitchen towel at her brother's head. "Swine!"

Laughing, he rose to his feet. "A reminder that the oldest daughter in a family has the worst temper, so I should pick a younger one."

His sister shrieked and prepared to snap the towel again. He caught her in his arms. "I have missed you so, Beatrix!"

Mollified, she hugged him back. "It's good to have you home, my pig of a brother. May the other troops also be home soon."

"They will, but in the meantime, we must make San Gabriel stronger. Papá, Major Masterson? I shall collect the maps of the valley. When you have finished eating, come to my father's office and we shall begin our work." With a bow toward his mother and Athena, Gilberto left the room.

Will and Señor Oliviera finished their meals and rose. Will sent one swift, warm smile toward Athena before he followed Señor Oliviera to the office.

And that was the last she saw of him for a week.

CHAPTER 14

Justin Ballard frowned at his ledger book, wondering how long it would take for the port-wine-shipping trade to recover now that the war was over. Demand was still strong — fine wines were always popular. But supplies were scarce because many Douro Valley vineyards had been hard hit and new vines took years to become productive. In the meantime, Justin was not as busy as he would like to be.

A tap on the door was followed by the cheerful face of Pia, one of his maids. "Mr. Ballard, there is a Sergeant Murphy here to see you."

It took Justin a moment to place the name and remember that Murphy was Will Masterson's batman. Feeling a clutch around his heart, he rose and strode toward his front hall. "I'll see him now."

He found the young soldier admiring the painted tile mural of a terraced vineyard that covered one whole wall of the entrance hall. Not bothering with the pleasantries, Justin asked sharply, "You have news of Will Masterson?"

"Yes, sir, and Major Masterson is well," Murphy said reassuringly, a pleasant Irish roll to his words. He held out a sealed letter of several pages. "He sent me to deliver this message."

The thick bundle was much more than a standard letter. "Do you want to wait for a reply?"

"Yes, sir, you'll see when you read it."

"Then join me in my office while I read. Pia, bring refreshments for Sergeant Murphy." Gesturing for the sergeant to follow, Justin returned to his office and settled behind his desk. He broke the wax seal and started to scan Will's familiar clear handwriting.

Greetings, Justin!

With the war over, I should be sitting in your drawing room enjoying views of the Douro and drinking Ballard port while you quietly consider how swiftly you can persuade me to go on my way. However, my journey homeward has been delayed in San Gabriel. Have you ever visited here? It's a lovely little valley kingdom that was unfortunately in the path of retreating French troops.

Much help is needed. Details listed below, but labor and good quality grape vine cuttings are the most important. (Preferred varieties are listed separately.) I also need tools, hardware, and black powder for blasting. I'll pay well to get strong, reliable laborers. Send them with the cuttings and other materials needed.

I'm told the road is bad — Sergeant Murphy will have firsthand experience by the time he reaches you — so I imagine everything will have to be brought up on donkeys or mules. Buy the pack animals — they're needed here.

Draw on my Porto account to cover costs. If expenses exceed that, I hope you will advance the balance, to be repaid when I can contact my bankers.

Murphy can escort the laborers and mules, but I hope that if you have the time, you'll come yourself. This is an interesting place, and the wine might be up to your standards if the local river can be made navigable down to the Douro.

Sergeant Murphy will explain more of the situation directly.

With hopes to see you soon —

Will, most grateful for whatever you
can do

Justin's brows arched when he scanned
the listing of desired supplies, including
nails, saws, hammers, and other tools. This
would not be inexpensive. Will could certainly afford it, but the question was why he
wanted to. "What on earth is Masterson
planning to build?"

Murphy swallowed a bite of the sliced ham
that was on the tray of refreshments Pia had
just brought in. "A bridge. Among other
things. The French did a lot of damage and
took most of the pack beasts and tools and
anything else they could easily steal."

"I've never been to San Gabriel, Sergeant
Murphy. Can you explain why Will has
taken such an interest in the place?"

"It's a fine little valley with good people
and it does need help, but many places do
when armies have passed through." Murphy
grinned. "San Gabriel, though, has a lady."

"Masterson is interested in her?" Justin
said, surprised. Will enjoyed the company of
females, but he'd never been a womanizer.

"Yes, and a very fine lady she is. English
and well respected in San Gabriel and near
as tall as I am."

And Murphy was taller than Justin. She

sounded like a good match for Will. Beginning to smile, Justin said, "The lady and the country sound interesting."

"Aye, sir. A pretty place with many fine ladies."

From the gleam in Murphy's eye, Justin suspected he'd found a lady of his own. Justin studied the list more closely. It was a little late in the season for planting grapevines, but San Gabriel was high in the mountains, where spring came later, so the plants would probably establish themselves well enough. The listed grape varieties all flourished throughout the Douro Valley and its tributaries, and he knew farmers that always kept their extra cuttings after the annual pruning of the vines. They'd be happy to sell the surplus.

There were also plenty of men in Porto looking for work, and some of them were seasoned vineyard workers. None of the other requested supplies presented much difficulty, though he'd have to use personal connections to acquire black powder.

After a swift mental calculation, Justin said, "We can be ready to leave in three days. I hope you'll stay here, Sergeant Murphy, since I'll need your advice on some of these things and I also want to know more about the situation in San Gabriel."

Murphy's grin broadened. "The major will be right happy to have you, sir. The sooner we can leave, the better."

Smiling, Justin began scribbling notes in the margin of the letter. He'd been in need of an adventure, and now one had appeared.

CHAPTER 15

"Gently, gently!" Will called out as the huge waterwheel was guided into the millrace so that the axle could be inserted and secured in place. Ever since French troops had wrecked the mill, the wheel had been lying half submerged in the river.

Since Will didn't have the materials to rebuild the bridge yet, he'd proposed rebuilding the mill and had recruited a couple of dozen strong young men to do the heavy lifting. Millstones and waterwheels were hard to destroy, so mostly this was a matter of putting the pieces back together.

Inside the thick-walled stone building, the massive millstones that would grind the grain into flour had been remounted earlier in the morning. Will and the mill owner, Señor de Sousa, had repaired and repositioned the complicated gears that transmitted the power of the river to the millstones.

The last step was raising and remounting

the waterwheel. Will had calculated where to anchor pulleys on the wall of the mill, and the young men were now hauling on them to pull the wheel upright so it could be remounted in the millrace.

With a squeal of wet wood on metal, the wheel was secured in place and immediately started turning as the river current pushed against the blades. The workers cheered and splashed more water at each other.

Will held his breath while Señor de Sousa engaged the gears. The runner stone on top began turning against the stationary bed stone below. Success! The gristmill was back in business. The mill owner gave a whoop of joy. "Praise the Blessed Mother and all the saints! And thank you, my friends, for aiding me. Now, we feast!"

Will found the mill repair a satisfyingly physical project after a week of canvassing the valley with the Olivieras. Memories of the French invasion were still vivid, so most Gabrileños welcomed the proposal to form small military defensive districts to provide safety and swift reactions if there were more attacks.

As Will had told Athena before the journey began, he stayed in the background and let the Olivieras do the explaining and persuasion, but his uniform was welcomed. The

British were popular in San Gabriel. Quietly he evaluated the defensible merits of manor houses and caves, and also inventoried water sources, weapons, foodstuffs, and other supplies that would be needed to create safe refuges.

The work kept him busy and so tired that thoughts of Athena didn't keep him awake all night. Instead, he dreamed of her, and woke up yearning. And burning.

Reinstalling the waterwheel was wet work, and Will was saturated. Luckily, the day was warm. He was drying his face with a small, ragged towel when Gilberto approached. "A good day's work, eh, Major?" the younger man called.

"Indeed it is. Now it's time to return to Castelo Blanco," Will said. "The supplies I ordered should be here in the next day or two."

"Later to the castle, but as Señor de Sousa said, first we feast to celebrate rebuilding the mill," Gilberto said. "See, coming down the castle road are carts and ladies. Such a celebration is traditional when many work together for the common good."

Will looked back along the road that led to the castle. His pulse quickened when he saw Athena and the princess riding in front of the carts. There were a dozen other females, all dressed in their festive best. Thinking that Athena was a sight for hungry eyes, Will said, "I like this custom!"

When the cart reached the mill, both ladies and food were greeted with enthusiasm. Gilberto's mother and sisters had come with several girls from the town. Amid much laughter, knee rugs were spread out on the shaded embankment and baskets of food and jugs of wine were unloaded from the cart under the supervision of Señora Oliviera.

Will skirted the crowd and headed to Athena, who was admiring the churning waterwheel from atop her horse. She used a sidesaddle today and her green riding habit made her complexion look like delicious cream. He wanted to lick her all over.

"Good day, Lady Athena!" He couldn't stop himself from grinning. "I'm told this kind of celebration is customary. What a very civilized country San Gabriel is."

"True, but don't discount the lure of seeing a large number of handsome young men in their shirtsleeves and wet to the skin!" She was regarding Will with undisguised approval, and he was abruptly aware of how his wet white shirt clung to his shoulders and torso. Barely decent, in fact, but he liked the expression on her face.

"Behold an engineer in his native habitat," he said with a sweeping bow.

"Is your current state typical of a military engineer?"

"Usually there's more mud. I enjoy splashing around on a pleasant day like this one." Freezing water and artillery fire had made such projects less appealing in places like Badajoz. But that was the past. Now was better. "May I help you dismount?"

She hesitated a moment. Athena was perfectly capable of dismounting on her own and they both knew it, but a gentleman's offer to help a lady from her horse was an excuse to touch. Will was pleased when she nodded and slid down into his waiting hands.

For just an instant he continued to hold her slim waist. She had a delicious tangy scent of rosemary, and he saw in her eyes that she remembered their evening on the rooftop as clearly as he did.

As he stepped away, she said a little breathlessly, "I've realized that the relationship scale needs another category. Flirting. Enjoying each other's company with a bit of romantic awareness, but no intention of going beyond."

This was promising. "An excellent idea. Let us restructure the scale into four categories. Friendship, flirting, a love affair, and marriage."

She tethered her mount. "Indifference and enmity are still possibilities."

"I could never be indifferent to you," he breathed. "And I'll do my best to insure you never look on me as an enemy."

She blushed and looked down to tie up the trailing skirts of her riding habit. "You are certainly flirting now, so the new category must be accepted."

He smiled. "I am definitely flirting. I have been waiting all week for the opportunity to do so."

"That goes beyond flirting to shameless flattery," she said, amused. "Was your work this past week successful?"

"Yes, no one has forgotten General Baudin, so just about everyone liked the idea of strengthening their ability to resist marauders of various sorts."

"Good! I want to hear details." She turned to her horse and took a lightweight, coarsely woven knee rug from her saddlebag. "The custom at these informal celebrations is to sit on rugs and chat and eat. The ladies bring their own rugs and usually stay in one place while the gentlemen tend to move around. It's interesting to watch."

Will took the rug and shook it out in a

patch of shade from a clump of spindly trees. The striped pattern was in natural shades of sheep wool with a few grass stains from prior usage. "Since many of the young men are recently returned home, I imagine there's a great deal of flirting."

Athena gracefully seated herself on one end of the rug, her knees tucked to one side. "I'm a chaperone and my job is to insure that the flirting stays within acceptable bounds. Gabrileños love a good time, and celebrating community efforts is a perfect excuse. Of course there's also the exhilaration of the war ending."

"Am I allowed to share your rug?"

"If you are willing to align yourself with a staid chaperone, please do." Her words were prim, but her hazel eyes danced.

He laughed and settled on the rug, which was large enough for two tall adults to sit without touching. He wished it were a bit smaller, but then he might be less welcome.

"Were the districts you tentatively sketched out workable?" Athena asked.

"Yes, Señor Oliviera seems to know every hill and field in the entire country, so his original estimates were accurate. In a couple of places, access to water meant adjustments might be made, but, overall, the organizing went very smoothly."

"What is needed most?"

"More weapons and more food supplies that will keep indefinitely, like beans and rice," he said promptly. "Bringing in food is easy and not very expensive, and I hope we have time to do it. Weapons are another matter."

Her brow furrowed. "How well can the strong points be defended?"

"That depends on the kind of assault," he said. "The Gabrileños' traditional construction style of high stone walls around a house, a well, and outbuildings makes it very easy to lock out casual bandits who want to sweep in and steal what they can. But a larger, better-armed, more determined gang of brigands is much more dangerous, especially if they're willing to lay siege."

Athena frowned. "I hope your itchy feeling of trouble coming means casual bandits, not the more determined kind. The weapons situation will improve when Colonel da Silva and the rest of the troops return."

"Yes, and that can't be more than a few weeks off," he said reassuringly. But his sense of danger suggested worse than casual bandits, and in the not very distant future. He'd like to think he was wrong, but his sixth sense had been very reliable in the past.

A laughing girl from the town approached and offered them a tray that held clay cups and a mound of warm little pastry pockets rather like English Cornish pasties. Will accepted wine and three of the little pies. "Thank you, señorita," he said. "Rebuilding gristmills is hungry work."

"Our thanks to *you,* Major Masterson. My mama was almost out of flour." She bobbed a curtsy and darted away.

The pies had a spicy filling that was mostly beans, onions, and peppers with garlic and sharp, interesting herbs. Will demolished the first in two bites. "I gather this is the Gabrileño version of the empanada, but with different spicing? Tasty."

Athena handed him one of several napkins she'd brought along. "Yes, though in more prosperous times there would be some meat, probably smoked pork, mixed in with the vegetables." She ate her empanada more neatly, but with enthusiasm.

The red wine was cool and sweetly tangy with bits of chopped fruit. "And this is the Gabrileño version of sangria?"

"Yes, this particular wine is rather coarse, not the best quality, so adding fruit disguises its faults. It's lovely on a hot day like this."

Thinking how freely wine flowed in the valley, he asked, "How long till the wine reserves are exhausted? Existing supplies won't last forever."

"There were several years of very good grape harvests before Baudin's invasion, so supplies were high," Athena replied. "There isn't a household in San Gabriel that didn't have a few barrels of wine stored in the back pantry or cellar. But you're right, reserves are running low. If the wine storage caverns can be opened, the barrels there will last quite a long time. Ideally, until the local wine production is back to normal."

Exquisite in a blue-and-gold habit, Princess Sofia was moving among her people, thanking the men who had volunteered their time and chatting and laughing with everyone. Will's idle gaze followed her. "Sofia takes her responsibilities seriously."

"She does indeed. During the time you were gone, there were three days of open court at the castle. It's another Gabrileño custom," Athena explained. "Anyone in the kingdom can present a petition or bring a dispute to the ruler. Since Prince Alfonso is no longer capable of presiding, Sofia has taken over. She's very patient and listens carefully before rendering her verdict."

Will gave Athena a quizzical glance. "Surely, you're there to help."

"Sofia confers with me before rendering

judgment," Athena admitted. "She tends to be a little too soft, so I encourage practicality. But I stay well in the background. She's the princess and she mustn't seem to be overinfluenced by a foreigner."

"We and our aid are warmly welcomed here," Will said quietly. "You've been a godsend to San Gabriel. But ultimately we're outsiders."

"I've always been an outsider everywhere," she said in an almost inaudible voice.

He wanted to wrap an arm around her shoulders and tell her that with him, she'd always have a place she belonged, but not yet. It was too soon. He said only, "But less of an outsider in England, surely."

She smiled with determined cheer. "I hope so."

Caught by movement in the distance, he shielded his eyes with one hand and peered along the road that led into Portugal. A slow smile spread over his face as he saw a compact, dark-haired man leading a well-loaded pack train. "I do believe our nails and beans and black powder have arrived."

"Ballard is here already?" Athena almost bounced with excitement. "Wonderful!"

Will got to his feet. "Are there enough empanadas and sangria to refresh Justin and the men he brings with him?"

Athena laughed. "There is never a shortage of food at Gabrileño festivities."

"I'll bring him to meet you." With a grin, Will headed to his horse. Real progress was being made; and the sooner he'd done what he could for San Gabriel, the sooner he could go home.

Preferably with Athena beside him.

CHAPTER 16

The road to San Gabriel was as rough as promised, and Justin and his train of workers and pack animals were grateful to be through the mountain pass and descending into the valley. It was a larger and greener place than Justin had expected. Perhaps some trick of the mountains brought them more rain than other areas. He studied the terraced hills where so many well-established vines had been destroyed, and was glad he'd been able to acquire plenty of good cuttings to restore the vineyards.

The road wound downward; and when Justin emerged from a sunken stretch, he saw the river not far ahead. A cluster of men and brightly dressed women was picnicking on the bank. It was a peaceful scene that made the war seem very far away.

High above and to the south, Justin saw a massive structure of pale stone that must be the Castelo Blanco. He was about to seek

out Sergeant Murphy when he saw a horse-
man galloping up from the gathering on the
river: a large man on a large horse.

Grinning ear to ear, Justin urged his
mount faster. He and Will met halfway
between the pack train and the river. Will
pulled his horse up alongside Justin and
shook his friend's hand enthusiastically. "It's
been too long! Damn, but it's good to see
you."

Justin laughed. "I can say the same! I'm
glad you've survived long enough to return
home, Will."

He jerked a thumb over his shoulder to
indicate the long train of pack animals. "I
reduced your Porto bank account to almost
nothing, but you are now the proud owner
of all sorts of hardware, grapevine cuttings,
foodstuffs, and various other things, as well
as the employer of a couple of dozen very
capable, hardworking men."

Will chuckled. "Would it surprise you to
learn that a project dear to the hearts of the
Gabrileños is clearing away the landslide
that sealed off the wine storage caverns?"

"These are my kind of people," Justin said
with a grin. "I look forward to trying the local wines."

"I don't think you'll be disappointed," Will
said. "But I look forward to having a few

pints of good English beer when I get home."

"Beer is for peasants," Justin said loftily. It was an old debate.

Will grinned as he turned his horse back the way he'd come. "Guilty!"

"What is the gathering by the river?"

"We repaired a gristmill this morning, so the ladies of the castle came down to feed us and celebrate," Will explained as they resumed riding. "I'm told there should be sufficient empanadas and sangria for you and the men you've brought."

Justin's mouth watered at the thought. "That's a good way to win the loyalty of everyone who came on this trek." He turned in his saddle and made a sweeping gesture to indicate that everyone should follow them down to the river. The mules and donkeys would like it as well as the men.

"Where's Tom Murphy?" Will asked.

"Acting as rear guard," Justin said. "Keeping the stragglers from getting lost while watching out for trouble. A very competent fellow. We had no problems, though. The trek up the Douro and over the mountains was rugged but straightforward."

"Does the road follow the San Gabriel River closely enough that you could see whether it might be made navigable?" Will asked.

"No, that will require a special survey," Justin said. "But from the glimpses of the river I saw now and then, improving the channel might be possible."

"Good." Will chuckled as he saw a pair of riders moving toward them. "Ladies are as curious as cats. Two of them are riding this way."

Justin saw a very tall woman in green, and next to her a petite girl in blue and gold. "Surely, the woman in green is the tall English lady I've heard about?"

"I suppose Murphy couldn't resist telling you," Will said dryly. "Yes, that splendid creature is Athena Markham, but don't admire her too much. She's mine."

Justin shot his friend a startled glance. "Really?"

"It's more accurate to say that I'm working on it," Will explained. "We're good friends, and I'm trying to lure her into becoming more."

Will would never speak of a woman like that unless his intentions were honorable, which made Justin eager to meet the lady. Will's friends had worried that the devastating loss of his young wife might have broken his heart forever, but apparently time had worked its healing magic.

Justin himself had no reservations about marriage, though he had yet to meet a woman who would fit well into his complicated, two-nation life. Now that the war was over, it was time to start seriously looking, perhaps on his next journey back to Britain.

Athena Markham and her young companion both rode superbly. Justin supposed that was necessary in this mountainous land with rough roads and few if any carriages.

Athena looked strong and graceful and competent, an Amazon well suited to Will Masterson. Though not a striking beauty, she was very attractive, with intelligence and humor in her expression. Justin looked forward to getting to know her better, but his first impression was that she was good enough for Will.

The ladies arrived and reined in their horses. "Welcome to San Gabriel, Mr. Ballard!" the young woman in blue said in fluent English enhanced by a slight, charming Gabrileño accent.

Justin had barely noticed the girl because he was studying Miss Markham, but now he turned his full attention to her — and felt as if a giant wine cask had just rolled over him, squashing him flat and rendering him unable to breathe. She was petite and beautiful, and under the shadow of her elegant riding hat, she had exquisite features, a sweet, direct expression, and a smile that scrambled his wits.

Will spoke before Justin's silence became noticeable. "Princess Maria Sophia, allow me to present my friend Justin Ballard of Edinburgh and Porto. Miss Markham, Justin Ballard. Justin, meet the leading ladies of San Gabriel."

Princess Maria Sofia? Justin swallowed hard. So this was the royal princess and heir presumptive to the throne of San Gabriel. Princesses were only supposed to be stunningly beautiful in fairy tales, not real life.

He bowed forward in his saddle. "Your Royal Highness, I am honored to meet you." He barely remembered to add, "And you also, Miss Markham."

"The pleasure is mutual, Mr. Ballard. We have been awaiting your arrival with great anticipation." There was amusement in Miss Markham's eyes. She was probably used to seeing men struck witless when they met the princess.

When Maria Sofia's gaze met his, her eyes widened for such a brief instant that he wasn't sure if he was imagining it. Then the polished manners of a royal princess took over and she offered her hand. "On behalf

201

of San Gabriel, I give thanks for your willingness to help us."

Her gloved hand was delicate, but her grip was firm. This was a girl who had learned to be more than a demure maiden of no opinions. He supposed that princesses learned early to deal with whatever and whoever came their way.

How old was she? Seventeen, perhaps eighteen? Too young for him. And a *princess*, for heaven's sake! The Ballard family was well-off, but not remotely royal.

Putting inconvenient attraction aside, he released her hand and said seriously, "The war has cost so many people so much. I'm glad to contribute to San Gabriel's recovery in some way."

"Your men can be accommodated in the military barracks, but you must stay at the castle. We have a great deal of space, and I'm sure you and Major Masterson have much to catch up on."

"Indeed we do." Could he sound any more vapid if he tried?

Thankfully, Will said, "Empanadas and sangria await. Later we can determine which projects to undertake first, now that the supplies have arrived."

"The grape vine cuttings must be planted as soon as possible," Justin said, glad to have a subject he was knowledgeable about. "It's already rather late in the season for planting. The sooner they're in the ground, the sooner they can begin to grow."

"Very true," the princess said as she turned her horse back toward the river. "The vines must be a priority. But now that you have the nails and hardware you need, it is time for you to build the bridge you promised us, Major Masterson. How soon might that be possible?"

"I think planting and building can be started at the same time," Miss Markham said. "But there remains the question of the long timbers needed for the bridge."

"I've calculated the amount required," Will said. "Now all we need is to locate usable lengths of seasoned wood."

The princess glanced at him. "I believe I have a solution, Major. Señor Oliviera and I have discussed this. Two castle outbuildings that were constructed with long timbers can be spared. If you believe they will suit, the buildings can be torn down and the wood used for your bridge. That will work, yes?"

"I've been thinking along those lines myself," Will admitted. "Once in Spain we tore down a nearby inn for its timbers when an emergency bridge had to be built, but it's not a popular solution. The innkeeper wasn't happy, even though he was compensated."

"We need the bridge more than we need so many barns, particularly since much of our livestock was stolen by the French and it will take time to rebuild the herds. Tonight, the four of us must dine together and discuss how best to proceed, now that Mr. Ballard has arrived with the supplies and workmen." The princess gestured for Justin to ride beside her. "And, please, sir, tell me about the wine-shipping business. This may be information San Gabriel can use."

"I can talk about the wine trade all day and into the night, your highness," Justin said, absurdly pleased. "You are warned!"

She laughed. "Please call me Sofia. This is a very small kingdom, after all."

He'd never been on a first-name basis with a princess, even a very young one. "I'm honored. In return, I hope you'll call me Justin. Now about the wine shipping . . ."

As he began to explain how the business worked, he gave thanks that he'd decided to come to San Gabriel himself. He'd wanted an adventure, and he'd found more than he'd dreamed of.

Athena and Will fell behind Sofia and Justin. When they were out of earshot, Will said in a low voice, "Was it my imagination, or did those two both light up like lanterns when they met?"

"Not your imagination," Athena said, her brow furrowed. "I trust Justin Ballard is an honorable man?"

"Without question," Will said as he studied the other couple. "They seem to have skipped friendship and gone straight to flirting."

"Which is as far as they can go." Athena had never seen Sofia react to a man so strongly. Granted, Ballard was very attractive, with the dark hair and suntanned complexion of a Gabrileño, but with bright blue Scottish eyes that sparkled with humor and an air of worldly sophistication.

Still, he could never be a suitable match for the queen of San Gabriel.

CHAPTER 17

Athena entered the family sitting room early, and found Will already relaxing there on the sofa while he studied a sheaf of papers. He'd removed his water- and mud-spattered clothes and wore a well-tailored navy blue coat, buff breeches, and polished black boots.

She stopped dead as icy shock jolted through her. He looked too much the fashionable London gentleman. Worse, he was dressed like her father on the one ghastly occasion when they'd met.

Her brief recoil vanished when he looked up and gave his wonderful, warm Will smile to her. He set aside the papers and rose to greet her, so she relaxed and stepped into the sitting room, closing the door behind her. "I'm glad Sofia suggested a small private dinner tonight. I'm not up for a full Oliviera meal, and your friend Mr. Ballard must be even more tired after his trek from Porto."

"Justin has always had excellent stamina." Will gestured toward the papers. "I've been going over the packing lists and he exceeded my expectations."

"I look forward to seeing the lists after dinner." Athena shook her head. "For months, we were barely staying afloat. Now San Gabriel can begin to move forward, thanks to you and Mr. Ballard."

"I look forward to sharing a brandy with him later tonight while we catch up with months of gossip." Will moved across the room toward her, a mischievous light in his gray eyes. "But at the moment, I'm interested in defining 'flirtation.' Does it include a well-mannered kiss?"

"I suppose it would depend on how well mannered the kiss is," Athena said as she watched him a little warily.

"Very well-mannered indeed." The brush of Will's lips on her left temple was feather soft, but at the same times his arms encircled her with warm thoroughness. "What about hugs? Is a well-mannered hug acceptable as flirting?"

Athena smiled, unable to resist relaxing against his broad, strong body. "Hugs are dangerous territory, but I'm exceptionally fond of them."

She tilted her head against his as tension flowed out of her. He smelled of fresh soap and his own appealing self. Though passion could be as close as the next breath if they allowed it, this embrace was pure, simple affection. She'd be happy to be held like this forever.

"I'm liking flirtation," he said thoughtfully as one hand stroked slowly down her spine. "Though I'm unwilling to accept that flirting can never go any further."

Athena was also having some trouble accepting that. At moments like this, it was easy to imagine that there could be more. That *they* could be more. And yet . . .

She made a face and backed out of his embrace. "It's easier to flirt with a wet, muddy engineer than the rather alarmingly fashionable gentleman I saw when I entered the room," she said with rueful honesty.

"I can take off this well-tailored coat and pour water over my head if that would help," he said earnestly.

She had to laugh. Will was so down-to-earth that it was easy to forget he was a landed gentleman. Though not a peer like her disdainful grandfathers, he could move easily in that level of society. From comments he'd made about highborn friends, she was sure that he did. It was best to enjoy flirtation and not yearn for anything more.

Though when she studied that powerful, masculine body and his laughing eyes, it was impossible *not* to yearn for more. "I shall forgive you the well-tailored coat, since I'm sure it's an accident that you look fashionable."

"Once, long ago, a valet informed me that it was impossible for a man built like me to look fashionable," he said seriously. "I'm too big. Excessive shoulders, excessive muscles. So I gave up on any thoughts of fashion and now settle for respectable."

"I have no complaints about your size. It's an exotic pleasure for an overly tall female like me to look up at a man," she said mischievously.

"I think you're exactly the right size," he said, a gleam in his eyes. "Deliciously huggable." Fortunately, laughter and footsteps sounded outside the door before Athena could decide whether to step toward him, or back away.

Athena and Will moved apart just before Sofia entered with Justin Ballard right behind her. The two were laughing together and Sofia had a bright happiness in her face that Athena hadn't seen since the French invasion. It was wonderful to see Sofia happy again, but not for a reason that guaranteed pain. *Be careful of your heart, little sister.*

After greetings all around, Sofia raised a bottle of red wine that she'd brought with her. "Justin kindly did not mention the quality of the sangria this afternoon."

"It was delicious and most welcome," Justin protested.

"But only a barely acceptable table wine underneath the fruit," Sofia said bluntly. "So I brought a wine that better shows what San Gabriel is capable of. Justin, will you open the bottle so it can breathe? It should be ready by the time dinner is served."

Justin obliged with the skill one would expect of an experienced wine merchant. After the cork was removed, he poured a very small amount into a goblet. "Don't drink it yet!" Sofia ordered.

He smiled at her. "I know better than to do that." He swirled the wine in the goblet, then sniffed carefully. "But it does smell most promising."

Two Oliviera girls arrived with trays of food. After laying out bowls and platters on the sideboard, the girls bobbed curtsies and withdrew.

There was a variety of hearty dishes, including dried cod that had been stewed with potatoes and onions, small garlicky sausages, corn bread, chicken with rice, cheese, bean salad, and the inevitable olives. It was peasant food, which was what San Gabriel could afford now, but cooked by a talented royal chef. Everyone attacked the sideboard with enthusiasm, and serving themselves made for an easy atmosphere.

Then Sofia poured the wine, careful not to disturb the sediment on the bottom of the bottle, and everyone paused to watch Justin's reaction. He chuckled. "It's hard to evaluate a wine under such pressure!"

Sofia started to apologize, but he waved off the apology. "Of course tasting it matters. I must be honest, you know. Mere politeness won't do in this case."

"I understand," Sofia said, her gaze unwavering.

He sipped at the wine, tasting it carefully, then drank more, his expression thoughtful. After a deeper swallow, he said, "This is excellent. As good as anything produced in the Douro Valley and with an extra quality all its own. I hope a way can be found to ship it to Porto and beyond."

Sofia and Athena exhaled with relief. The problem of transport was major, but it should be solvable. Now that they knew the valley had the potential for valuable exports, they'd find a way.

Though Gabrileños usually didn't believe in mixing business with anything as important as dining, all four of them were eager to start planning, so the lists of materials were passed around as easily as the wine bottles.

Athena studied the quantities of new food supplies. Will and his friends had not stinted. "I'll take charge of distributing food, since I learned where supplies were most needed during the winter. I assume that some of the staples that keep well, like beans and rice and dried cod, will be stored in the refuges, while other foods can go to people who need it now?"

"That was my thought," Will said. "No one should go hungry while waiting for the new season's gardens and crops to ripen."

Sofia nodded approval. "Justin, you and I and Señor da Cunha, the castle wine master, should distribute the vine cuttings. The royal Alcantara vineyards are the largest and suffered the most from the French, but there are many other growers in the valley who also suffered damage."

"Royal Alcantara," Justin said thoughtfully. "That would be an appealing name for the best Gabrileño wines."

Sofia sucked in her breath, her eyes shining. "What a splendid idea! We must use every advantage we have to rebuild San Gabriel."

Blushing under his tan, Justin asked, "How much help will the vineyard owners need with the planting? All the laborers I hired have experience with the vines, and most have other skills as well."

Sofia considered. "All vineyards have family members and often servants who are skilled in working the vines, but the larger farms will need extra help so the work can be done swiftly. I'll ask Señor da Cunha how many laborers are likely to be needed for the plantings. Not all of them, I think."

"I'll need a few of the larger fellows to help tear down the castle barns and prepare the timbers for use in the bridge," Will said. "By the time we're ready to build, more men should be free to help."

Sofia clapped her hands together, so excited she looked ready to bounce up and down in her chair. "In two or three weeks, the vines will be taking root and we will have our bridge! By then, the first garden vegetables will be ready and the town markets can open again. No one need go hungry this coming winter!"

"After the planting and the bridge, we can reopen the wine caverns," Will said. "Justin, I'm tempted to use some of the black powder you brought to blast our way in, but Athena doesn't want to risk ruining the wine."

Justin sat back in his chair, laughing. "Lord Masterson, you look entirely too eager to blow things up. How will you bear the tedium of the House of Lords when you return home?"

The ice Athena had felt when she saw Will as a fashionable gentleman returned a thousandfold. Feeling her blood drain away, she asked carefully, "Lord Masterson?"

"Hasn't he mentioned that?" Justin asked with mild surprise. "He's Major Lord William Masterson, sixth Baron Masterson of Hayden Hall. You are the sixth baron, aren't you, Will? Or is it the fifth?"

"The fifth," Will said, his brow furrowing as he regarded Athena.

Athena took a sip of wine to moisten her dry mouth. "No, you hadn't mentioned that, Lord Masterson."

Catching her gaze, Will said, "Having a title isn't something I think much about. It's not the most important thing about me, and completely useless on a battlefield."

"Being Lord Masterson won't stop a bullet," Athena agreed. "But so very useful socially. You are definitely among the grand sheep, not the humble goats."

Feeling ill, she got to her feet. "I'm tired and ready for bed. In the morning, I'll start delivering food where needed. I'll enlist some of the castle servants and perhaps Mercedes da Silva also. She likes riding and people." With a blind nod at Sofia and Justin, she collected a candlestick and opened the door to the corridor.

"Athena!" Will said sharply. Ignoring him, she closed the door and walked swiftly toward her rooms.

He moved faster, tearing through the door and running along the corridor. He caught up with her just before she reached the safety of her rooms. "Athena, please!"

He caught her arm and turned her to face him. In the dim light of her candlestick, his face was worried. "Why are you so upset? I'm no different than I was."

"You are a peer of the realm with a seat in the House of Lords." She wrenched her arm free. "If you enter a room in London, people will whisper that Lord Masterson has arrived. Yes, *that* Lord Masterson, the military hero. You will be high on any eligibility list of the Marriage Mart. You are likely far wealthier than I realized. You may not have changed, but my perception of you has."

She drew a shuddering breath. "It's time to end the flirtation. You'll finish your work in San Gabriel soon and go back to your real rank and your real life. A life that has nothing to do with me."

He started to reply, then stopped, his eyes narrowing as he studied her face. "I can only imagine the pain and persecution you suffered growing up," he said slowly. "Even your mother would not have really understood. Though she chose to live scandalously, she had the confidence that comes with being born Lady Cordelia. You had no such choice, and were condemned to bear the consequences of her actions."

She looked away, unable to meet his eyes. "You're perceptive, Lord Masterson. I grew up with sneers and insults, both to my face and behind my back. An aristocratic young man was my first and only calf love and eager to kiss me, but he was revolted by the idea that I could ever be anything more to him than a mistress. Those years at a horrible school where I was made to sew a sampler that said that the sins of the mother are visited on the daughter. I was never allowed to forget who or what I was. *Never!*"

He sucked in his breath. "I hate knowing you had to endure so much condemnation. But being illegitimate doesn't define who you are any more than my having inherited a title defines me."

"No? You may have been a lonely little boy until your brother came, but you always knew you were heir to a barony and would someday be a lord yourself. My mother had that aristocratic confidence, and so do you. I do not. I never will."

"You're right," he said, his brow furrowed. "Yes, titles can be useful. I can give you one. Marry me and you'll be Lady Masterson. Over time, surely that will heal some of the wounds of the past."

She closed her eyes, aching. "Your offer is the greatest honor I've ever received, your lordship, but I must decline. You can't have run into many English women on the Peninsula, so I suppose flirtation was inevitable under these circumstances. But the novelty of my being English and tall isn't enough. Go back to England and find yourself a lovely, well-born English girl who will be a suitable lady to your lord."

"Your opinion of me is shockingly low," he said tightly. "As is your opinion of yourself. Can't you see me as plain Will Masterson, a competent soldier who likes building things and splashing in the mud, and who thinks you're the most fascinating woman he's ever met?"

She opened her eyes and studied his forceful, handsome face. He was a good man, and she would not be a good woman if she took advantage of his innate decency. "I can't see you as plain *anything,* my lord. The gap between us is vaster than you can imagine. Return home. Someday soon you'll be grateful that I turned you down."

"Athena, don't throw what we have away!" He pulled her into his arms and kissed her with a desperate intensity that incinerated her senses. They'd kissed before, but she'd not felt the full force of the passion that lay under his easygoing exterior. For delirious moments she kissed him back, aroused to a madness she'd never known before.

For a wild moment, she was able to convince herself that he was right, that they could join their lives happily ever after. Then the tilting glass chimney of her forgotten candlestick pitched over and smashed on the floor.

She jerked away from Will, hot wax from the candle burning her hand as she remembered all the reasons they should stay apart. "Do you want to hear the full extent of my shame?" she said in a shaking voice. "My mother wasn't only Lady Delilah. She was also called Lady Whore, and I was Lady Whore's Daughter. Every girl in that hellish, sanctimonious school I attended knew, and they weren't ashamed to call me that.

None of them ever had their mouths washed out with soap for using that term, either. Because that wasn't bad language, it was *truth*."

"Dear God, Athena!" His face was white. "I don't know if it will ever be possible to make up for such abuse, but give me the chance to try!"

She sighed wearily. "I don't doubt your sincerity, but you haven't thought this out. Do you want to hold a ball or a dinner party in London and have the guests refuse to attend so they won't have to be under the same roof with Lady Whore's Daughter? Do you want to have people cluck their tongues and feel pity for you because it's a shame that such a nice, well-liked man married a scheming woman who must be as big a slut as her mother? Do you want to have to fight duels to defend my name? Or worse, believe that rumors of my profligate behavior might be true? Do you want your children shadowed by their grandmother's wicked reputation?"

His gaze was anguished, but he didn't look away. "You paint a bleak picture. It couldn't possibly be that bad. Memories are short, and once people get to know you, they'll forget the old scandals. I'm willing to take the risk of social disapproval."

"That's a credit to your good heart if not your good sense." She peeled the spattered drops of cool wax from her hand. "You've never been the target of such hating and disdain and you underestimate how hurtful it is. Since I know, I will not allow you to take on such a burden." The wax was peeled away, leaving angry red marks. Raising her gaze to him, she said, "We should be only the most distant of friends, my lord. You can have any woman you want, so find one who fits you and your life, and . . . and be happy."

Unable to bear any more, she bolted into her room. As she closed the door behind her, he said in a low, anguished voice, "You're wrong. Obviously, I can't have any girl I want."

His words were a knife slash to her heart. She closed and locked the door with shaking hands, then leaned against the heavy wood panels as she fought tears. She wished she believed that together they could build a good life. But when he wasn't holding her, all the slights and insults of her past sprang to stinging life.

Will might not mind that she was a bastard. But everyone around him would.

CHAPTER 18

Stunned, Will stared at Athena's door. He didn't have to hear the bolt snapping into place to recognize finality. They'd been enjoying each other's company so much till tonight, and now a few words had changed everything.

He'd never felt so helpless in his life. Mind reeling, he returned to the family sitting room. Sofia had tactfully withdrawn, leaving Justin. When Will entered the room, his friend asked, "Bad?"

"I asked Athena to marry me." He drew a shaky breath. "Apparently, the lady would rather see me in Hades."

Justin lifted a bottle and poured a generous measure into a goblet. "I think you need some of the local brandy, which is quite fine." He handed the glass to Will. "I don't know any of the details, but Miss Markham was clearly shocked at the knowledge that you're a peer of the realm."

"An understatement." Will sank into the sofa, then accepted the brandy and swallowed deeply. The kick of alcohol steadied his nerves. "I was a damned fool to propose marriage when she was in a state of shock."

"She seemed to like you well enough until I made the mistake of revealing your grand origins." Justin frowned over his brandy. "I'm sorry. It never occurred to me that she didn't know your rank."

Will sighed. "You couldn't have known. Though I recognized that she wasn't fond of the aristocracy, I didn't deliberately keep my title secret. Being Lord Masterson has had very little to do with my life in recent years."

"Most women would be delighted to have a rich, titled gentleman interested in them, but obviously there is more going on here," Justin said gently. "Do you want to talk about it?"

Will needed to talk, and Justin was clear-sighted as well as a good listener. Swirling the brandy absently, Will debated how much he could say without violating Athena's privacy. "Athena is illegitimate. Her mother was a daughter of one of the grander aristocrats, but she chose a life of wanton scandal. She lived as a courtesan to the great and powerful and apparently chose to have an illegitimate child as a companion."

"Good heavens, Lady Delilah Markham?" Justin said, startled. "I didn't know she had a daughter."

Will's brows arched. "You knew Lady Delilah?"

"I never met her, but I once saw her at a distance in Porto. She was dazzling, the kind of woman a man stares at, and then tries desperately to learn who she is. I've heard any number of stories. She was said to be as wild as she was beautiful and charming. Now that I think of it, I vaguely recall that she had a very visible affair with one of the Gabrileño royals. The king?"

"No, Prince Alfonso." Since Justin knew the general facts of Delilah's life, Will added, "That was the basis of Athena's connection with San Gabriel."

"Who is her father?"

"A grand lord who was revolted by her very existence and supported her on the condition she never reveal who he was. After her mother died, Athena was entirely alone and her father had her sent to a vicious, bloody-minded school, presumably to have the wildness stamped out of her."

Justin whistled softly. "I begin to understand why she isn't fond of lords. Do you know her father's name?"

"If I did, I'd be tempted to find the wretch and break a few bones," Will said dryly. "Other than that, it doesn't matter to me what her bloodlines are. We just realized that we first met during the bridge of boats disaster in Porto five years ago. She was in the midst of saving a child from drowning, and almost drowning herself. She is who she is, and that's enough for me."

"I knew you were there, but it's remarkable that she was also!" Justin exclaimed. "Did she get caught in the middle of the battle on her way to San Gabriel?"

"Exactly. She was collecting Princess Maria Sofia, who was at a convent school in Porto. When the French invaded, she was instrumental in getting the nuns and students to safety. That's when I met her. Then she escorted the princess and another Gabrileña girl home. She's lived here ever since, but would like to go home to England. In some way that no one will notice her."

"Intrepid woman! Well suited to you," Justin said. "She reminds me of someone, but I can't place the resemblance. Maybe it will come to me."

"She's sometimes called Lady Athena here as a title of respect. She has earned that respect, just as I earned the right to be called Major Masterson. Being called Lord

Masterson is just a superficial accident of birth," Will said with exasperation. "Unlike actually having money, which can be useful. But if peerage titles matter, I did offer her one. She thinks there is an impassable gap between us. I don't."

"Do you intend to give up on winning her over?"

"Of course not. You know how stubborn I can be. Athena is . . ." Will shook his head. He'd cared greatly for her already, and the honor and vulnerability she'd shown tonight had made him care even more. "I've never met her equal. I'm not leaving San Gabriel till I've fulfilled my obligations here. That should give Athena time to recover from her shock and realize that I'm not on some bloody unreachable pedestal."

Justin poured himself more brandy. "But you are on a pedestal, though not an unreachable one."

"I don't *care* that she's illegitimate!" Will said explosively. "How can I get her to believe me?"

"She may believe that *you* don't care, but she has reason to believe that everyone else does." Justin's shook his head. "You're as fair-minded and tolerant a man as I've ever met, but you were born to privilege. You always knew that someday you'd be Lord

Masterson. As a fish in the sea doesn't recognize the water he swims in, I don't think you're fully aware of just how privileged you are."

"Athena said something similar," Will admitted. "I know that I've been fortunate, but that doesn't make me special in any way that matters. I'm legitimate and Mac isn't, but he's much brighter and more popular than I, and he's made a fortune by his own efforts. He's never lacked for confidence."

"I think Mackenzie learned early how to fake confidence well, probably to compensate for the bar sinister. Have you ever talked to him about the difference between your legitimacy and his lack of it?"

Surprised, Will said, "That was never necessary because it wasn't important."

"Not to you, but I'd wager anything you like that the difference mattered to Mac." Justin's brow furrowed. "Most of our classmates at the Westerfield Academy were as privileged as you. I was the only one in the first class who wasn't an aristocrat. Ashton was a duke at age ten, you and Kirkland and Wyndham always knew you would inherit titles, Randall inherited a substantial estate and is in line to inherit an earldom. None of you had easy childhoods, but you were all raised swaddled in privilege."

Will frowned at Justin. "Were you made to feel inferior? I wouldn't have thought so, but obviously I'm not very observant."

Justin grinned. "I'm a Scot. Why would I give a damn about the opinions of a bunch of Sassenach? That said, Lady Agnes created an egalitarian atmosphere at the school so there was little bullying or snobbishness."

"The Westerfield Academy is for boys of good birth and bad behavior, so how did you end up there?" Will asked, curious. "I know the reasons why our other classmates were sent, but not yours. You always seemed to get on very well with your parents."

"I did and do. I was incredibly fortunate to have them as parents. I attended Westerfield because of crass opportunism," Justin said promptly. "My father liked that the school was founded by a duke's daughter and thought it would be good for the business if I went to school with 'a pack of aristocratic brats,' as he put it. I wasn't keen on the idea at first, but he promised that if I hated the place, he'd send me somewhere else. But I liked my classmates, adored Lady Agnes, and settled in quite happily."

"Your father wasn't wrong," Will said with a flicker of humor. "The whole pack of us aristocratic brats now drink Ballard port."

"The friendships are real. The excellent

port is a bonus." Justin poured more brandy in their glasses. "I wonder. When Miss Markham told you about her illegitimacy and her notorious mother, did you have to tamp down an initial spurt of revulsion?"

"Not even for an instant." What Will had felt was profound tenderness. "I want to protect her from every wretched person who's ever hurt her."

"Not the sort of relationship to abandon lightly," Justin said. "For what it's worth, I think your plan of quietly waiting until Miss Markham has time to get used to the idea that you're a peer is reasonable. I have no better suggestions."

"I'm not giving up easily, but she's as stubborn I am." Will laughed suddenly. "One of many reasons I like her."

Justin raised his glass. "A toast to your success! From what I know of the lady, I think she'll suit you very well. Plus, the two of you look splendid together!"

Will clinked his glass against Justin's. "I hope I can persuade her as well as I've persuaded you."

After they'd both drunk to that, Justin said a little wistfully, "Because your feelings seem to be mutual, I think you have a good chance of winning her hand and heart. I rather envy that. At least you have hope."

It wasn't hard to interpret his words. "You and the princess both looked lightning struck when you met."

Justin smiled wryly. "That's a good description. One look and I felt as if I was falling off a cliff. But there's no hope for anything more than respectful admiration. She's likely to become queen, which means she must make a significant marriage that will benefit San Gabriel. No Scottish merchants need apply. And, of course, she's very young. By the time she's of marriageable age, she'll have long forgotten me."

"She's not as young as she looks," Will said. "She's almost twenty-four. Under Gabrileño law, she can take the throne at age twenty-five."

"So she's a young woman, not a girl," Justin said, startled. "Not that that changes anything. The gap between a royal and a foreign wine merchant is far vaster than the distance between you and Miss Markham."

Will poured more brandy into their glasses. "True. So let's make a toast to miracles!"

Justin laughed and complied. "To miracles!"

Will had experienced one or two miracles in his time. Now he must hope for one more.

CHAPTER 19

A princess should be ladylike, poised, and gracious. She should also be intelligent, compassionate, and have good judgment. Never arrogant, but always aware of her rank and responsibilities. In short, being a princess took serious effort.

But despite all the responsibilities, a girl could still dream.

Sofia stole a quick sideways glance at the man riding beside her. Justin Ballard had visited her dreams the night before, and she hadn't been entirely ladylike with him. Her mouth curved in an involuntary smile.

Justin's multiple facets enchanted her. Though British, he looked and spoke like a native of Portugal. She'd already seen that he could talk easily to anyone of any rank, a trait he shared with his friend Major Masterson. Though his manner was relaxed, she didn't have to ask if Justin was successful in his business because confidence was a bone-deep part of him. She'd never met a man like him.

And, of course, he was strikingly attractive. The incredible blue eyes set in his tanned Portuguese face were perceptive, as well as reflecting humor and intelligence. Those eyes made her want to swoon like a schoolgirl.

Proper princesses certainly did not swoon over pretty eyes and a fine pair of shoulders, but she was allowed private appreciation.

The day had started at foggy dawn as she and Justin and Señor da Cunha, the royal wine master, had examined the newly arrived vine cuttings. Nodding approval, the wine master had selected what was needed in the royal vineyards and had sent the cuttings off to be planted under the supervision of his chief overseer.

Then Sofia, Justin, and Señor da Cunha had set out with a short train of mules carrying the remaining cuttings to be distributed as needed. As they rode down the valley, the rising sun burned off the mists, revealing San Gabriel at its loveliest.

Bubbling with delight for the day, Sofia urged her horse into a canter up the hill ahead. At the top, she halted and made a sweeping, theatrical gesture that encompassed the whole valley. "Behold my land!"

Below, the river curved through the valley, and stacked on the steep, sloping hills were the quintas, the ancient vineyards that were the heart and soul of Gabrileño wine country. The owners lived and worked in the centuries-old stone farmsteads above the dramatically stepped terraces.

Justin pulled up beside her, his practiced gaze surveying the terraces and the many gaps in the rows of vines. "Beautiful. Very like the upper Douro Valley." He shook his head. "It was sacrilege for the French to destroy so many vines."

"Very shortsighted for a people who like wine almost as much as Gabrileños do," Señor da Cunha agreed as he joined them. "Yet there have been vines here since before the Romans came. The two or three years until we return to full productivity are the merest blink of time compared to that."

"So I hope," Sofia agreed. "But I am impatient!"

"The young always are," the wine master said indulgently. He glanced back at the lazily-plodding pack mules that carried the baskets of cuttings under the supervision of half a dozen newly arrived Portuguese laborers. "Pack mules are slow and good for developing patience, so I will leave them to you while I ride ahead to Señor Carnota's quinta. He can send his sons to bring men from the neighboring quintas."

"Very good, Señor da Cunha," Sofia said courteously.

As the wine master cantered toward the long, low buildings ahead, Justin said in English, "I expect he really wants to tell them about me, foreign wine shipper that I am, and to assure them that I am not totally ignorant about wine."

Sofia laughed and replied in the same language, "Wise of him to assuage their curiosity before you appear. They are bound to like you, though. You saw how pleased Señor da Cunha was when he chose cuttings for the Alcantara vineyards. He recognizes good stock."

"He knows his business." The road entered the Carnota vineyard and Justin reined in his horse and dismounted. As the pack mules ambled by incuriously, he knelt and took a large pinch of soil and tasted it.

Sofia halted, intrigued by his action. "What does the soil taste like?"

"Hard to describe." He stood and brushed off his hands, then unhooked the canteen from his saddle and rinsed his mouth out. "Sharpish. Very like the soils of the upper Douro Valley, though there's a difference I can't define that makes Gabrileño wines so

233

excellent."

She nodded. " *'Terroir.'* Señor da Cunha says that's the French term for the soil and climate and rain and everything else that makes the wine of a place unique."

"Exactly. The same is true for things like cheese, as well, and meat and fruit and other products of the earth." He gave her a warm, mischievous smile. "Would you like a taste?"

Sofia blinked. But farmers tasted soil with some regularity, and she'd never heard that anyone died of it. "Yes, please." She pulled off one glove.

Justin bent for another pinch and dropped it in the center of her palm. His fingertips brushed her bare skin, and it was like the snap of electricity sometimes felt in winter after walking across a carpet. But . . . nicer. Repressing the thought to consider later, she cautiously touched her tongue to the soil.

"As you say, sharpish," she said thoughtfully. "I've not tasted soil elsewhere, so I've nothing to compare it to, but I shall remember that this is the taste of Douro wine country. The taste of San Gabriel."

"You're a very intrepid princess," he said as he remounted his horse.

She rinsed her mouth with water from her canteen and spat it out. "This is my country,

234

my charge," she said seriously. "It is my duty to know as much about it as I can. And that includes the soil."

As they resumed riding toward the quinta, Justin said, "All great wines reflect their native soils and specific climate. Though San Gabriel is part of the Douro watershed, that doesn't necessarily mean the soil has the same composition. Given the taste of the local wine, I thought the soils must be very similar, and I just confirmed that."

"So all we need do is raise our productivity back to normal and find a way to transport the wine to Porto and beyond." Sofia smiled a little wistfully. "Strange to think that the fruit of our vines might travel to places I'll never see."

Justin gave her a searching glance. "You wish to visit distant countries?"

She nodded. "I never quite believed in foreign lands when I was a child. Then I was sent to Porto to a convent school. The first time I saw the sea . . ." She stopped, not wanting to reveal her useless fascination with ships and the dream of exotic places. "Tell me of your home, Justin. You look very Portuguese, except for the blue eyes. Do all Scots look like you?"

"Most are fair-skinned, but I have a Portuguese grandmother, and I spend much time in the sun," he replied. "Scotland is green and misty and rather magical. Also sometimes cold and wet and dismal!"

"Do you miss your homeland?"

"Yes, but I love Portugal. I also love London, where Ballard Port has a major office and warehouse." He smiled ruefully at her. "I supposed it's better to love several places than none, but I have trouble imagining settling down in one place forever. The shipping trade suits me for that reason."

"I would love to see London. Uncle Alfonso enjoyed his time there and used to tell us stories of it."

"It's a grand place, but the weather is better here," Justin said pragmatically. "You'll see for yourself someday. When the political situation is stable again, you'll be able to visit London. You could stay at Ballard House. My mother and sisters would welcome you."

She sighed and looked across the valley. "If I become queen, which every day seems more likely, traveling so far will not be possible. At least not until I am old and have grown children to succeed me."

"You think your father and brother are not coming back?" Justin asked quietly.

"Hope refuses to die," she said, her voice tight. "But I am not a fool. There has been

236

no word since Baudin carried them off in chains. He might have had them shot and buried them in a shallow grave on the other side of the mountains. Or left their bodies to feed the crows." Her voice caught and she ducked her head to hide the shameful tears.

Justin moved his mount so close to hers that the horses were almost touching, and stretched out his hand to clasp hers. He held it for a long moment before letting go and moving away. "I can only imagine how difficult this last year has been for you. But from what I've seen, you are doing admirably. Your father would be proud if he could see you now."

"I'm trying to become the ruler San Gabriel needs. I don't know what I would have done without Athena." Sofia's mouth twisted. "I rely too much on her. A year ago, the main thought on my frivolous mind was whom I might marry. Athena did her best to teach me more serious subjects, but I didn't take those lessons seriously until Papá and Alexandre were taken. Now I listen when Athena teaches me how to carry the responsibilities of a queen."

He gave her a sidelong glance. "I suppose your father would have arranged a political marriage for you?"

"Since I wasn't the heir, Papá was willing to let me choose my own husband within reasonable limits. I couldn't marry a poor nobody, of course — it would have to be a husband who would bring some benefit to San Gabriel — but I would have had more choices." She made a face. "Now I'll likely have to marry some beastly grand duke with warts and three chins."

Justin laughed. "Surely, there are better grand dukes than that!"

"I hope so!" Turning serious, she said, "How my husband looks is not important. What matters is finding a man who will not try to take over San Gabriel because I am a mere weak woman. I'll marry Grand Duke Toad if he respects the fact I will be queen and this is *my* country. He will be my consort, not the king."

"Such a man will be difficult to find," Justin observed. "Men who are born to power often crave greater power."

"I know." She made an exasperated gesture with one hand. "And I don't even know how to go about looking for a suitable husband! I will discuss it with Colonel da Silva when he returns to San Gabriel. He is an intelligent and worldly man. I'll probably make him my chief minister. He will have some useful thoughts, I'm sure."

"A prosperous foreign merchant who is uninterested in power would be a good choice in some ways," Justin said softly as he glanced at her, his eyes intense. "But, of course, that would be impossible."

Emotion pulsed between them, hot and demanding. *If I were free to choose, I would choose this man and never regret it.* The knowledge was vivid and undeniable. She would think it absurd, except that her mother and father had felt the same certainty when they met.

Perhaps love at first sight was a mark of the passionate Gabrileño temperament, except that Justin was British and she saw the same certainty in his eyes. Maybe that ability to love in an instant came from his Portuguese grandmother.

But her mother had been the well-dowered daughter of a Spanish nobleman, a good match in terms of worldly rank and wealth. Sofia was a royal princess with the weight of her small kingdom on her shoulders, while Justin was a foreign merchant. Though she was popular, most Gabrileños would be horrified by such a match. It would damage the country, and that she could not allow.

Trying to keep her tone light, she said, "Quite impossible, alas. I shall be required to wed one of the Archduke Toads of the world."

"There are sometimes royal love matches. I hope you have one," he said, his eyes filled with regret and acceptance. Turning back to the quinta, he remarked, "It appears that Señor Carnota has done a good job of rounding up neighbors."

"That will save us some time," Sofia said, hoping she sounded normal. Today's oblique conversation was as close as she and Justin could come to discussing the impossibility of becoming more to each other. Her duty must come before personal happiness, and that reality hurt her heart.

Yet there was some comfort in knowing that he also cared for her. That comfort would have to be enough.

CHAPTER 20

A week of riding across San Gabriel, distributing food and assessing needs, had restored Athena's control. She wished she hadn't broken down and told Will about Lady Whore, one of the worst nightmares in her private chamber of horrors, but she trusted him not to reveal it to anyone else.

Though he'd reflexively claimed that illegitimacy and her mother's reputation didn't matter to him, he'd clearly been shocked by the picture she'd painted of social ostracism for him and any children they might have together. He was too much a gentleman to withdraw his offer, but by now he must be feeling relief.

A week of observing the problems of others had put the situation in perspective for Athena. She'd visited homes that had lost sons and husbands to the war, and hovels where the inhabitants were near starvation, but always she had been greeted with warmth and welcome. Her bruised heart was a mere bagatelle by comparison.

After visiting virtually every hamlet and farmstead in San Gabriel, she turned her small party and unburdened pack mules and headed back to the castle. She now felt capable of treating Will Masterson as a friend and no more.

With luck, he'd soon be heading for home and she'd never have to see him again.

As Will and Tom Murphy surveyed the churning waters of the San Gabriel River, the batman asked, "How old do you think this bridge is, sir? Might the Romans have built it?"

"I suspect that the bridge would still be standing if it was Roman work. My guess is that it's three or four centuries old." He glanced at the younger man. "You've worked on your share of bridges. Which were the worst?"

"The ones where the French were shooting at us as we splashed around in the mud!" Murphy said feelingly.

Will grinned. "Hard to argue with that. As bridge-building projects go, will this one be difficult or easy?"

Tom's eyes narrowed as he studied the banks and the flow of water. "It should be easier than most," he said cautiously. "The stone piers on both banks are intact, and now that the spring snowmelt has gone down, another stone pier in the middle of the river is visible and that will give good support for the center section of the bridge."

"The middle pier will make the job enormously easier," Will agreed as he calculated lengths and designs. "The beams we pulled out of the royal barn are sturdy and long, close to sixty feet each. Half of them can be used to stretch from this bank to the middle, and the other half will reach from the middle to the far bank. How should we go about this?"

"Use the barn beams to make two sixty-foot-long pontoons," the batman said promptly. "Luckily, we also salvaged plenty of planking from the barn and it should be enough to make the pontoons really solid."

"Which is important for a bridge that needs to last indefinitely, not just months. How should we get the pontoons in place?"

"To begin with, someone will need to swim out to the middle pier and pull over some heavy cable to connect the bank to the pier."

"Are you volunteering to do that, Sergeant?"

"No, sir, you're a much stronger swimmer!" Tom retorted. "Once there are cables in place between all three piers, the first pontoon should be slid in the water upstream and floated down, then raised to rest on the center and east-bank piers. Once that pontoon is secure and planked over, we can carry the second pontoon to the middle, then haul it over to bridge to the west bank. Will that work?"

Will nodded approval. "Very good. Do you think railings should be installed on the sides?"

"With people and carts and livestock crossing, definitely some sort of railing to keep them from falling off," Tom said. "Sheep aren't very clever. Be a pity to lose them to the river."

"Do we have enough wood for railings?"

"Not just now, but we could put uprights every couple of yards across both sides of the bridge and string rope between them from one end of the bridge to the other," Tom said thoughtfully. "Two levels of rope at least. Three if there's enough strong rope. Not as good as a solid railing, but it could be put in place quickly."

"That will work," Will agreed. "How long do you think it will take us to rebuild this bridge?"

"Sir, are you giving me an examination?"

Tom asked suspiciously.

Will chuckled. "Of sorts. If you decide to stay in San Gabriel, it will be useful to have a skill, and I think that a good builder could be well employed here."

"Would I be able to stay here without being considered a deserter, sir?" the younger man asked, surprised. "I enlisted for twenty-one years so I'd get a pension if I lived long enough, which I didn't expect to do."

"With the war over, I can make it right for you to return to civilian life, though you won't get any pension." Will thought about that "privilege" Justin had explained to him. Yes, Major Lord Masterson could make it easy for a young soldier to stay in San Gabriel if he wished. "No reason for you to travel all the way back to Britain, unless you wish to return to Ireland?"

Tom sighed and his accent became more Irish. "It would be a fine thing to see the green fields of Ireland again and no mistake, but there's not much for me there. My mum is dead, my father has probably drunk himself to death by now, my brothers and sisters don't know how to read and write, so I've not heard from any of them in years. I don't know what I'd do with myself there."

"While San Gabriel has Maria Cristina."

Tom blushed. "It does indeed, sir."

"She seems like a lovely young woman," Will said encouragingly.

"That she is, sir. You might not know this, but the French killed one of her younger brothers when they invaded. Señora Oliviera has been hinting that another son would be welcome. Señor Oliviera seems to like me, but he'll not let Cristina marry a man who can't support her properly."

"Do you find all this approval wonderful or alarming?"

The batman grinned. "Mostly wonderful, sir. They're a fine family and they've been very kind to me, at least after they found out I was Catholic. But if Cristina and I marry, I'd like us to have a house of our own."

"That would be wise," Will agreed. "Coming from two different countries, you'll need time to adjust to each other's ways and that will be easier without in-laws staring over your shoulder and taking sides when you disagree. Noisily."

Tom made a face. "I've thought of that, but I haven't the blunt to buy a house."

"If you decide to stay and settle down, you'll be due a wedding gift after all you've done for me. A house sounds about right."

Tom turned and stared at him. "You'd do that for me?"

Will nodded, wondering if wealth and privilege were the same thing. To some extent they were. He could buy a fine house for Murphy and his bride and not even notice the cost. "You don't have to decide this minute, but think about it."

Tom's gaze swept the valley in a new way. "I won't talk to Cristina just yet. I need to consider a little more to be sure. But this is a happy country despite what they've endured." After a pause, he added softly, "It's easy to imagine living a long and rewarding life here with Cristina."

Someone might as well be happy, Will thought wryly. "You can think about it while we rebuild the bridge. Then on to the wine caves!"

"There will be a festival then and no mistake!" Tom said exuberantly.

Anything that kept Will busy was welcome. How long could her mission keep Athena away from the castle?

Too bloody long.

"I wonder where everyone is," Maria Mercedes da Silva said as they rode through town on the way to the da Silva home. A bright-eyed, energetic young woman, she was Princess Sofia's best friend and had been looking forward to a good gossip at the end of their weeklong sojourn. "Do you suppose my father and the others have returned and there is a festival?"

"Not yet," Athena said, sorry to quash Mercedes' hopefulness. Besides missing her father and brother, she and one of her father's young lieutenants were sweethearts and the girl was almost jumping out of her skin with eagerness. "We'd certainly have seen signs of a large group of men coming down the road from Spain. But perhaps there is a different festival going on."

"Maybe the bridge has been rebuilt!" Mercedes guessed. "That would be worth a celebration." Seeing the elderly gatekeeper at the da Silva entrance, she called, "Diego, where is everyone?"

"The wine caves are about to be opened!" he called back, his weathered face wreathed in smiles. "The bridge is finished and very fine it is. So the British major put the men to digging their way into the caves. They will break through at any moment and all Gabrileños are waiting to celebrate!" He sighed with elaborate regret. "All but poor Diego."

Laughing, Mercedes said, "Alas, poor Diego! I shall see that one of the servants who is at the caves will return to relieve you before the fiesta ends so you can join the celebration."

He sighed again, even more loudly. "That will have to do, Señorita Mercedes. You are kind to a useless old man."

"You are a master at sounding ill-used, Diego! But that won't work with me. We are off to the wine caves!"

And Will Masterson would be right in the middle of things. The prospect made Athena wonder just how good her control would be when they met face-to-face; there would be no way to avoid him entirely. "I'll take the pack mules up to the castle, and the rest of you can go to the caves."

"Nonsense!" Maria exclaimed. "You and Sofia closed the caves to keep our wine safe from those wicked Frenchmen, and it is only right that you be there when they're opened again."

Athena turned to the royal servants, who rode behind and managed the now-unburdened pack mules. "Does anyone want to return to the castle now?"

A chorus of "No's!" rang out. Everyone was in the mood for a fiesta.

"The mules can be left here for now," Mercedes said. "Our splendid Diego will take them to the stables and see they have hay and water."

The gatekeeper raised his face to heaven

and muttered a prayer or curse. Athena knew that this was an old game for Diego and members of the da Silva family, so she resigned herself to the inevitable. Collecting her reins, she said, "Then onward we go!"

If she couldn't avoid seeing Will, she hoped he'd be looking magnificent in his uniform. That would be compensation for her nervousness.

By the time they reached the wine caves, her nerves were under control again. Part of the population of this end of the valley had gathered and already had begun celebrating. Food and drink were laid out on improvised tables; children ran shrieking; dancers twirled to the sound of buoyant music; a tantalizing scent of roasting meat filled the air.

"A pig roast!" Mercedes exclaimed rapturously. "No fiesta has been so fine since the coming of the French."

It was a mark of how much Gabrileños cared about their wine that a precious pig had been slaughtered for the celebration. With so many people present, no one would get more than a small piece, but the pork was a symbol of better times to come. And it smelled *delicious*.

The great mound of fallen earth and stone that covered the original entrances was now pierced by a surprisingly large dark rectangle with a wisp of dust puffing out. No sign of Will. She should have realized that he'd be digging away in the shaft rather than supervising from a lordly distance.

Sofia and Justin Ballard were near the entrance. Seeing Athena, Sofia waved madly to summon her to the excavation. One of the royal servants said, "Go to the princess, Lady Athena. I shall care for your horse."

Athena thanked him and dismounted to make her way through the crowd. When she reached the small, cleared area around the entrance, Sofia greeted her with a hug. "So much has been done in the last week, Athena! The bridge and now this!"

She gestured at the mouth of the shaft. The entrance was framed with crooked but sturdy timbers, and a strange contraption stuck out of the opening. Puzzled, Athena studied the wheels, the broad leather band, and the workman who was turning a massive crank that caused the band to move outward from the shaft. "What on earth is that?"

"Will calls it an 'earth conveyor,' " Justin explained. "He saw something like it in a Yorkshire mine. He cobbled this one together with old wheels and tanned cowhides so the dirt could be removed more quickly."

Sure enough, two buckets filled with dirt approached the end of the conveyor. The man turning the crank stopped and removed the buckets and passed them to another worker, who carried them away to a pile well clear of the mining operation. The empty buckets were stacked and carried back into the shaft.

"Ingenious!" she said. "Have they reached the door into the first cave?"

"Yes. I wanted to see, but Will wouldn't let us in," Sofia said. "He said he didn't want us to be squashed if there is a problem."

"But it's all right if he's squashed?" Athena asked skeptically.

"There's not much risk," Justin assured her. "Will is just being careful with the safety of Her Royal Highness."

He and Sofia shared a glance rife with intimacy. Athena's heart contracted. There wasn't a hint of anything improper, but she could see that their closeness had grown while she was away. So much tender emotion, and no legitimate way to express it.

Despite the noise of the feasting Gabrileños, she could hear clinking sounds from inside the shaft. She contemplated the entrance, her curiosity alive. She'd never regretted starting the landslide that kept the wine treasury of San Gabriel away from the French, but she'd prayed that those casks and barrels could be salvaged.

There was only one way to learn how the project was going. "I'm not royal," she said, and marched into the shaft.

Athena had to duck her head a little, but not as much as she'd expected. The shaft needed to be large to allow the largest casks to be removed. The earth conveyor ran along the wall on her right, and every dozen or so feet, a lantern hung from one of the beams shoring up the roof.

The conveyor ended at what she guessed was the midpoint of the tunnel. A short, sturdy fellow walked toward her, a bucket of earth in each hand. He grinned cheerfully, his teeth white in a dirty face. She didn't recognize him, so he was probably one of the workmen from Porto.

She heard a voice speaking Portuguese and glanced back to see that Justin Ballard had followed, and he'd greeted the workman. He smiled at her. "I'm not royal, either, and I'm irresistibly curious to see whether the wine has survived."

"I'm sorry you aren't royal," she said obliquely.

He grimaced. "So am I. But I can't regret coming to San Gabriel."

A philosophical man. That was a useful trait in his situation. She'd been more philosophical once, but Will was playing Hades with her detachment.

The end of the shaft was now visible and Athena saw in the dim light that Will and Señor da Cunha, the royal wine master, were using trowels to scrape away earth around the massive wooden door. Will had spared his scarlet coat and was in his shirtsleeves, the white linen smeared with dirt. She smiled ruefully. He looked magnificent anyhow.

"You found the entrance!" Justin exclaimed.

"Thanks to Señor da Cunha." Will gave a barely perceptible flinch before he veiled his reaction to seeing her. "You two really shouldn't be here."

"We couldn't resist," Justin said cheerfully. "Besides, I have great faith in your mining abilities."

Will shrugged. "Of which I have few, but this was a relatively easy job, being on a level site and through fallen earth rather than tunneling through rock. We were able to follow the line of the road straight in. Simple."

"Will it be difficult to extend the tunnel to the second cave?" Justin asked.

"The caves are connected inside," Señor

da Cunha said. "God willing, we'll be able to enter the second cave without more digging."

Athena crossed her fingers. "I hope the landslide didn't cause damage inside."

"I hope so also," Señor da Cunha said. "But you and our princess did what was needful. Better to lose all our wine than to let the French have it!" He spat after saying "French."

Will finished revealing the seams around the door, cleared the keyhole with a thin metal rod, then stepped back. With a grand flourish of his left hand, he said, "Señor, the honors are yours!"

Chapter 21

Sofia managed to control her curiosity about the excavation until Justin followed Athena into the shaft. Exasperated, she slipped in after him. A sizable amount of the stored wine was hers, or at least her family's, which surely gave her license to view the proceedings.

The clinking of the tools at the tunnel end covered her quiet footsteps. She passed a workman who recognized her and made an awkward attempt to bow. She waved that off and touched a finger to her lips in a request for silence. He bobbed his head in understanding and continued on with his buckets of earth.

She came up behind Athena and Justin just as Will Masterson finished clearing the door and yielded to Señor da Cunha. Being small, she could easily lurk unseen. Her wine master ceremoniously produced a massive iron key and inserted it into the lock.

As he worked to open the lock, Will ordered, "You two retreat at least a dozen feet. This isn't a mine, so probably there won't be explosive gasses, but there's no telling what your landslide might have stirred up."

His warning sent Athena, Justin, and Sofia a dozen feet back. The wine master jiggled the key until he was able to turn it. When that was done, Will locked both hands on the wrought-iron handle and pulled hard. The door opened with a grinding squeal.

A blast of heavy, wine-scented air poured into the tunnel. The smell was so intense that Athena sneezed and Sofia almost coughed.

"The angel's share!" Justin exclaimed fondly. "The intoxicating aroma of a wine warehouse. Amazing how much evaporated alcohol can accumulate when a cave has been shut for the better part of a year."

Sofia had always loved the term "angel's share" for the alcohol that evaporated from storage casks while wine was aging, so it seemed a good time to announce her presence with applause. When Athena and Justin turned, surprised, Sofia said brightly, "I couldn't resist watching, either. After all, much of the wine belongs to House Alcantara."

The wine master, who had taught Sofia almost everything she knew about wine, clucked with indulgent disapproval. Handing her one of the lanterns, he said, "You may have the honor of being the first in, your highness."

Sofia took the lantern in one hand and used the other to clasp Athena's hand. "Come, my friend, we shall see what we wrought that dangerous day."

"Not much damage, I hope!" Athena said fervently.

Side by side, they stepped through the broad doorway into the wine cave. From the intensity of the scents, Sofia had feared seeing broken casks, but everything looked miraculously intact. Here and there, small piles of dirt showed where earth had been shaken loose from the roof by the landslide, but all the casks were far enough from the door to have avoided damage.

She lifted the lantern above her head and the light revealed racks and racks of casks disappearing into the darkness. Each cask was marked with the name of the quinta that produced it. A third or so were stamped with the royal Alcantara arms.

"All is well!" she called to the men behind

her. "The cave looks just as it did before the coming of the French."

Awed, Justin entered the cave and asked, "How much wine is stored here?"

"A great deal," Señor da Cunha said. "We'd had several excellent harvests, so more wine was produced than San Gabriel could drink. Behind this chamber are several more storage chambers, and the new cave is larger than this one."

"Which is a very great amount of wine indeed," Sofia remarked. Enough to help San Gabriel financially if she could get it to market.

"About half is regular wine, and about half has been fortified by ardent spirits for a longer, more potent life." The wine master raised his key ring and selected a different heavy key. "Now to see if the newer vault survived equally well."

He walked halfway down the chamber before halting at a massive door set between two racks of casks. This lock turned more easily. He swung the door open and stepped back as another wave of intense aromas was released. When the scents were mostly dissipated, Señor da Cunha raised a lantern and stepped inside with everyone else close behind him.

" 'Tis a miracle," the old wine master

whispered as the lantern revealed peacefully-resting casks. A glint of tears showed in his eyes. "A miracle of Saint Deolinda."

As they returned to the first cave, Justin asked Sofia, "Saint Deolinda?"

"A local legend. I'll tell you about her later. For now, would you like to taste some of the wine? That's the true test of how well it has survived."

"An excellent idea," Señor da Cunha said. "I'll draw samples for us."

A table near the entrance had a dozen small tasting glasses turned upside down. A couple had been shaken off the table and broke, but the rest were intact. The wine master pulled a clean handkerchief from his pocket and wiped them all clean in case there was dust, then studied the casks. Making a decision, he carried a stack of five little glasses to a large cask marked with the Alcantara arms.

"If you will forgive me, your highness." He drew a small amount of wine from the chosen cask and tasted it himself instead of offering it to Sofia. It would not be good to offer a visiting wine merchant a wine that had gone off.

After the first cautious sip, Señor da Cunha gave a gusty sigh of pleasure. He drew another sample. "Your highness, I believe this is suitable for royalty."

She tasted and gave a nod of approval. "Very fine and smooth. It has aged well here free of disturbances. Justin?" She offered him her own glass, liking the small, private intimacy.

He accepted with a smile, his fingertips brushing hers as she handed him her glass. She cherished even these small touches, and tried not to think what it would be like to kiss him when she watched him taste the port. He had a beautiful mouth, mobile and sensuous.

First he sipped; then he finished the glass with pleasure. "Truly a fine port. We need to find a way to get some down to Porto."

Both Athena and Will were tasting the wine, concentrating on their glasses and keeping a careful distance apart. They were not looking at each other with an intensity that was palpable.

It was maddening to watch. Sofia knew they cared for each other and there was no obvious reason why they couldn't be together. There must be unobvious reasons, since Athena was not a fool. She spoke little about her past, but it was obvious that her illegitimacy and unusual upbringing had left their mark.

Athena deserved a splendid fellow like Will. Instead she'd bolted when she'd learned that he was Lord Masterson.

They needed to be thrown together, and a way to do that occurred to Sofia. "This is the last of the engineering projects you proposed, Lord Masterson, but before you return to England, I hope you'll consider one more."

Will gave a swift, almost imperceptible glance at Athena. "It would be my pleasure, Sofia. I'm in no great rush to leave San Gabriel."

"I propose that we ride down the San Gabriel River to survey its course and see if the channel can be improved enough for shipping," Sofia said. "You and Justin and Athena and I can camp along the river while we consider what might be feasible."

Athena looked appalled. "I'm not needed on such an expedition! I know nothing of engineering."

"But I need you as a chaperone," Sofia pointed out.

"There are other possible chaperones," Athena said tartly. "Or Major Masterson and Mr. Ballard could go on their own. They would surely be faster and more efficient without us slowing them down."

It was time to bring out the heavy guns.

Sofia said softly, "Wouldn't it be a pleasure to ride out into the mountains? The last time we did such a thing was the day the French came. Ever since, we've been too busy. Too tired. Too worried. Now that the country's affairs are in better case, we deserve a bit of a holiday."

"A low blow, little sister!" Athena smiled ruefully. "But you're right. After a hard year, finally San Gabriel's future is looking brighter. I always enjoyed our long rides. I supposed it's time for another. It will be . . . interesting." Her gaze flicked to Will, then away.

"Thank you for agreeing! It will be lovely to be away from the palace and the need to act as a princess at all times." Sofia gave Athena a swift hug, then continued, "Now we will choose two small casks of Alcantara wine for the fiesta, one red and one white. None of the fortified wine, because we don't want anyone to celebrate too much!"

Laughing, she led the way outside to the fiesta. Life was good, and surely she and Justin would dance before the day was done.

While Athena had never regretted burying the cave entrances, she was greatly relieved to know that the wines, the treasure of San Gabriel, had survived intact. That was good

263

for Gabrileño morale, and perhaps also for the badly strained exchequer.

The fiesta kept expanding as people heard the good news and came from farther away. More casks of wine were produced, dance music began to play, and soon everyone was feeling merry.

As a lady of mature years, Athena was watching the dancing from the sidelines when Will's batman, Tom Murphy, approached her with a devastating Irish grin. "Dance with me, Lady Athena?"

She laughed. "But there are so many beautiful young Gabrileñas who would love to dance with a handsome soldier!"

"But you're a proper height," he explained as he took her hand and led her into a lively Gabrileño country dance. "And Señora Oliviera won't let me partner Maria Cristina for every dance."

"There is that, and you don't want to raise the hopes of other girls, since Cristina might be *The One.*"

Murphy's fair Irish skin turned rosy under his tan. "I think she is, Lady Athena. Being a soldier makes a man cautious, so I'll think for another day or so, but . . ." His gaze went to Cristina, who was dancing with her father. She glanced up as if she felt Tom's regard, and they smiled dotingly at each other. He exhaled in a happy sigh, saying, "Cristina makes me feel wonderful. If we decide to marry, the major has said he'll buy us a house as a wedding gift!"

The blasted major is painfully decent, Athena thought with exasperation. But he was generous to give a young couple a good start in life. Many lords would never think to do such a thing, she suspected. It would be a good match, too. Cristina was as intelligent as she was beautiful, and she had imagination, a good trait if a girl was going to marry an Irishman.

Putting thoughts of Will out of her mind, Athena relaxed into the dancing. Murphy was indeed a convenient height, almost as tall as Will, though not as broad, and he liked dancing as much as she did.

The dance involved multiple couples spinning around and sometimes changing partners, so she shouldn't have been surprised when she turned to clasp hands with her next partner and found herself face-to-face with Will.

He smiled and took her hands and led them into a spin. A jolt of reaction moved through her as their bare hands linked warmly. Her pleasure was immediately followed by the recognition that he was *Lord* Masterson.

Feeling her stiffen, Will said in a quiet voice under the music, "You decided we could still be friends, and friends dance together, don't they?"

Unable to resist his smile, she said ruefully, "Yes, but it's surely a mistake to enjoy it too much!"

His smile widened. "I'll be around a few more weeks. We're living under the same roof, and your minx of a princess has organized a camping trip, so won't it be better if we're relaxed with each other? I won't do anything you don't wish."

Better to be relaxed, but not easier. Yet, now that she'd recovered from the shock of knowing marriage would never be possible, she realized that she wanted to savor his friendship for what time they had left. She smiled up at him. "Very well, we can be dancing friends."

"And camping comrades. Excellent." His gaze intensified. "I recognize that you won't have me, but I would . . . deeply regret if we couldn't be dancing friends."

"As would I," she whispered, and then it was time to change partners again. Dancing friends. A new category, and one that she liked.

CHAPTER 22

Though Athena knew this river expedition would have awkward moments with Will, she felt bubbling anticipation as the four of them assembled in the castle courtyard. Sofia grinned mischievously at her, then allowed Justin to help her into her saddle. She and Athena both wore their practical split skirts so they could ride comfortably astride, and their saddlebags contained whatever else they'd need for a trip of two or three days.

Athena checked the condition of her carbine, then slid it into the holster on her saddle. Will was tightening the girth of his saddle, but he glanced up and said, "I've been wondering what happened to the rifle you had in Porto."

"The French officer who escorted us to safety in the church looked at the rifle, looked at my nun's habit, then took the rifle, no questions asked. Since it was a

French weapon, I didn't argue." She grinned. "Besides, I was out of ammunition."

"A rifle without ammunition is no more than a club. Though sometimes a club is very useful." Will holstered his own very business-like carbine. "Would you be mortally offended if I offered to help you mount?"

"No, but it's really not necessary." She swung into her saddle. "Being unnaturally tall has its advantages."

"There is nothing unnatural about being tall!" Will also mounted his horse. "The effect can be quite magnificent."

She arched her brows. "I believe that falls in the forbidden category of flirting."

"Never!" he said piously as he set his mount into motion. "It's pure truth."

Athena laughed, in charity with the world. She had sunshine, warmth, the best of companions, and she was taking a holiday from her usual responsibilities. Sofia was right: They both needed this period of relaxation. And while traveling with the men they wanted but couldn't have might be stressful, it would also be a joy.

As they rode down into the valley, Will asked Sofia, "Which side of the river will we follow?"

"The south side, along the Porto road. It's close to the river for much of the way," Sofia replied. "Justin, did you study the condition of the river as you rode up here?"

"Yes, Will had told me to pay attention, but the road swung away during the steepest part of the climb up the mountains," Justin said. "I expect those are the parts of the river that make it impossible to take a boat down to the Douro."

"Yes, there's a narrow gorge with dangerous rapids and a major cataract," Sofia said. "I've only seen that waterfall from a distance, but it's a formidable obstacle."

"I haven't ridden that far lately," Athena said, waving back at several children beside the road who were waving enthusiastically. "If I recall correctly, there's a rough track that follows the river when the main road swings away. Is it close enough to get a clear view into the gorge?"

"I think so," Sofia replied. "We'll see!"

"I'm dead keen on blowing a few things up," Will said helpfully. "I had Justin bring in black powder especially, and I haven't had a chance to use it yet."

The others laughed. "You may get your explosive wish," Athena said. "I apologize for depriving you of the chance to wreck the wine caves."

"That would have been a crime against humanity!" Justin declared, laying a dramatic hand over his heart. "Good wine should be cherished, not blown up!"

"Bad enough to just shake it," Sofia said loftily. "It takes days for the sediment to settle again."

"And that is bad," Justin said gravely. "I try to avoid upsetting my wine."

"One doesn't want angry wine," Sofia agreed before breaking into infectious giggles. She needed this holiday from responsibility as much as Athena did.

The four of them continued their bantering as they reached the river and headed west toward Portugal. Turning serious, Justin said, "The river is swift and could be dangerous here. How much is the flow reduced during the dry months?"

"There's always enough water for small boats to travel through the valley," Sofia replied. "Even in high summer, it's risky to ford the river in the central valley, which is why rebuilding the bridge was so important."

They traveled at a steady pace, with Will taking notes about the more difficult areas of the river. By early afternoon, they moved beyond the cultivated areas of the valley and into pasturelands, where occasional groups of sheep or goats grazed placidly under the relaxed eyes of young herders.

The river became narrower and rougher, but when they stopped for a companionable lunch of bread and cheese and wine, Justin said, "The rapids are challenging, but so far, the river is no worse than some of the upper reaches of the Douro. The riverboat men who sail the *'rabelos,'* the wine boats, are very skilled at steering through rough waters."

"Some of the boulders could be shifted to make a smoother channel," Will said thoughtfully.

Athena laughed. "Anything to use your black powder!"

"Very true. Though it won't be worth doing unless the lower reaches of the river can be improved sufficiently." He finished jotting notes about what he saw in the river, the food and wine was packed away, and they continued on their way.

Soon the main road swung away and they continued on the narrow track that followed the riverbank. The track grew rougher and steeper and the increasing number of tumbled boulders gave the landscape an eerie, unnatural look. But the mountain-bred Gabrileño horses were sure-footed and no sections of the track were impassable.

The track leveled off and to their right the river cut deeper into the mountainside, creating the gorge Sofia had told them about. As the track started to descend, the rim of the gorge was no longer visible because mounds of boulders blocked the view.

The thunder of falling water intensified as they continued. Will pulled his horse in and studied the mounded boulders and loose stones. "From the sounds of the water, we must be right opposite the cataract. I could climb to the top and look down into the gorge."

With visions of the scree shifting under his weight and pitching him into the gorge, Athena suggested, "Why don't we continue along the track? We might find a place with a clear view."

"Athena is right," Sofia said. "My brother told me there is a place where one can look down on the cataract. He . . . he promised to take me there one day." She swallowed hard as she thought of that unfulfilled promise.

After a last longing look at the piled stones, Will said, "In that case we should continue on. If we can't find such a spot, I can always come back here."

"If that's necessary, I'll do the climbing,"

Justin said. "I weigh several stone less than you and I'm less likely to create a rock slide."

They continued along the track, which wound between more boulders and occasional tough, piney trees. Then the track swung around a particularly massive boulder into a small, grassy clearing — and there was the cataract.

Athena caught her breath at the high, powerful waterfall. Even this far above, particles of cool water brushed her face. She was equally enchanted by the beauty of the plunging waters and dismayed at how very *not* navigable the river was. "You'll not be getting any *rabelos* over that!"

Justin studied the gorge and the height of the cataract. "This is like a smaller version of the Valeira Gorge. That was cleared, but it was a very expensive proposition and it took years."

Sofia bit her lip. "There isn't enough money in San Gabriel to undertake such a vast project."

"It would be far too expensive to put in a system of locks, but I think it's possible to build a portage trail around the falls," Will suggested. "If the *rabelos* can transport casks from San Gabriel to a station above the falls, mules and men could carry the wine to different *rabelos* on the river below."

"That might work," Justin said, intrigued. "If the river below is navigable until it flows into the Douro, the only really impossible area is the gorge and cataract. We'll have to survey the lower river, but carrying the wine around the falls could be a simple, practical solution that will make it possible to get the Gabrileño wines to market."

"Won't a portage raise the costs significantly?" Athena asked.

"Yes, but I think the quality of Gabrileño wine will persuade people to pay more," Justin said. "There are a goodly number of English aristocrats who pride themselves on how expensive their wine is, as long as the wine is good enough to justify the cost."

"I like the idea of creating jobs for Gabrileños," Sofia said thoughtfully. "Many of the men who will be returning from war will want work beyond cultivating fields and vineyards. But boats and mules and men must be paid for before we can earn any money from our wines."

"Might it be possible to raise foreign funds to invest in this?" Athena asked. "Form the Alcantara Wine Company. Will and Justin must know Englishmen who would consider investing in it."

"I know men who might be interested,"

274

Will agreed. "Justin?"

"Once I transport samples down the mountain so San Gabriel wines can be tasted, I know I'll find investors," Justin said. "I'll put in money myself. I think it will be a decent investment."

Sofia gave Justin a dazzling smile. The connection between the two was so strong, Athena could feel it. It hurt to know that her little sister of the heart had found love with a man worthy of her, yet they could never marry.

Might San Gabriel accept a royal consort who was a Protestant Scottish merchant? Impossible to imagine. Sofia needed a husband with wealth and rank and influence beyond anything Justin had. Her marriage prospects had been a subject of Gabrileño speculation for years.

Her thoughts were interrupted by Will saying, "I think it's time to set up camp for the night. This is a decent location. There's good grazing grass, a spring for watering horses and people, and boulders to protect us from the wind. There are also enough trees scattered among the boulders that firewood shouldn't be a problem."

"I'm ready to call it a day," Sofia said. "I haven't spent this long in the saddle for months."

"But you ladies haven't slowed us down at all," Justin said as he dismounted and helped Sofia from her horse. "You're both bruising riders."

"Today, more bruised than bruising," Sofia said teasingly as she came down into his arms.

Athena swung from her horse. "I haven't camped on the trail like this since we traveled up from Porto five years ago. It will feel odd sleeping under the stars again."

"At least it doesn't look like rain!" Sofia removed her hat and brushed back the dark tendrils that had escaped from her neatly bound hair. "Remember how wet the journey from Porto was? We looked like drowned rabbits by the time we arrived home. I never wanted to see another tent in my life!"

"Neither did I," Athena said fervently as she removed saddlebags and saddle. "Yet here I am, camping again and without even a tent!"

Will dismounted and began tending his horse with the ease of long practice. "Where did the two of you stay when you hid in the hills from Baudin?"

"A high-country cave," Athena said. "We had a good view of the valley, and there was a spring inside, so we had water."

"We shared the cave with our horses so

we wouldn't be seen," Sofia added. "Have you ever slept with horses in tight quarters?"

"Actually, I have," Will admitted. "It's not my favorite situation. But worse for you because of the suddenness of the invasion."

Athena tried not to remember the helplessness, confusion, and sheer terror they'd felt in those days. They'd been on the verge of riding over the mountains into Spain when the French had moved out, traveling on the main eastbound road. "We spent much of our time talking about what, if anything, we could do. Without success."

Expression compassionate, Justin asked, "Did you consider riding off for help?"

"Where would we go? And who would help us?" Sofia replied starkly. "San Gabriel is so isolated. It's a long ride to the nearest towns, and anyone we found would surely have been worrying about their own survival. After Baudin and his brutes left to rejoin the main French Army, I fell on my knees and gave thanks to the Blessed Mother for their departure."

"We were worried they might stay," Athena said in a low voice. "A pleasant valley with a strong castle and good wine. A soldier's paradise."

"Luckily, the French Army's loyalty to Napoleon is strong," Will said gravely. "If they'd dug in here, they would have been very hard to dislodge."

They shared a glance, and she knew that he was thinking of their early discussion about the possibility of a well-organized guerilla band deciding to move in. She had been having nightmares about such an invasion.

They had done all they could to prepare for an attack and the Gabrileño army would be home soon, so she told herself to stop worrying. Worry wouldn't help and it shouldn't be allowed to interfere with this brief holiday. "When the horses are taken care of, will someone gather firewood? I'll start on our dinner."

"What's on the menu?" Will asked with interest.

"Wait and see," Athena said as she untied one of her saddlebags. "But wine will be served with our meal."

"Now you've spoiled the surprise!" Sofia said with mock dismay. As the others laughed, she continued, "I'll gather firewood. Justin, will you help me?"

"It will be my great pleasure, your royal highness." Justin pulled a small hand axe from his saddlebag in preparation. "You locate, I'll chop."

"I shall make you carry the wood. You are

warned!" Sofia said as she marched off between a pair of tall boulders.

The muted roar of the nearby waterfall covered Athena's voice as she watched Sofia and Justin disappear into the maze of boulders. "I'm not being a very good chaperone."

"Neither will cross the line," Will said quietly. "But they deserve some time alone."

"That was my thought," Athena said, remembering the sweetness of first love. Sofia deserved that even if she and Justin didn't have a future. "If we're lucky, they may even remember to bring back some firewood."

Will grinned. "There's some kindling over by that boulder. I'll get a small fire started. Maybe we can have some good English tea before dinner and wine?"

"You're a mind reader," she replied. "Or perhaps just English. There is indeed tea."

As she pulled food and cooking utensils from her saddlebags, a chuckling Will moved across the clearing to collect the kindling. Her gaze followed him. She loved watching him move. He was all smooth, efficient power, both purposeful and relaxed. And she would never, ever tire of admiring those broad shoulders.

She gave a small, private smile as she

pulled out the packet of tea leaves. Even if they didn't speak or touch, it was satisfying to breathe the same air.

CHAPTER 23

Sofia. Justin's fond gaze rested on her elegantly curved form as she led the way through the maze of boulders. He'd wondered how a princess would deal with trail conditions, but Sofia was obviously having a wonderful time. Not only was she a splendid rider, but she demanded no special treatment. That was rare in well-bred young ladies, much less princesses. Though admittedly, he hadn't met any other princesses.

He was glad to see that the stiffness that had been between Will and Athena was gone. There was a different kind of tension that both kept firmly tamped down. He saw no sign that Athena Markham was inclined to accept Will, which was regrettable, but he did understand her reservations about an unequal marriage that would take her into the heart of the British aristocracy.

His own family was regarded as vulgar nouveau riche in some circles. They laughed about it among themselves. The Ballards had worked hard, with energy and intelligence, and they had a fortune to rival that of most aristocrats, but they took pride in being hardheaded Scottish merchants. They could afford to laugh at aristocratic arrogance because they had success and, even more important, loving family bonds.

Athena Markham had none of that, and he suspected she carried more than her share of hidden scars. If he could wave a magic wand to heal those scars and bring her and Will together, he'd do it in a heartbeat, because they seemed so well suited.

He smiled wryly. At least he and Will would be able to commiserate with each other about the loss of the women they loved. Because Justin did love Sofia, and knew he always would. Neither of them had said a word or made an improper touch, yet when she was near, he felt . . . happy. More whole.

"That dead tree can supply all the wood we need." Sofia pointed at the gray skeleton of one of the scrubby trees that grew among the boulders. "I trust your axe is sharp?"

"Like me, the axe is ready to serve." With a couple of swift chops, Justin severed a branch. "Nicely seasoned, too. Not many people come this way looking for firewood."

Sofia gathered fallen branches as Justin chopped more from the tree, then cut them to manageable lengths. When they had a good-sized pile, he straightened and brushed bits of wood from his hands and clothing. "That's enough wood to last all night. I'll have to make two or three trips to get it all back to our campsite."

"I'll help." Sofia stared at him, her dark eyes huge and shy. "Justin?"

"Yes, my princess?" he asked, puzzled.

"Will you kiss me?"

He felt as if she'd clubbed him with a heavy branch. After swallowing hard, he said, "There is nothing I would like better, but is this wise?"

"No. But it is necessary." Sofia bit her lip before continuing to speak. "If I was not who and what I am, our situation would be very different. But San Gabriel must come first. My marriage prospects are being discussed all over the country, and no one less than the son of a high-ranking Spanish or Portuguese nobleman is being considered. When Colonel da Silva returns home, a short list will be chosen and negotiations will begin to find the best and most appropriate royal consort for the queen of San Gabriel."

His heart tightened. "So soon?"

"I'm twenty-four. It's time I married and began a family, because it isn't right that the direct line of the Royal House of Alcantara has dwindled down to me." She raised her chin, her gaze defiant. "I shall do my duty, but I want one kiss with you to . . . to cherish through the long years and nights ahead."

Awed that she shared his feelings, he said, "I want to kiss you too much, *meu anjo,* my angel. Perhaps it's best if you kiss me instead."

She nodded and stepped shyly forward. He was no more than average height, but her petite frame made her seem rare and fragile. Having seen her ride, he knew that she wasn't fragile at all, but rare she was. So very rare.

She placed her hands lightly on his shoulders and studied his face intensely, as if to memorize his features and this moment. Then she rose on tiptoes and touched her mouth to his. Her lips were exquisitely soft.

Unable to resist, he clasped his hands on her waist below her short jacket, holding her in kissing distance. She was ripe with life and sensuality; her mouth sweet as strawberries. Knowing they must not allow the mood to intensify dangerously, he murmured, "We both smell of horse."

Instead of being insulted, she laughed. "Since both of us do, I didn't even notice." Then she leaned forward into another kiss, and this time her lips parted against his.

Their tongues touched and desire jolted through him. *"Meu anjo,"* he whispered again between nibbling kisses across her lips, her satin smooth cheek, her delicious little ear. "My bonnie, bonnie lass."

She whispered endearments back, moving closer and closer so that she was pressed against him. His hands moved of their own volition, shaping the curves of her waist and hips. She was exquisite, perfect, and, for this brief moment, *his.*

Realizing how close he was to losing control, he hid his face against her sleek dark hair and enfolded her in his arms, inhaling her scent, feeling her heart beat against his. She sighed and relaxed against him, her arms going around his chest.

"You know I'd marry you if I could, don't you?" he whispered.

"I know." After a long silence, she said hesitantly, "I've wondered if this is what the English call 'calf love' and if it would last. I've not had the opportunity to meet many interesting, attractive men. You're the only one I've met that I wished I could marry."

She was seven or eight years younger than

he was, and though in some ways, she was wise beyond her years, in others she was an innocent. "I can't speak for the depth of your feelings, *meu anjo,*" he said, choosing his words carefully. "For your sake, I hope what you feel is infatuation that will pass and that fate grants you a husband you can love completely and forever."

"I've hoped for that, too," she said wryly. "But princesses are seldom so lucky."

"Then I shall pray you have good luck." He moved back, still holding her but able to look down into her dark eyes and exquisite features. "But for me . . . I've had the usual experiences for a man of my station. That has included calf love and brief infatuation. But I've felt nothing like what I feel for you. I believe it's the forever sort of love." In fact, he was sure of it.

Tears glinted in her eyes. "My hope for you is that you marry for love and have strong, beautiful children."

He brushed a kiss on her hair. "I hope that, too, my princess. But you will always be in my heart."

"And you in mine." She closed her eyes for a moment, then stepped away, her expression composed. "I've considered making you a count of San Gabriel to make you more eligible," she said teasingly.

"Uncle Alfonso would agree to such a charter if I asked him."

"Lord Ballard of Porto?" Justin chuckled. "I suspect that no one would be persuaded that would make me a suitable consort. My father is likely to be made a baron soon for his services to Britain — in other words, running several successful businesses — but that is even less likely to impress anyone in San Gabriel."

"British titles don't count, I fear. Only ancient Iberian titles will do," Sofia said with a smile. "Now we must return to the campsite before Athena sends a search party."

"Agreed." He bent and scooped up a large armload of firewood.

Sofia added more pieces, then lifted a smaller load for herself. "One more trip after this should suffice."

They retraced their steps. Carrying a pile of firewood made holding hands impossible, which was just as well.

When they reached the camp, Athena glanced up from a small fire. "Good timing. I was about to run out of firewood."

"About the same amount of wood is waiting to be brought here." Justin released his load in a pile by Athena, then transferred Sofia's kindling to the pile.

"I'll go with you to bring it back," Will said.

Knowing he shouldn't be alone with Sofia again, Justin led the way back to the rest of the firewood. As they picked up pieces, Will said with mild amusement, "You cut a lot of wood, considering how short a time I heard chopping sounds."

"I worked fast so Sofia and I could have time to talk."

"Talk," Will murmured. "Of course."

"I've done nothing to compromise her," Justin snapped.

Will looked surprised. "Of course not. It's obvious that you're yearning for each other, but you're both too wise to do anything foolish." He reached down for more wood. "Only a high stickler would consider a kiss to be ruination."

"You know me too well," Justin muttered as he picked up the last chunk of firewood. Straightening, he said, "Are we going to end up as two old men mourning over our glasses of port about the girls who got away?"

"Quite possibly," Will said as he started back toward the camp. "I haven't entirely given up hope yet, though I suspect it will take a miracle to persuade Athena that she wouldn't regret marrying me."

Justin grimaced. "I need rather more than a miracle, I fear."

And yet, it was impossible to suppress a faint whisper of hope.

As Athena built up the fire with the new kindling, she asked, "Did you find anything interesting while foraging for fuel?"

"Only more rocks and boulders and a few sad little trees." Sofia settled on her folded blankets, her legs tucked to one side. Athena had arranged their saddles and blankets around the fire, the two men on one side and the women on the other. Quiet chaperonage. She added, "I didn't do anything very shocking."

Athena glanced up with a smile. "I didn't say a word."

"My conscience is bothering me," Sofia admitted ruefully. "Attending a convent school left me with the belief that a single kiss outside legal matrimony is a mortal sin, and one shouldn't enjoy kisses too much even if married."

Athena sat back on her heels. "Passion is powerful and can have dire consequences," she said seriously. "Young people in particular burn with desire, so churches do their best to keep unruly passion under control. But desire is natural and without it, there would be no humankind. As with so much in life, it's finding a healthy balance." She grinned. "I'm told that marriage eventually reduces mad passion from a fever to a more manageable part of life. Not that I'd know about that."

Sofia sighed and pulled the pins from her hair, then massaged her tired scalp with her fingertips. "Do you think there is any chance that San Gabriel would accept Justin as a royal consort? It will take my country years to recover from the damages of war and lost young men. I couldn't bear to set my subjects at war with each other."

Athena considered before answering. "Your country values tradition greatly, but you are very popular, so people might be more accepting of your choice. The world is changing. I won't say it's impossible that he could be accepted. You should discuss this when the time comes to weigh the possibilities."

"But the chances are vanishingly small. Being popular means people want 'the best' for me, and to many, that means a Duke Toad." Sofia stood and dusted off her riding skirt. "Is there anything I can do to help?"

"Slice the cheese and bread and ham." Athena pulled a large cast-iron griddle from her saddlebags and set it over the fire on three piles of stones she'd stacked outside the coals. "A griddle is too heavy for a serious trip, but I thought that for only a night or two on the trail, it was worth bringing. These will be special days for both of us, Sofi. I'm glad you suggested this holiday."

"So am I." Sofia ducked to hide a blush as she pulled a large chunk of cheese and a loaf of bread from her saddlebags. She and Athena had divided food and utensils between them. For two days, she could enjoy being a kitchen maid rather than a princess.

By the time the men returned, Athena had the simple dinner prepared. Admittedly, Will in his scarlet uniform coat was stunning, but it was Justin who held Sofia's gaze. His eyes widened when he saw her loose hair spilling around her shoulders. The nuns would say she was tempting him. Sofia was glad that she could.

As Will added his load of wood to the pile, he said, "I believe I'm seeing a sandwich of some sort, but one that smells particularly fine. Will you explain, or make me guess?"

She laughed. "It's more or less what you've been eating since you arrived in San Gabriel, only toasted on a griddle." She flipped two nicely browned sandwiches onto a platter, where half a dozen were already stacked. "Slices of bread layered with smoked cheese, smoked ham, and a Gabrileño pepper sauce, then heated on the griddle till the cheese melts and the bread is toasted. After, toasted almonds to round out the meal."

"The wine is a light red that will go nicely with these sandwiches," Sofia added as she passed filled tumblers to the men. "This would be a modest meal in the castle, but quite nice for trail food, don't you think?"

Will settled on a folded blanket in front of his saddlebags and bit into one of the hot sandwiches, then swallowed a mouthful of wine. "Excellent! I didn't realize that you're a good cook, Athena."

"I've had to cook often enough that I've learned a few dishes that are more or less foolproof," she explained as she sat cross-legged in front of her own saddle and belongings. "This is one of them."

"Simple pleasures are so often the best." Justin raised his tumbler of wine in a toast. "To good food and good company!"

Everyone leaned forward to clink their wineglasses. Sofia wished this expedition with friends could last forever. Since that wasn't possible, she'd enjoy every moment they had. "To friendship and Saint Deolinda!" She tossed back half of her wine.

Justin drank the toast, then reached for one of the sandwiches. "Sofi, you said you'd tell me the story of Deolinda. The name means Beautiful God?"

She nodded. "It's the story, perhaps only a legend, of the founding of San Gabriel. Many, many years ago, the beautiful Deolinda was a Portuguese girl of high birth married to Prince Alexandre, son and heir to the king of Alcantara."

"This was a Spanish kingdom where the city of Alcantara is now?"

"Yes, *alcantara* means 'the bridge,' and that name suits the story. An evil rival for the Alcantaran throne marched his men into the city by night and murdered the king." Sofia paused to finish consuming her sandwich. "Prince Alexandre bravely fought to his death to allow the escape of his beloved wife."

"No doubt it was a dark and stormy night," Justin said solemnly.

"But of course," Sofia said with twinkling eyes. "In a legend, one never flees for one's life on a sunny day! Great with child, Deolinda and a loyal guardsman fled north into the mountains and ended up in this valley. She gave birth to her son in a cave near the site of the Castelo Blanco. The archangel Gabriel appeared and said that she and her son would both be made saints, and they would rule a land of peace and plenty, where all could live in safety."

"It sounds like the legend might be based on a true tale," Justin said, intrigued.

"I've always thought so, for the angel's prediction came to pass," Sofia said pensively. "Refugees from Spain and Portugal made their way to the valley, which is why we have names and words from both countries. It was said that only those led by the angels could find their way here." Her mouth tightened. "And it *was* a land of peace, until the French came."

"There will be peace again," Athena said gently. "Already the valley is healing."

"It's a fine tale," Will said as he finished his third toasted sandwich. "If the princess was Saint Deolinda, who was her son?"

"San Gabriel de Montana. Saint Gabriel of the Mountains," Sofia said. "Named for the archangel, of course, and the country is named for both of them. Because Gabriel came of royal blood, San Gabriel is a kingdom rather than a duchy or a principality, even though it's so small."

She rose grandly, took several steps away from the fire before pivoting and saying with exaggerated hauteur, "Kneel before me, peasants, for the royal blood of Alcantara,

Spain, and Portugal runs in my veins!"

Her companions laughed at her antics.

Then the clearing erupted with gunfire and danger.

CHAPTER 24

Athena was relaxed and a little dreamy from wine, food, and discreet contemplation of Will's splendid physique when gunshots exploded across the clearing. Multiple bullets ricocheted from the boulders, and the ear-numbing blasts echoed over the gorge and the stony landscape. As she froze in shock, a hoarse voice bellowed in French, "Grab the girl — we haven't had a camp whore in too long! Kill the British officer and the others!"

Gunshots were still echoing when Will leaped to his feet, yanked his carbine from the saddle behind him, and shouted, "Take cover!"

A bullet kicked up dust where he'd been sitting an instant before. As he dropped to one knee, cocked his weapon, and aimed upward at a sniper atop one of the boulders, he barked, "Athena, grab your gun and *move*!"

Will fired and a scarlet blossom of blood appeared in the center of the sniper's chest. With eerie slowness, the man and his rifle fell separately to the ground. The weapon discharged harmlessly when it struck. Athena smelled the sharp sulfur scent of black powder and felt the fierce compression of air from the blast of the weapons.

Her brief paralysis ended and she scrambled to her feet as two men in shabby blue French uniforms burst into the clearing. One grabbed Sofia and the other had his rifle aimed at Will from point-blank range.

The Frenchman's finger was tightening on the trigger and Will was still reloading. Terrified, Athena grabbed the griddle from the fire, spilling toasted almonds from the surface, and pitched the heavy, cast-iron utensil at the rifleman.

The scorching-hot metal disk smashed into his face. He shrieked and pitched backward, dropping his gun and pawing at his eyes. Will's bullet ended the man's struggles before he hit the ground.

Athena grabbed her carbine and took cover behind a boulder opposite the French attackers. As she gulped for breath, her gaze swept the clearing through the eye-stinging smoke from the shots that had been fired.

In the seconds that had passed, Sofia's

captor had started to drag her away, but she kicked and screamed and fought like a furious wildcat. Swearing, he lifted her high so her feet were off the ground.

"Sofi!" As the Frenchman tried to subdue her, Justin lunged after them. His right fist punched into her captor's jaw as his left hand locked onto Sofia's arm.

As Justin tried to wrench her from her captor's grasp, the man swore in filthy French, pulled a pistol from a side holster, and shot. Justin twisted away, but from the way his body jerked, he'd been hit. Even so, he didn't let go of Sofia.

Still swearing, the Frenchman shoved his pistol back in its holster and pulled out a wicked dagger. Sofia screamed, *"Justin!"* and kicked at her captor's knee, but she couldn't prevent him from stabbing Justin.

Justin managed to wrap his arms around Sofia's waist. His weight dragged her free of her captor's grip and they fell together, Justin protectively on top.

With the two of them on the ground, Sofia's captor was a clear target. Grimly, Athena aimed her carbine and shot. She aimed for his chest, since it was the largest target, but the bullet tore into his throat instead. He made a horrible gasping sound and collapsed against the boulder that had concealed him earlier.

Will had vanished. Since he hadn't fallen in the clearing, he must have gone after their attackers. Swearing at herself, Athena realized that she'd left her ammunition pouch with her saddle and she'd fired the ball loaded in her carbine.

She was about to run to her saddle for her ammunition so she could help her friends when a man charged out from behind the boulder to her left. He was carrying his rifle, but skidded to a stop just before colliding with Athena. His eyes widened with shock, possibly from the surprise of running into a woman taller than he.

Not waiting for him to recover, she gripped the barrel of her empty carbine and swung at his head with all her strength. The heavy stock smashed into his temple and dropped him in his tracks. Will was right — an empty firearm made a good club.

More gunshots were fired from not far away. Three or four, it was hard to tell with the echoes. After enough time to reload, another two or three shots.

Then, silence.

Athena grabbed the fellow's rifle and cautiously emerged from her refuge behind the boulder. A bloodstained Sofia knelt over Justin, sobbing his name as she rolled him over to examine his wounds. As she crossed to join Sofia, Athena scanned the clearing.

No French soldiers in sight except for the fallen; no sounds of men approaching, though with the background noise of the cataract it was hard to be sure. The sounds of water were how the French devils had managed to sneak up on them, she realized.

Athena reloaded her carbine while keeping a wary eye out for new threats. "How is Justin? How are *you*?"

"I . . . I'm fine," Sofia said in a choked voice. "Justin is breathing, but there's so much *blood*!"

Athena joined her, kneeling on Justin's other side and setting the carbine and French rifle within grabbing distance. The pistol shot had wounded him in the head, and blood poured from his scalp, as well as the knife injury. To her relief, Justin's eyes fluttered open. "Still here," he whispered. "But I've . . . been better."

Relieved that he was coherent, Athena ordered, "The head wound doesn't look serious. Sofi, bring towels from your saddle-bags, my cooking knife, and a basin of water from the spring."

Sofia gulped and scrambled to her feet. Her white shirt and tan riding skirt were garish with bloodstains as she raced to obey.

While she waited, Athena ripped open Justin's shirt along the slashed linen. A bloody laceration started at his right shoulder and cut halfway to his waist.

When Sofia handed her several small towels, Athena rolled one and pressed it along the knife wound to slow the bleeding. Then she sponged the head wound clean so she could examine it better. "The ball only grazed you, Justin," she said calmly. "Head wounds bleed dreadfully and you'll have a beastly headache, but it doesn't look like there was serious injury."

"Scots have . . . hard heads," he managed before his eyes closed again.

Athena used the knife Sofia had brought to slice a towel into smaller pieces. "Did you bring a flask of brandy on this trip? We need some to clean the wounds."

"No Alcantara travels without brandy." Sofia tried to smile before returning to her saddlebags for a silver flask engraved with the Alcantara arms. When she returned with it, she sat on Justin's other side and gripped his hand with hers as if she could heal him by sheer force of will.

Athena cleaned Justin's head wound again, then opened the brandy flask. "Justin, this will hurt, but it's necessary to prevent infection."

"Save some . . . for me to drink," he whispered.

"You're a credit to your Scots ancestors." She trickled the brandy over the head wound, then bandaged a fabric pad over it.

Turning her attention to the knife slash, she cleaned it first with water. The bleeding had already slowed. "Like the head wound, this is messy but not deep, Sofi," she said reassuringly.

"That's because the French soldier didn't know the proper way to knife a man." The voice was Will's and Athena looked up to see him striding across the clearing toward them.

Easygoing Will had been transformed into a cool, lethal officer, a man who could react to danger in a heartbeat. An officer with blood staining the white shirt under his open red military jacket. Athena's heart almost stopped at the sight. Even though he was walking easily and had several long French rifles in one arm, she could barely breathe.

He said reassuringly, "Not my blood, but how is Justin?" He frowned at the sight of his friend.

"A bullet graze on the head, a knife wound down my chest, neither very serious if Athena is to be believed," Justin said in a thin, rasping voice. "What, pray tell, is the correct way to knife a man?"

"Hold the dagger underhand and strike upward," Will explained as he set down his carbine and the collected French rifles. "One is much more likely to strike vital organs that way. Your attacker stabbed downward and hit mostly bone over your shoulder and ribs. Poor training, for which we can all be grateful. I agree with Athena. Your injuries look messy and painful, but no lethal damage."

"Thank *God*!" Sofia breathed out; her face was ghost pale.

Athena felt much the same. When this was over, she wanted to find a place where she could quietly faint. Or scream.

Later. Over the years she'd had experience treating injuries and those skills were needed now, but there was no reason for Sofia to see her beloved being treated for wounds that could have killed him. "Justin is doing well, Sofi," Athena said. "You don't need to watch the rest of the bandaging process."

"You're right. It isn't good for a princess to tremble like a blancmange," Sofia said with unsteady humor. After brushing a light kiss on Justin's forehead, she stood and moved to her saddlebags, then folded onto the ground and buried her head on her crossed arms as she drew deep, slow breaths.

When Will moved closer to help with Justin, Athena saw that he had a nasty powder burn on the left side of his neck. She swallowed hard and tried to sound calm. "The blood might not be yours, but I see you were almost shot in the throat."

"*Almost* doesn't count with bullets," he said with a shrug. "Do you need more brandy, or is Sofia's flask sufficient?"

"Save yours for drinking," she advised. "We'll all need some."

"Use Will's brandy for medicinal purposes," Justin murmured, his eyes closed. "Sofi's is better for drinking."

"I am corrected by the expert," Athena said, amused as she twisted the top back on the royal flask. "Will, besides getting your brandy, do you have some old garment that can be used for a bandage around Justin's chest? The towels aren't long enough."

Will foraged in his saddlebags and produced a worn brandy flask and a long white cravat, which was well suited to bandaging. As he returned with them, he said, "I didn't know that treating the wounded was one of your many skills, Athena."

"I don't faint at the sight of blood, so I've been pressed into service before," she explained as she patted a clean towel along the knife wound. Justin's bleeding had largely stopped.

"My brother faints at the sight of blood," Will said as he opened his more humble brandy. "Mac is a big, broad fellow like me, so he finds it a great embarrassment."

"I've seen other big, broad men faint like that. I'm glad you're not one of them." She smiled crookedly. "That would be inconvenient."

As Athena applied brandy along the knife slash, Justin jerked before forcing himself to calm. "Can I have some of Sofi's brandy?" he asked in a strained voice.

"You're a brandy snob," Will said as he opened the Alcantara flask and carefully poured a small amount into Justin's mouth.

Justin swallowed. "It's my job. Just like yours is remaining vigilant as you're doing now." He took the flask from Will's hand and sipped more.

Athena realized that Justin was right. Though Will was relaxed enough to banter, at the same time he was keeping sharp watch on everything around them.

As she finished bandaging Justin's chest and spread a blanket over him, she asked, "Will, do you know how many attackers there were? Were they all wearing French uniforms? If so, don't they know the war is over?"

"All the men I saw wore shabby, battle-worn uniforms. My guess is that not everyone in the army wanted to surrender, so this lot turned to banditry," he said with a frown. "As to how many, there are five dead men that I know of, but I found six saddled horses back along the track and I see that you collected a French rifle. What happened?"

"One came after me when I took cover behind that boulder," she said. "My gun was empty, so I bashed him with the stock. He went down hard, but I don't think I killed him." She hoped to God that she hadn't. Shooting Sofia's captor was more than enough death dealing for one day. "I'm sorry, I forgot all about the fellow."

"I hope he didn't wake up and run off. It's time we got some answers." Will rose and went in the direction indicated, returning a few moments later hauling Athena's victim with a strong grip under the fellow's arms.

The French soldier was groaning and starting to move. Will propped him against a boulder in a sitting position, then tied his wrists with a handkerchief. He was skinny and underfed, more boy than man. Athena gave silent thanks that he was still alive.

In fluent French, Will asked, "Who are you and why are you in San Gabriel?"

The boy groaned again and didn't answer. Across the clearing, Sofia rose and claimed the basin, scooped it full of cold spring water, then dumped it over the French soldier's head. As he sputtered and swore and thrashed about, Sofia withdrew and watched him with narrowed falcon eyes.

Will gave Sofia an approving nod. "Now that we have your attention, I ask again. Who are you and what brought you to this remote area to attack innocent people?"

The Frenchman stared at Will hopelessly. "Why should I talk? You will kill me anyhow."

"Not necessarily," Will said calmly. "Let us begin with names. I'm Major Will Masterson. And you are . . ." When the Frenchman hesitated, Will asked, "What harm can it do to tell me your name?"

Reluctantly the boy said, "Jean Marie Paget."

"Thank you. Your uniform has the markings of a corporal. Is that accurate?"

"I was to be made a sergeant after . . ."

When Jean Marie stopped, Will asked, "After what? I have a powerful desire to find out why French soldiers are so far from home. Or do you no longer consider your-self a soldier of France?"

"Always!" the corporal spat out.

"Even though your emperor has abdicated and disbanded his forces?"

"Why should soldiers accept the command of a leader who has surrendered? One who sent countless Frenchmen to death and then made a cowardly escape to safety. A true emperor would have died first!" The words sounded like the boy was quoting someone else.

Will's intuition sharpened. "So because he was angry at Bonaparte, your commander decided to turn his men into bandits."

"Not bandits!" the corporal said hotly. "The general has a plan. The valley of San Gabriel has only a weak, helpless princess as heir with no man to care for her. The general will marry the princess and give the valley the strong leadership it needs. All of us who have loyally supported him will receive land and women. I can be a man of consequence as I never could have been if I had stayed in Bordeaux!"

As Sofia gasped, Will said acidly, "How very generous of the general. Did it not occur to him that the Gabrileños have plans of their own?"

"Half the women in the valley are widows from the wars," Jean Marie retorted. "They will welcome having real men in their beds and a strong leader on the throne. Once General Baudin marries the princess, all will be legal. Even she will surely welcome a real man to care for her and her country."

The name Baudin electrified the clearing. The Frenchman's plan made damnable sense, Will realized. Baudin had seen this safe, remote valley and recognized that it would make a good retreat if and when Napoleon surrendered. By removing the king and hereditary prince and leaving San Gabriel in the stewardship of an ailing old man, he'd left the country ripe for conquest. If Baudin married Sofia, no other country would bother to interfere, not when all were busy binding the wounds of war.

Eyes raging, Sofia joined Will and stared down at the French soldier. "The royal princess of San Gabriel will *never* welcome a swine like Baudin into her bed," she spat out. "If he tries to force her, she'll slit his throat. I guarantee it!"

CHAPTER 25

Jean Marie stared, entranced by Sofia's glossy dark hair and exquisite features. "The general said the princess is just a weak, silly young girl," he said uncertainly. "He told us she will welcome his strength."

"I am Her Royal Highness Princess Sofia del Rosario de Alcantara," she said in a steely voice. "If your general tries to lay a hand on me, I will cut it off. He devastated my land once before. I will not allow that to happen again!"

"You can't be the princess!" the Frenchman gasped.

"Because I am not weak and helpless?" She smiled sweetly. "I was once, but that is no longer true. Your general is responsible for turning me from a butterfly into a lioness. And we lionesses protect and defend what is ours."

"He said that the princess lives in a great palace in the valley," the boy faltered.

"And . . . and princesses wear crowns!"

"I have several tiaras, and at my coronation, I will wear the royal crown of San Gabriel. My people managed to hide the crown jewels from your general when he invaded my country last year." Her brows arched delicately. "Normally, I live in the Castelo Blanco, but now my advisors and I are studying ways to strengthen my land."

Jean Marie's eyes widened with horror as he realized that he and his fellow soldiers had attacked the royal princess and her advisors, and whoever commanded the French party had wanted to make her a camp whore. "N-no insult was meant, your highness," he stammered. "General Baudin has the greatest respect and care for you. He would never want a hair on your head harmed."

"Then he should not have sent murderous scouting parties to my country. That is what you are, yes? Scouts?" When he nodded, she commanded, "Tell me your general's plans for invasion."

White-faced, the corporal said, "I have already said too much."

Having watched Sofia with pure pleasure, Will said in a voice of command, "On the contrary, you have said too little. How far behind you is General Baudin? How many men does he have?"

Jean Marie swallowed hard, his Adam's apple bobbing. He stared at Sofia with hopeless worship, but his conflicting loyalty to his general was obvious.

Changing her tactics, Sofia laid a gentle hand on his arm. "Corporal Jean Marie Paget. Your parents gave you the middle name Marie to invoke the special blessing of the Virgin Mother, yes?"

When he nodded weakly, she continued, "San Gabriel is a land where the Blessed Mother is honored. Your General Baudin ravished my country last summer. He stole the sacred, beloved statue of the Queen of Heaven. Were you part of that assault?"

He shook his head. "His brigade suffered many casualties and I was sent as a replacement after he rejoined the main army. Men who had been in San Gabriel told me what a pleasant place it was, how much they had enjoyed visiting. They said the country was ours for the taking."

"*Visiting!* I'm sure they liked that we could offer no resistance and we had plenty of food to steal," Sofia snapped, unable to keep anger from her voice. "Did they tell you of the death and destruction they brought? The innocent Gabrileños who were killed? The burning of the vines and fields and homes? Why in the name of all that's holy would they think they would be welcomed back?"

He shrank back from her fury. "The men who had come through the valley made it sound like paradise. They said we would be greeted happily. We . . . *I* . . . wanted that. My family is dead, so I have nothing to return to in France. If you released me so I could go home, I'd be butchered by Spaniards who hate all Frenchmen." He closed his eyes, saying bleakly, "Nothing. I have *nothing*. No life, no hope. Go ahead and kill me now as payment for the sins of my comrades! A British officer will surely kill more quickly than a Spanish guerilla."

Yes, very young, Will thought. *And melodramatic with it.* While he considered what approach to take, Sofia ordered, "Corporal Jean Marie Paget! Look at me!"

When the young man's eyes opened, she caught his gaze and said, "If you will give San Gabriel your loyalty, you can indeed have a life here, but only as yourself, not as part of a conquering army. You will have your freedom and I will find you work on the Alcantara estates. In time, you may win a wife and have a home and family of your own. In return, you will swear allegiance and tell us what you know about Baudin's planned invasion."

When he hesitated, Athena approached with a tumbler of wine and the last two toasted ham-and-cheese sandwiches she'd made earlier. "Will, untie his hands so he can eat while he considers, because this is a great decision that will determine his life. You won't try to hurt anyone, will you, Corporal Paget?"

"No, ma'am," he said meekly. "Not when you've been so kind to me."

Will sat back on his heels and watched in amusement. He had been prepared to do whatever was necessary to get vital information from the prisoner, but he much preferred the charm offensive of Sofia and Athena.

Paget was clearly as dazzled by Athena as by Sofia, though in a different way. The young man almost inhaled the first sandwich. Even cold, it was probably the best meal he'd had in weeks.

Then he took a swallow of wine. After a startled moment, he took a second swallow. "Your wine is very fine, Princess! As fine as the Bordeaux wines of my home, but with its own soul."

"Indeed it is fine," Sofia said. "We are developing a means to transport our wines to Porto and then to Britain and beyond.

When that happens, new lands higher in the valley will be cultivated. Men who know how to make good wine and work hard may become owners of their own vineyards."

"That could happen to me?" Jean Marie whispered.

"It might," Sofia said judiciously. "As heiress to the throne, I swear you will have opportunities to better yourself. But only if you pledge fealty to San Gabriel with a whole heart. And then work very hard. These are the same opportunities native-born Gabrileños have."

His resistance collapsed. "Forgive me for my sins against your country, Princess," he whispered as he made the sign of the cross over his heart. "I swear loyalty to San Gabriel and to you. I will help you in any way I can."

Now that Sofia had won the young man's heart and soul, it was time for more military matters. "How many men does General Baudin command?" Will asked. "How well armed are they? Do you have field artillery?"

Jean Marie frowned. "Less than a battalion. Between five and six hundred men. General Baudin commanded a full brigade, but the casualties were heavy at Toulouse, and when he decided to head west to San

Gabriel, he had to move out very quickly and he could not wait for more men to join him."

He paused to bite into the second sandwich. This time he ate more slowly, savoring the smoky taste of the cheese and ham and the crunch of the toasted bread. "All the troops are armed with rifles and there is a good supply of ammunition, but the field artillery pieces were lost fording a river in Spain."

That was a definite plus. Will asked, "When does Baudin plan to invade?"

"In . . ." The corporal paused to calculate. "Five days. At dawn on Sunday because the general thinks the Gabrileños will be at church and easily caught unaware."

Every fiber in Will's body tensed. Five days until the arrival of the doom he'd been sensing. "How does he plan to enter the country? The main road from Spain?"

"Yes, we scouted the mountain passes and that is the only route that will allow us — him — to march in fast enough to take the country by surprise."

Will had come that route himself. His mind spinning with possibilities, he said, "It's time for a council of war. Corporal Paget, I do not wish to suggest that I don't trust your solemn oath. But you need time to adjust to becoming a Gabrileño. I will not ask you to fight against your comrades."

Jean Marie breathed a sigh of relief. "I thank you for that. My loyalty is now to San Gabriel, but I do not want to shoot at men who were friends."

Will glanced at Sofia. "Assuming her royal highness agrees, you are no longer a prisoner. You may leave if you wish, but you'll go without your horse, your rifle, or any other weapons."

"I agree," Sofia said firmly. "If you stay, it must be of your own will, Corporal."

The young man grimaced. "The Portuguese are no fonder of the French than the Spanish are. San Gabriel is my best chance for life. I will not betray my vows to you."

A sensible young man, Will thought. He guessed that in six months, Jean Marie would be fluent in the Gabrileño dialect. He was also good-looking, or he would be when he wasn't all bones. When the time came, he should have no trouble finding a wife and creating the home he longed for.

"While we discuss our plans," Will continued, "scout around the area to see if you can find a place that can be easily used to bury your fellow soldiers. I don't want to leave their bodies to be eaten by wild beasts, but neither have I time for digging graves.

Find something suitable for their final resting place."

Jean Marie looked stricken. "You alone killed all the others?"

Will glanced at Athena. "I had help. I'm sorry if they were your friends, but they attacked us without warning and sought to kill us out of hand. Except for the princess, whom your leader wished to capture and . . . dishonor." Will gestured to where Justin was resting a few feet away. "My friend was injured saving her."

Jean Marie paled. "I was circling your camp and did not hear that. The lieutenant who commanded our squad was a . . . a coarse man."

"Justice was visited on him and the others," Sofia said coolly. "As children of God they deserve a proper burial, but I will shed no tears for them."

"You are generous not to leave their bones for wolves to gnaw on." The corporal stood. "I will find a decent burial place. With your permission?"

Will nodded and the Frenchman left the clearing, his face determined. Sofia asked quietly, "Do you think he will return?"

Athena said, "Yes, with nowhere else to go and on his own and without a horse or weapons, he'd never survive the trip across

Spain to France. It was wise of you to offer him new hope, Sofi. You turned him from an enemy into an ally."

"I did not want to see him executed, and we needed that information," Sofia said practically. "But Holy Mother of God, Will! What can we do against hundreds of well-trained and well-armed enemies? Our militias are small, we haven't enough firearms, and we have only a handful of seasoned soldiers."

"Since we know the *when* and *where* of their invasion, we'll ambush them," Will replied. "I came over the mountains on the road from Spain, and there is a sizable stretch of sunken road at the crest of the route into San Gabriel."

Seizing on the idea with relief, Sofia said, "That sounds like an excellent plan! Will, may I appoint you commander in chief of San Gabriel's military forces? I can make you a general if you like. Or a field marshal — that's an even higher rank, isn't it?"

Will smiled a little. "I never had the ambition to be a general, but I will accept the temporary appointment of commander in chief, since I'm best qualified. I'd like to make Gilberto Oliviera and Tom Murphy brevet captains, since they're both experienced and very capable."

"Do as you think best, Will." Sofia smiled ruefully. "My contribution to the defense of San Gabriel will be prayers. First to give thanks that you're here and willing to help, and then even more fervent prayers for victory."

"What are the chances of success?" Athena asked quietly. "We have at best half the men and less than half the weapons, and only the veterans you led back from Toulouse have faced combat."

Will hesitated, not liking what he had to say, but Sofia and Athena needed to know the truth. "The odds may be about even." At best.

Sofia asked hopefully, "Might Colonel da Silva and the rest of the Gabrileño Army return by then?"

"It's not impossible," Will replied. "But they must march the full width of Spain with men recovering from wounds. I don't know how much they'll be slowed down."

Sofia raised her chin. "I shall pray for their swift journey home, and I'll remember Will's instructions on the best way to knife a man in case Baudin tries to bed me."

"It won't come to that, Sofi," Athena said. "You are the golden prize that would legitimize Baudin's conquest. If he gets close, you'll be out of the castle by tunnel and hidden safely away in a cave." She laughed a little. "All the work that was done to clear the wine caves! We did it too soon."

"Speaking of swift passages home," Will said, "will Justin be in any shape to ride hard back to Castelo Blanco tomorrow?"

Before Athena could answer, Justin replied in a thready voice, "He will. Tie me to the damned horse if you must. There is no time to waste. If I bleed, I bleed."

"We'll ride as fast as we can without actually killing you," Will promised. "San Gabriel needs you alive for shipping Gabrileño wine."

Sofia winced, but Justin gave a laugh that turned into a cough. "I've always liked your common sense, Will," he managed when he regained his breath. "But don't make me laugh again! It hurts."

With her brow furrowed, Sofia suggested, "Perhaps you should ride ahead, Will, since you're vital for San Gabriel's defense. The rest of us can follow at a slower pace."

He shook his head. "We travel together. None of us can be spared, and as we found out today, this country is more dangerous than we thought."

To his relief, no one argued the point. He'd had quite enough combat for one day.

CHAPTER 26

Jean Marie Paget found a water-scoured hole in the stony landscape that was a good fit for five bodies; next to it was a pile of stony scree. Together he and Will wrapped the fallen Frenchmen in their blankets and carried them to their final resting place.

Though the burial site wasn't visible from the clearing, Athena could hear the sounds of earth and stones falling on the grave. It was another reason to be grateful that Sofia had persuaded the young Frenchman to change his loyalties. If he'd been killed, Athena would have had to help Will, since Justin wasn't up to the effort and it was unthinkable to ask a princess to bury bodies. Though Sofia would have helped if asked, honorable princess that she was.

After the burial came a brief service for the dead. Jean Marie spoke their names and told a little about each man. Will gave a quiet soldier's requiem. Sofia prayed for their souls. Justin didn't go to the graveside, saying he needed to preserve his strength. Though Athena attended, she didn't speak, but mentally she damned the old men who created wars in which young men died.

She was grateful that by the time they returned to their campsite, the sun was setting on the long summer day and they could retire for the night. Jean Marie was wrapped up in a ragged blanket a tactful distance away from the others, near the horses. Sofia dug her two blankets from her saddlebags and said defiantly, "I'm going to sleep by Justin."

Athena smiled. "I wouldn't dream of arguing about it. If his condition worsens during the night, wake me, but I hope you both sleep well."

Justin laughed, then coughed again. "I hope so, too. And you needn't worry, I'm in no shape to compromise anyone, even if she is the most beautiful girl in the world."

Sofia's tension dissolved into a giggle. "There is nothing wrong with your flattery, Mr. Ballard." She fussed over Justin's blankets until they were smooth and even, then lay down on her own blanket within touching distance.

Justin took Sofia's hand and said in a soft voice that wasn't meant to be overheard,

"No matter how long I live, I shall never forget the night I slept with a beautiful princess." His words elicited another giggle.

Athena moved out of hearing range so she couldn't discern their soft voices over the rush of the waterfall. They would have a simple breakfast of bread and cheese and head out in the morning as soon as there was enough light to ride, so she packed away everything that wouldn't be needed.

After she'd done the essential packing, she glanced around for Will and saw that he'd settled against the boulder nearest the fire and was feeding wood to the flames. Wondering if his nerves were as frayed as hers, she approached and said, "I was thinking of making tea. Would you like some?"

He gave her a tired but welcoming smile. "Indeed I would. After the day we've had, we're all in need of a soothing cup of tea."

The last light of sunset had gone and they seemed to be alone in the night, even though three other people were resting nearby. The constant low roar of the cataract made their location seem even more private. As she hung the small water pot above the fire to heat, she said, "I gather you're standing guard tonight?"

He nodded. "Jean Marie said he didn't think any other French scouting teams were in this area, but there might be other brigands around." He gestured to the stack of French rifles to his left. "Cleaning those weapons, as well as mine, is a good way to pass the time."

She frowned. "My carbine needs cleaning. Ordinarily, I would have done it by now, but it's been a distracting day."

"Bring it over and I'll do the cleaning while you make tea."

She brought him her weapon and he cleaned it while she relaxed and waited for the tea water to heat. "It's hard to remember that we set out from the castle just this morning," she mused. "The day seems to have lasted a week."

"A long, hard week at that," he agreed. "I have bruises I don't remember acquiring."

"So do I!" The water came to a boil, so she added tea leaves and set the pot on the ground to steep.

Will caught her hand and tugged her back to sit on the folded blanket beside him. "Your day has been particularly beastly," he said in a low, serious voice. "How are you faring?"

She started to say she was fine, then stopped, unable to speak. She tried again to talk and began shaking violently. Will's right arm wrapped around her shoulders and he drew her close against him.

"I . . . I hope you don't mind me having strong hysterics," she said in a choked voice. "When I think of how close we all came to dying . . ." Her voice broke.

Will's arm tightened, lending her warmth and strength and support. "You've earned the right to strong hysterics," he said firmly. "What you did today was quite extraordinary, you know. If not for your courage and quick thinking, we'd all be dead. Or worse."

Athena thought of what the French wanted to do to Sofia and barely refrained from throwing up. "It all happened so quickly, I'm not quite sure what I did."

"Let me remind you." He exhaled roughly. "I was a damnable fool and allowed myself to be lulled by the apparent peacefulness of this country, and that almost got us killed. I barely avoided being shot by that sniper up on the boulder. I managed to get out of the way and take him down, but I would have been killed by that other fellow while I was reloading if you hadn't thrown your hot griddle into his face."

"Sheer instinct." Her screaming nerves were starting to ease thanks to Will's warmth and closeness. "I grabbed and threw without even thinking."

"Thank God you have good instincts! You

would have made a superb soldier. Though that would have been a great waste." He began stroking his palm down her right arm. She felt like a cat being petted.

"I went after the other attackers, which had to be done, but you're the one who saved Sofia from being dragged off."

"Justin is the one who saved her. I just took advantage of a clear shot when he managed to free her from her captor." Athena shivered again at the memory.

"I don't think it's the first time you've killed a French soldier to protect the ones you love," he said softly. "But that doesn't make it easier to do, or to live with after."

She remembered the French soldier she'd killed in Porto when he invaded the convent, and buried her face against Will's shoulder. "I'd rather not get in the habit of killing marauders," she said, her voice muffled against him. "But with what lies ahead for San Gabriel, who knows?"

"Who knows indeed?" he said wryly. "I give thanks for your courage and quick thinking because you may need them."

His words confirmed her earlier suspicions. "How bad is the situation? I suspected you were simplifying earlier when we had our war council."

He frowned. "It's hard to predict how well

the ambush will work. We'll have to be in position at the right time and place, which will mean good scouting to know the exact time. Our men will have to arrive early, and likely they'll have to lie in wait for hours through a chilly night. They'll need to be very still and very quiet. The French are seasoned troops and they'll be wary of the sunken road precisely because it's an obvious ambush hazard. The least sound or sight of one of our men will put them on full alert and ruin the advantage of surprise."

Reluctantly she moved away from his comforting arm and poured the tea in pewter mugs, then added chunks of sugar. Handing him his mug, she said, "You know the troops you have to work with. What do you think is the most likely outcome?"

"If all goes well, we'll reduce the numbers of French troops substantially, but as they fight back, there will be serious casualties on our side. Some of the militiamen will flee because they've never been in battle. They'll be terrified," Will said bluntly. "The worst case is that virtually the whole militia breaks and runs and the retreat will turn into a bloodbath."

Athena gripped the pewter mug between both hands, needing the warmth. "If that's the worst, what do you consider the most likely?"

"Each small militia unit is built around one of the soldiers who served with da Silva. I hope there are enough such men to steady the others so there won't be a mass retreat," Will said slowly. "But the French will fight back hard and well. They've marched a long way to take San Gabriel, and they will not easily turn and run. Like Jean Marie, where do they have to go? Since they didn't lay down their arms with the abdication, they're now outlaws in the eyes of the Allies. They'll fight like cornered rats."

Athena took a deep swallow of the half-cooled tea as she thought about the possibilities. "Surely, there will be opportunities to use that black powder you've been yearning to explode."

Will chuckled. "Yes, and after I've surveyed the ambush territory, I'll know how to use it to maximum effect. But five or six hundred troops marching along a narrow mountain road will be strung out a great distance. I haven't anywhere near-enough black powder to blow them all to hell at once. I can improve our odds, but explosions alone won't be enough to win the battle."

"What if enough French soldiers survive

to overrun the country?"

Will shrugged his broad shoulders. "We pray that the safe houses and caves will protect most of the population until Colonel da Silva returns. My best guess is that the army will arrive in two to three weeks."

Athena wished it would be sooner. "So the situation isn't good, but it isn't hopeless."

Will swallowed the last of his tea. "Prospects are better than when you were fleeing the French across the collapsing bridge of boats and I was in a cellar waiting to be executed at dawn. We both survived then against the odds, and we'll do the best we can to survive this time. It's all anyone can ever do."

"Hear, hear!" Athena swallowed the last of her tea, then covered a yawn. "All of a sudden I can barely stay awake. I need to sleep for a few hours, and so do you. Wake me up when we're halfway to dawn and I'll take over."

"If necessary, but I don't need a lot of sleep." He smiled with quiet intimacy. "Lie down beside me, Athena. My thigh will make a tolerably good pillow."

"That's an offer that I should but won't refuse." She covered another yawn. Then she rolled into her blankets, resting on her side with her head on his right thigh. "You really are comfortable," she murmured. "But I can be relocated if you need to move. And wake me up so you can get some rest!"

He rested his hand on her shoulder and could feel her muscles relax as she slid quickly into slumber. Part of his mind listened for any sounds that didn't belong to the river or the stealthy creatures that moved through the night, but mostly he thought of how very peaceful it was to be here with Athena sleeping trustfully against him.

She was a remarkable woman who would have made a superior soldier, but it was so much better that she was female. Under her blankets, he could see the lovely length of her strong, graceful body. Such wonderful, long legs. Such courage and resilience. So little confidence that they could build a life together.

Tonight the possibility of a life together seemed moot. San Gabriel was going to war, he was commander in chief of its very limited forces, and a good officer did not lead from the rear.

If he'd refused Duval's request to come to San Gabriel, he could have been safely back in England by now. But then he wouldn't have met Athena, and he could not be sorry to have her in his life, even if it was for too short a time.

"Sleep well, little owl," he whispered. "Sleep well."

Athena slept soundly and woke early enough to force Will to rest for a couple of hours. She also made a good pillow, he informed her before dozing off.

She loved having his head on her lap, though it was a powerful temptation to caress every part of him within touching distance. The man needed his rest.

In the dark hours before dawn, she thought of the brief, magical days she and Will had known each other. Her resistance to his courtship had deep, anguished roots. But now the two of them faced an invasion that was a mere four days away. Life was fragile. A single lead ball could have destroyed the bright spirits of Will or Sofia. The ball that had grazed Justin's skull would have been lethal if it had struck half an inch closer.

They had survived today, yet they might be dead in a week.

She studied Will's handsome face, weary with responsibility even in sleep, and swore she would not waste any of the precious moments remaining.

CHAPTER 27

The long ride back to the Castelo Blanco was agony for Sofia — not for herself, but for Justin. He was clearly in pain, yet being an abominably stoic Scot and refusing to admit that anything was wrong. Not that much could be done to ease his pain when they needed to return to the castle as quickly as they could. Sofia rode at his side and prayed that his wounds wouldn't reopen and begin bleeding again.

Interestingly, Jean Marie was equally solicitous, riding on Justin's other side and keeping a keen eye on him. He had the instincts of a really good personal servant.

Will also cared about his friend's welfare, but even more, he cared about San Gabriel and its defense, so he took Justin at his word. They rode at a brisk pace with few breaks, and those more for the horses than the riders.

Sofia was intensely grateful when they

finally reached the castle. Justin was gray with pain and fatigue and in danger of pitching headlong from his horse. Will helped him to dismount safely and held him upright until both grooms emerged from the stables, looking worried.

"Mr. Ballard was wounded in an attack," Sofia explained. "Miguel, help Corporal Paget get Mr. Ballard up to his room. Sancho, ride into town and bring Dr. de Ataide here as quickly as you can."

The grooms stared at Jean Marie in horror. "A French soldier!" Miguel said, aghast. "Have you gone mad, your highness? Is this brute threatening you?"

"Señor Paget is no longer a French soldier," Sofia said flatly. "He has pledged a solemn oath to San Gabriel. He will help you guide Mr. Ballard upstairs to his room."

Miguel opened his mouth to say more. Sofia cut him off sharply. "Do you question my judgment?"

Miguel swallowed hard. "No, Princess." He moved to Justin and slid an arm around his waist, while Jean Marie took a similar hold on Justin's other side.

Speaking English, Justin said with a whisper of mischief, "You sound more like a queen every day, my princess. The frightening sort."

As the men started moving him toward the castle, Justin's coat fell away from his torso and she saw fresh bloodstains on his bandaged chest. Horrified, she said, "That means I can give you orders, you Scottish peasant! You are going up to your room and you will stay there until the surgeon pronounces you fit!"

"Or you'll have me beheaded? Yes, your majesty," he said meekly, but his eyes glinted with humor before he started up the steps and had to suppress a gasp of pain.

Biting her lip, Sofia followed Justin and his helpers up to his room. He groaned as they laid him gently on the coverlet of his bed and his eyes closed. He was still gray with exhaustion, but at least he was lying down rather than jostling along on horseback.

Sofia thanked the two men, adding, "Miguel, you're needed with the horses. You saw that we came back with more than we left with."

He nodded. "Skinny beasts, but with proper care they'll be useful. What happened to their riders?"

"Six renegade French soldiers made the mistake of attacking our party," she said tersely. "Five of them didn't live long enough to regret it. Jean Marie, will you

335

help Mr. Ballard take his coat off?"

Miguel left for the stables and Jean Marie gently raised Justin enough to remove the coat. The bleeding seemed to have stopped, but Sofia wouldn't be happy until the surgeon had examined his wounds and given him fresh bandages.

When Justin was resting again, Sofia said, "Jean Marie, you'd best take off your French uniform coat now. No one has forgotten the French invasion last year, and I don't want you to be killed by accident."

"I don't want that, either, Princess," he said fervently as he peeled off his worn blue coat.

Eyes still closed, Justin said, "If you don't mind removing the bloodstains, you can have the one you took off me. It will be a little large now, but should fit well enough once you've put on some weight."

"You would give me your own coat, sir?" Jean Marie examined it. "It is a very fine coat."

"Made in London with good fabric and cut," Justin agreed. "But I won't be able to wear it again without thinking of being shot and stabbed, so you're welcome to it."

"Thank you, sir!" Jean Marie pulled it on. The material was a dark brown so the stains didn't show too badly, and it would fit well when he got some meat on his bones.

"Welcome to civilian life, Señor Paget," Sofia said.

He stroked the fine wool of his left sleeve. "I was conscripted into the army against my will. I will not miss it."

"I think you will like being a Gabrileño much more," Sofia said. "For now, go down to the stables and help with the horses. After, ask where to find Señor Oliviera and tell him I said to put you to work and find you a room and meals." She waved a hand tiredly. "For the next few days, life will be rather chaotic."

"Anything you wish of me, you have but to ask, Princess." He bowed deeply, then left the room.

As he did, a small furry gray shape darted inside the room. Sofia breathed out her tension in a long sigh as she scooped up the cat. "*Querida* Sombra!" she said as she rubbed her cheek against the soft, striped fur.

"Someone else is your *querido,* my princess?" Justin's rusty voice asked.

Smiling, Sofia perched on the edge of the bed. "My watch cat has arrived. When I'm not here, he spends his time in the kitchen, where he works diligently on the mouse patrol, but he always knows when I've returned and he finds me." She held the cat out and talked to him seriously. "*Mi* Sombra, stand guard over this man. Keep him company, offer comfort, and if he tries to get up, bite him!"

She set the cat on the bed. Sombra promptly marched up to the pillow and began licking Justin's chin. "Sombra thinks you need a shave," Sofia said. "He's right."

Justin laughed and began scratching Sombra's head and neck. He was rewarded with a mattress-rattling purr. "I see I have a rival for your affections. Your bedmate, I presume?"

"Indeed he is." She took Justin's hand. "I'll stay here until the surgeon arrives. With an invasion on the way, I have much to do. I have a thought. Would you accept Jean Marie as a body servant? You're going to need extra care for a few days."

Justin considered. "I like the idea. He seems inclined to please, and he knows a well-made coat when he sees one."

"He is also desperate to find a place where he belongs," Sofia said softly. "If he is treated well, he will serve you all his days."

Justin squeezed her hand. "You have a gift for inspiring loyalty, my princess. As Athena said, you turned an enemy into an ally."

"Would that I could do that with the rest

of the French!" She sighed. "I'm frightened, Justin. *Terrified.* Baudin returns with many soldiers at his back and a desire to claim San Gabriel and me. If he becomes entrenched here before Colonel da Silva returns, he will be hard to dislodge. There will be a war with many deaths."

"Don't underestimate Will. He's a fine officer, skilled at getting the most from his men." Justin paused to catch his breath. "And your people are fighting for their homes. That gives them extra strength."

She hoped Justin was right. She *prayed* he was right.

"Justin? How are you feeling?"

Will's quiet voice drew Justin from his tangled dreams. He woke and blinked at the canopy over the bed. "I ache," he said muzzily. "The blasted surgeon must have given me laudanum. I wish he hadn't. Sofia probably insisted."

Will chuckled as he moved into Justin's line of sight. "I have the same reaction to laudanum. It's nice the pain is reduced, but the scrambled wits are a nuisance."

Justin glanced at the window. "How long have I been asleep?"

"Only a couple of hours." Will leaned against the heavy post at the foot of the bed, looking tired. "Just long enough to miss the storm of horror and shock that blazed through the castle when people learned of the imminent invasion."

Justin frowned, wishing he could think clearly. "How widespread is the news?"

"Mostly just the royal household. We don't want to risk the general population knowing too soon in case the news should somehow reach Baudin. Without the element of surprise, San Gabriel hasn't much hope of staving off the invasion." Will moved to the table by the bed and poured a glass of water. "You look thirsty."

Justin downed the whole glass in one long swallow. "I was and didn't quite realize it." He held out the glass for a refill. "That cleared my wits a bit, as well as removing the laudanum aftertaste from my mouth. I assume that you and Sofia's people have been working on more detailed plans?"

"Yes, we'll evacuate the farms near the Spanish road and move as many people as possible into the sanctuaries on Friday. Guards will be set on the road to Spain to prevent anyone from leaving the valley heading east, as well as to watch for Baudin."

Justin drank the second glass of water more slowly, then cautiously pushed himself up to sit against the pillows. His head didn't seem bad except for a dull ache, and the knife wound was merely painful, not agonizing. "I'll be ready to join your forces by Saturday night."

Will shook his head. "You're not going to be part of the ambush."

Before Will could continue, Justin's usually mild temper flared. "I'm a tolerably good shot, and I've had enough experience with war and bandit attacks that I'm unlikely to break and run. You're going to need every steady soldier you can find, damn it!"

"Yes, sorry, I know you'd be valuable," Will said apologetically. "But I have a more important task that you're best suited for."

"What is more valuable than fighting off the French?"

"Getting Sofia out of San Gabriel and down to Porto," Will retorted. "If we fail to stop the French from overrunning the valley, the first thing they'll do is try to capture her and drag her to Baudin's bed."

Justin gagged at the thought. "The castle is virtually impregnable."

"Yes, but if she's besieged inside, Baudin can take his time securing the rest of the country, and he may set up an ambush of his own to attack Colonel da Silva and his men when they return. If you take Sofia to

Porto, with your help she can rally British and Portuguese support if that becomes necessary. I assume you know high-ranking Portuguese officials. You can also send word to our influential British friends to drum up support for the gallant and beautiful princess in exile." Will grimaced. "I hope it won't come to that, but it's best to be prepared."

Justin hesitated. "I see the value of helping her escape, but it feels like cowardice. You have even better connections with the British establishment, and you would be a bodyguard without equal to get her safely away."

"If the situation gets that desperate, I'll be dead," Will said tersely. "You're the best hope for Sofia and San Gabriel. She won't want to go for the same reasons you don't want to go. She would die for her country. Your job is to persuade her to *live* for her country. Between you and Athena, you can convince her to leave if necessary."

"That would get Athena away to safety also," Justin observed.

"A thought that hasn't escaped my attention," Will agreed. "You'll have noticed that Athena is also an effective bodyguard. Along with a couple of Gabrileños with combat experience, you'll be able to travel fast and light."

"You've persuaded me." Justin smiled wryly. "To be honest, dying nobly doesn't really appeal to me that much."

Will laughed. "Once I thought it would be noble, but no longer. Yet ever since I joined the army, I've assumed I'd die fighting. If my time has come . . ." He shrugged. "At least it won't be a surprise."

"A soldier's life produces a rather shocking degree of fatalism," Justin muttered, trying not to show how rattled he was by Will's calm acceptance of likely death. "I think you'll survive because you and your brother are both apparently unkillable."

Will grinned. "Would that were true."

Justin threw back his covers. "Pull out the chamber pot. I may need help not to keel over. Damned laudanum!"

Will caught his arm as Justin slid from the bed. "I'll tell Jean Marie to make sure no one gives you any more. He's appointed himself your personal attendant. The only reason he's not here is because I sent him off to find some food and assured him I wouldn't let you die on my watch."

"I'm becoming fond of the lad," Justin said, swaying a little. "I may keep him."

One of his laudanum dreams slid across

his mind. An image of a petite woman who reminded him of Athena. He blinked and considered the image. "I've been thinking about friends back in England, and I may know who Athena's father is. . . ."

CHAPTER 28

The day had been long and tiring and it might already be too late, but Athena couldn't delay any longer. She might not have another chance. She undressed and donned her long night robe, then unpinned her hair and brushed it loose over her shoulders and back.

Quietly she stepped from her room into the long corridor that led from one end of the floor to the other. The castle was silent, and enough moonlight entered the windows at both ends of the passage that she didn't need a candlestick to light her way.

Soft-footed as Sofia's cat, she made her way to the far end of the corridor and tapped on Will's door to alert him, since she was sure that startling an experienced soldier wasn't a good idea. When she got no response, she tried the handle. The door opened easily and she stepped into the bedroom.

A wide swath of moonlight splashed across the bed, limning Will's bare, powerful torso with silver light. He lay on his side, one arm over a pillow and the lower part of his body covered by a blanket. "Will?"

He came awake instantly. "Athena, what's wrong?" He pushed himself up to a sitting position. As the blanket slid lower, it was obvious that he was quite gloriously naked. "It's too quiet to be the French invasion come early."

Her lips twisted ruefully. "A different kind of invasion."

She stepped forward into the moonlight, wishing she had a tenth of her mother's allure. "We could easily have been killed on the trail. It made me recognize how foolish my doubts and fears are. I discovered that I don't want to die without . . . without sharing your bed." Her voice faltered. "That is, if you still want me. I wouldn't blame you if you've lost interest. . . ."

"Want you?" His smile lit up the room as he extended his hand. "My dear girl, I can't imagine a day when I won't want you. Come to me."

Weak with relief, she stepped forward and clasped his hand with her shaking fingers. Unsure what he believed about her, she said uncertainly, "I'm not a virgin."

"Neither am I." He pulled her down onto the bed and embraced her, his arms enfolding her with strength and tenderness. "Please tell me this isn't a dream." He buried his face in the loose waves of her hair, his warm breath teasing her throat. "No, if it is a dream, don't tell me. I don't want it to end."

She laughed a little, relaxing in his welcome. "This is real. You're *very* real. I have trouble remembering why I resisted you so intensely when I wanted you so much."

"From what you've said about your childhood, your doubts were understandable." He pulled back a little so he could study her face in the moonlight, his gaze probing. "Danger has a way of stripping away lesser concerns, but when danger has passed, it's easy to regret actions taken when death seemed imminent. If you think you might have regrets later, now is the time to retreat." His mouth twisted. "I don't want you to go, but neither do I want you to have any regrets."

"The only regrets I'll have is that I've waited so long," she said honestly. "Don't hold anything back, Will."

His brows arched. "Maybe you should clarify what you mean by that?"

With difficulty, she said, "I told you that I

would never want to bring an illegitimate child into the world, but I've realized that I want rather fiercely to have your baby." Her smile was self-mocking. "In other words, I'm as selfish as my mother. Though I think what she craved was any child, and I want only yours. That's unlikely when we have so little time, but I will rejoice if it happens."

He sucked his breath in. "That's the greatest compliment I've ever received. If you're sure . . ."

"I'm sure." Growing impatient, she rolled forward and pressed her lips to his.

He responded as if she was a spark and he was tinder. "Athena," he breathed. *"Goddess . . ."*

He kissed her more deeply, drawing her against him so that their bodies pressed together and his great, warm hands roamed over the curves and valleys of her back and sides. "So elegant and strong," he murmured. When his exploring hand slid under a fold of her robe, his voice changed. "And you are most interestingly naked under your robe!"

She ducked her head in embarrassment. "One of the alarming pieces of maternal wisdom Delilah gave me was that very few men can resist a naked female body. Perhaps that's how she seduced my father, the dreadful duke. I'm sure this method was more reliable in her case, but I . . . I thought that if you were undecided, I could take off my robe. Just to make my humiliation complete if you still rejected me."

She could joke about it, since he hadn't rejected her. She hadn't even had to drop her robe.

Will laughed. "There is truth in her words, but not the whole truth. Female nakedness is always interesting, but even more important is that the female be interesting. And you, little owl, are the most interesting woman I've ever met."

"I'm not a *little* anything!" she protested.

"A long and lovely owl? True, perhaps, but not as good a pet name." He gently pushed her onto her back and untied the sash of her robe. "You are a banquet, my lady," he said, his voice thickening. "Strong and lithe and exquisitely female."

He caressed her bare body from shoulder to hip before returning to her breast. She gasped as he thumbed her nipple. It hardened instantly, sending jolts of sensation to deep, secret places.

His hand moved to her other breast and he leaned in for a kiss that began with warm lips and sliding tongues, then moved. "A banquet of irresistible taste and texture," he said huskily.

Wherever his mouth touched, he brought every fiber of her being to shocking life. His tongue traced her ear. Who knew that ears were so insanely sensitive? Her throat arched against his lips, utterly vulnerable. A delicate nibble along her collarbone. Her breasts, dear God, her *breasts*!

She felt the powerful length of his arousal against her thigh and rubbed against it, loving his gasp and the jerk of his reaction. She did not want to be alone in this spiraling madness. As sensation drowned her rational mind, she simultaneously wanted this intimacy to progress, and to last forever.

When his mouth resumed its downward path, she panted, "I . . . don't know how much longer I can bear this. I may burst into flaming embers."

"That's rather the point." He laughed softly, with his warm breath stirring the lightly tangled hair at the juncture of her thighs.

Then his wicked, sinful mouth and tongue reached her most sensitive female places and she did burst into flames. Her hips churned and her fingers dug into his shoulders until the inferno faded, leaving her limp and stunned. "Oh, my . . . ," she breathed. "Oh, *my* . . . !"

He hummed with satisfaction as he rested his head on her belly. His breath was almost as ragged as hers. "Are you still sure about wanting all of me?"

"Oh, yes. *Yes!*" She had a fierce need to give him equal pleasure so this mating would be burned into his soul as intensely as it was burning into hers.

He shifted to brace himself above her, his powerful thighs between hers. She skimmed her hands over his beautiful, broad shoulders, down his chest, and over his ribs. So much power and strength and masculinity revealed, and for these precious moments, they were all hers. "If I'm Athena, you are Hercules, a man so splendid that he was transformed into a god."

He laughed. "Moonlight glamorizes. Except in the case of you, where it enhances the beauty that is already there."

Supporting himself with one arm, he let the fingers of his other hand drift to the still pulsing folds of her most intimate places. She'd thought she was beyond sensation, but found that wasn't true. Her hips began moving again as she yearned for a different kind of completion.

Daring, she reached down and clasped him. He gasped and froze for an instant. Then he leaned into her, sliding forward slowly but with inexorable power. "It's been a long time for you, hasn't it?" he said raggedly.

"Very." She shivered with rich satisfaction and raised her hips, taking him deeper inside her. He was so powerful and male and *right.* "This was worth waiting for."

He began to move and she found that responding to each other's rhythms was a new kind of profound pleasure. She absorbed his strength and need and returned it with all the passion she'd suppressed so long.

She was so attuned to his body that she didn't recognize the increasing urgency of her own until she experienced another shattering culmination as he groaned and poured himself into her. Her body thrashed convulsively as she broke and was remade. Never again would she be the woman she had been, nor did she want to be.

Tension eased out of him and he rolled to his side so he wouldn't crush her. As he gathered her against him, he murmured, "That was even more amazing than I had dreamed possible." He kissed her forehead. "I am so very glad you're here."

"So am I. And *very* glad I gave you a guest room with a large bed!" She loved the intimacy of this skin-to-skin touching. She loved how the dim light sculpted the planes and muscles of his beautiful male body. Most of all, she loved the intimacy and sense of rightness between them.

Will murmured, "What are you thinking? I do hope it's not that you've made a ghastly mistake."

"Never that!" She laid her hand on his chest, feeling the sturdy beat of his heart. "I was wondering if Delilah felt like this with her lovers, if that was why she had so many. But how could she possibly feel this way with multiple men?"

"It's an interesting question," Will said thoughtfully. "There is great pleasure in the pure animal satisfaction of mating with a well-matched partner. But emotional mating adds so much more. She might have loved the physical pleasure, but never found the deeper emotional connection. Maybe she had many lovers because she was looking for more than the physical satisfaction."

"Perhaps. I'll never know. But she had a restless disposition. Maybe the satisfactions she found were always fleeting." Her brow furrowed. "I'd hate to think that was true with you. I want more, not less."

"As do I. You realize that now I'll start nagging you to marry me."

Athena rolled to her side so her back was

to him. "I overcame my qualms about becoming lovers, but marriage is another matter."

Will rolled over behind her so they were spooned together, his arm around her waist, his legs warming the back of hers. "Wouldn't you like to sleep like this every night for the rest of your life?" He brushed a kiss on the side of her throat.

She reached back to pat his bare flank. "We'd freeze in England."

He promptly reached down and pulled a blanket up over them both, then settled behind her again. "We'll adapt. There's something very fine about being cuddled together in a warm bed while wild storms rattle the windows."

A brittle edge sounded in her voice. "That does sound rather nice, but I'm still Lady Whore's Daughter."

"Our past is part of who we are, but you'd be Lady Masterson," he pointed out. "There might be some difficult moments, but I will not let any man insult you, and I guarantee that my closest friends and family will be entirely on your side."

"I've lived as an outcast too long to be easily persuaded that I can become part of the privileged establishment," she whispered, her throat aching. "And such questions are moot when we may not survive the next week."

"There is that," he agreed, his hand coming to rest on her breast. "But we might both survive. You're much more likely to do so than I am, so tomorrow morning I'll write my brother and tell him who you are and what you are to me. He will stand your friend, and be an uncle to your child if you have one. You'll never have to fear poverty again."

She drew a shaky breath. "It must be lovely to trust someone so much."

"I would trust Mac with anything. If you need to find him, he's Sir Damian Mackenzie, his club is named Damian's and it's on Pall Mall. His London house is right next door. Remember that."

"Damian Mackenzie, Damian's, Pall Mall," she repeated dutifully.

His arm tightened around her waist. "Or we could invite the priest up from the town and have him marry us in the morning so you and any possible child will have the protection of my name and fortune. A daughter would be well dowered, and a son would be the next Lord Masterson."

"You're relentless, aren't you?" she said, more amused than irritated.

"Yes," he admitted. "At least, when the

goal is worthy. As you are, little owl."

The endearment almost destroyed her defenses. Deciding they needed a change in topic, she asked, "What was your wife like? Unless you can't bear to speak of her."

After a lengthy silence, he said, "Lily was bright and pretty and full of life and optimism. I've always been dull and sober. . . ."

"That is *not* how I would describe you!"

"You didn't know me at twenty-one," Will said dryly. "But we were young and ripe to fall in love and we tumbled happily into marriage. I didn't realize how delicate her health was. She knew her heart was weak, but she never told me. We were delighted to learn she was with child. But she began fading before my eyes.

"I called in the best physician in London and he said she should never have tried to have a child, but by then, it was too late. All I could do was watch her grow weaker and weaker. She gave birth prematurely and . . . she and our son did not survive."

Athena rolled onto her back so she could study his face. "I'm so very sorry, Will. Life is too often cruel."

She was trying to think what else she might say when he blurted out, "I should have known she wasn't strong enough! The evidence was there, but I didn't see it. I was a damned fool. I wanted to believe that we were too young and happy for tragedy to strike."

Athena took his hand, gripping it tightly. "Such optimism is part of being young. It's not a sin."

"If I had been more aware, she needn't have died," he said flatly.

Taking a guess, Athena asked, "Is Lily why you feel you need redemption?"

After a long silence, he said, "She was my responsibility, and I failed her."

The dark side of being a leader was bearing the guilt of everything that went wrong. Choosing her words with care, Athena said, "From what you say, Lily knew her health was weak and that she wouldn't make old bones. I suspect that she decided to seize life with both hands while she could. She wanted to love and be loved. She wanted passion, and she found those things with you. When she was fading at the end, was she angry? Did she blame you?"

"No," he said slowly. "But I thought she must be concealing anger so as not to hurt me." His voice broke. "The last words she said were that she loved me."

"Oh, Will." Athena raised his hand and pressed it to her cheek. "That you loved each other was a great blessing, even if the

two of you didn't have enough time together."

Will exhaled roughly. "You're wise, little
owl. Perhaps you're right. All I've seen for
years is the loss and my failure to care for
her properly."

"Haven't you helped a great many others
over the years? For example, risking your
life pulling drowning nuns and children out
of a river? Didn't all your rogues in need of
redemption pitch in to help?"

"Yes, but that doesn't change the fact that
I failed Lily."

"That's debatable. Even if it were true, we
all make mistakes, and decent people punish themselves for things outside their
control," she said gently. "But you've done
much to balance the scales. Lily on one side,
many other generous deeds on the other.
Surely, those scales are even by now."

Will frowned. "I'll have to think about
that. In the meantime, it's my turn to ask
awkward and possibly painful questions. Tell
me of your love life. Did you have one great,
lost love?"

Reluctantly, she said, "An intense mad calf
love that wasn't fully intimate, and later one
great, mad misjudgment. The calf love died
when I realized that the object of my infatuation wouldn't dream of marrying Lady

Whore's Daughter, though he was quite keen on doing anything short of actually ruining me." She thought she'd discovered true love everlasting. Instead, she'd learned about betrayal.

Will whistled softly. "More and more I understand your low opinion of so-called gentlemen. What about the mad misjudgment?"

She hated having to reveal her stupidity, but she had to admit that Will's program of probing questions had given them a remarkable degree of emotional intimacy in a very short period of time. She'd never been able to talk to a man like this.

"It wasn't long after the calf love devastation. I decided I would be like Delilah and take lovers and enjoy wild, passionate affairs, then move on, heart whole." She sighed. "I liked the passion part, you see."

"Being passionate is one of your many admirable traits," Will said firmly. "But I gather that didn't work out well?"

"I found out I could not lie with a man without coming to care too much, and that way devastation lay," she explained, unable to keep bitterness from her voice. "That's when I realized I must resign myself to virtuous spinsterhood."

Will frowned. "Your lover wouldn't marry you?"

"He was married already. I was trying to be like Delilah. The affair made me realize I could never, ever be like her. I didn't even *want* to be like her." She caught Will's gaze. "We have come together as two adults, experienced and with our eyes open. That does *not* mean you must marry me, even if you think honor demands it."

"Honor bedamned, I *want* to marry you!" he said with exasperation. "But now it's time to sleep. Tomorrow will be another long, tiring day." He drew her into his arms and tucked the blankets around them, then brushed a kiss on her forehead.

"You aren't going to give up, are you?" She rested her head on his shoulder, enjoying the relaxed intimacy of this embrace, the feel of his arm around her.

"No, but for the next few days, other concerns will come first." He hesitated, then went on, "You're as stubborn as I am, so changing your mind might never happen. But if I'm killed, please, please, go to my brother even if you don't need help. Tell him about my time in San Gabriel. He'll want to know."

"I promise I will," she whispered. She

owed Will that much and more.

So much more.

CHAPTER 29

He was losing her.

Will woke up with his heart pounding, his brain a jumble of loss and panic, of fading Lily and vanishing Athena. His heart slowed down when he saw that Athena still lay sleeping in his arms. He studied her peaceful face and wondered if Justin had been right in his guess of who her father might be. She'd said "the dreadful duke," and there weren't very many dukes. Not that it mattered to him, but it surely mattered to her.

She woke and gave him a sweetly sultry smile before her gaze went to the window. Dawn.

"I have to go!" She started to swing from the bed. "I can't risk being caught in immoral behavior that might reflect badly on Sofia."

"Just a moment more. *Please.*" His arms locked around her. "I thought we'd wake earlier and have a little more time. I wanted to make love to you again." But could he have borne that if he'd known it might be the last time?

"That would have been a splendid way to greet the day," she said softly, her face against his throat, her embrace as tight as his. "But given how very long yesterday was, and how busy we were for much of the night, it's not surprising that we didn't wake early." She pulled away, smiling with a warmth and lack of reserve he'd never seen before. "I did sleep very, very well, though."

"I also slept well. You're good for me." He cupped her cheek, aching with regret for all they might have had. "We might not have another chance to be together. I'll spend the day organizing the militia, scouting out the ambush area, and planning how to best use my black powder. I might not make it back to the castle tonight. Tomorrow night we'll be settling into our ambush positions and waiting for the French."

She bit her lip. "I'll be equally busy helping to evacuate as many people as possible to safer places, as well as making sure they all have the supplies needed to hold out until the troops return."

"It's going to be a busy day, but surely we can fit a short little wedding ceremony in after breakfast?" His tone was light, but he was in dead earnest.

She kissed him and slipped away. "Our schedules are far too busy, my dear Major Masterson." She scooped her robe up from the floor and pulled it on quickly. As she tied the sash, she whispered, "Keep yourself safe, Will! The world needs you." Then her graceful figure silently slipped from the room and was gone.

He lay back, staring up at the ceiling, his hands clenched at his sides. He might never see Athena again, and the thought ripped his heart from his chest.

Then he rose, washed and shaved, and donned his uniform. He had a war to fight. And then, by God, he'd come back and change her mind about marriage.

Breakfast with the Olivieras was somber but not panic-stricken. At least this time, they had warning of the French invasion. Justin was at the far end of the table, bandaged but looking reasonably well. He gave Will a thumbs-up and a smile. Athena wasn't present, and neither was Sofia. He wondered if they'd already eaten and set off on their tasks, or if Athena was trying to avoid him.

His new captains, Tom Murphy and Gilberto Oliviera, were sitting at one end of the long table, with an empty chair between them, and they beckoned for Will to join them. Like him, they were dressed in their well worn uniforms,

"Where do we begin planning, Generalissimo?" Tom asked, grinning.

"For calling me that, Gilberto will be senior captain and my second in command," Will said as he took his seat.

"See, Murphy? The generalissimo recognizes superior skill," Gilberto said teasingly as he passed a plate of savory sausages to Will, followed by another platter of baked eggs with potatoes and peppers.

"It's just because you're a Gabrileño," Tom retorted. A large coffeepot was set in the middle of the table, so he filled Will's mug, then topped up his and Gilberto's.

Will took a grateful swallow of coffee. "You're right, Gilberto is second in command because he's Gabrileño and knows more about his country than you or I ever will. He is also not prone to lower his dignity by running donkey races."

"An Irish specialty," Tom explained to Gilberto. "And great fun."

Gilberto smiled, but his levity quickly faded. "We'll not have time for donkey races on this campaign. Major Masterson, what are my duties for the day?"

"You're in charge of organizing the militia-men, since you know which men are most reliable and who will be steadiest under fire. Your veterans will be the backbone of our forces and they need to be mingled through-out the ranks to steady the others."

"And me, sir?" Tom asked, also serious.

"You and I will scout the ambush area to figure out where to place our men and the best use of our black powder. Gilberto, can you recommend a scout? Someone to go up the road into Spain and give us warning of advancing troops."

Gilberto considered. "Joaquim Cavaco. My father says he's the best young poacher in San Gabriel. He's quick and clever and looks younger than he is, so if the French notice him, they might not think he's a danger. The French killed his father last year, so he will be eager to undertake the task. I'll summon him here so he can guide you up the Spanish road."

"He sounds perfect," Will said. "Tom, have you any thoughts about how we should proceed?"

Tom indeed had some thoughts. Most had been considered already, but he had a couple of useful new suggestions. The three of them discussed everything, bouncing ideas off each other. While the commanding officer always had the final word, Will would be a fool not to take advantage of his subordinates' experience and ideas.

By the time the discussion ended, Will had cleared his plate and was ready to leave. Then silence fell across the dining room as Sofia entered, looking very regal, a tiara on her head.

Athena followed quietly, her expression serious, but wearing a delightful sunshine-yellow morning gown. Just looking at her made Will smile. Her warm, swift return glance did not suggest that she had any regrets about the previous night.

Sofia raised her hand in a command for attention. "My friends, you all know the grave situation that faces us. We will work together to preserve San Gabriel and our way of life, but the burden will fall most heavily on our soldiers, who will face the enemy. William Masterson, Gilberto Oliviera, and Thomas Murphy, please come forward."

Surprised, the three men stood and crossed the room to face Sofia. "Gilberto Oliviera, you are now promoted to captain in the Army of San Gabriel. Step forward so I can attach the insignia of your rank."

Gilberto obeyed, saying under his breath,

"You're getting quite good at being royal, Sofi!"

She smiled at her old playmate and said equally quietly, "Behave yourself or I might accidentally stab you while I pin this on."

He stood at attention and saluted her, saying with complete seriousness, "Your royal highness, I will do my duty to San Gabriel, even if it costs me my life."

"See that it doesn't, you scamp!" his mother said in a voice that carried through the room and produced a ripple of laughter.

Suppressing a smile, Sofia said, "Thomas Murphy, you have embraced this land as your own. I now commission you as a captain in the Army of San Gabriel."

"I am honored, your royal highness," he said firmly. After the princess pinned on the insignia, he saluted her crisply.

Then it was Will's turn. "Major Lord Masterson, in the brief time you've been in San Gabriel, you have already done much to help my country rebuild from the devastation of war," Sofia said in ringing tones. "Now by virtue of your experience and skill, I appoint you commander in chief of the Army of San Gabriel. You said that you never wished to be a general, so I give you the rank of colonel."

She stepped up to him with the insignia

of rank. She was so very small.

"Any rank will do, as long as it's higher than the others," he said with a smile.

"Indeed." She had to stand on her toes to attach the insignia to his shoulders. Stepping back, she said, "For as long as you are commander in chief, you also have the right to carry the Royal Sword of San Gabriel. Lady Athena, pray present it to Colonel Lord Masterson."

Athena stepped forward and offered him a shining sword with both hands. Startled, he took the weapon from her, saying softly, "Athena, goddess of war indeed!"

"Would that the sword wasn't needed!" she replied. "It's Damascus steel, strong and supple and very old."

The hilt glinted with inlaid gold wire patterns, but when he took the weapon in hand and made several experimental thrusts, he found that it was beautifully balanced. He usually carried a larger blade better suited to his height, but this one would do very well.

He raised the sword and clasped its hilt to his chest in a salute. "It's a magnificent sword, your royal highness. I am proud to wield it on behalf of San Gabriel."

"I know you shall carry it with honor." Sofia's gaze swept across the room, touching the familiar faces of her friends. "And may God and the Blessed Mother keep us all safe!"

Joaquim Cavaco was a clever imp who enthusiastically agreed to scout beyond San Gabriel's borders to watch for the approaching French forces. He was sixteen, but looked about twelve; and in his shabby brown-and-tan clothing, he blended in well with the landscape.

With some regret, he refused the offer of a horse to ride, saying that a mule was more sure-footed and more likely to be ridden by a shabby boy. If he were Spanish, he'd have been a natural to join the Spanish guerillas. Without the guerilla bands, Wellington never would have been able to drive the French from the Peninsula.

Will and Joaquim and Tom rode together up the road to Spain. As they passed the shrine of the Madonna de las Rosas, Will noted that a bouquet of summer flowers had been placed in front of the crude statue of the Madonna so recently that they hadn't yet started to wilt. A prayer for divine aid against the French, perhaps.

As they continued along the road, Will said, "If I recall correctly, the section of sunken road isn't much farther."

"You've a good eye for the country, sir," Tom commented. "I barely noticed it when we came this way before."

"All the Gabrileños were mad keen to get home so we rushed through here." Will shaded his eyes as he studied the road ahead. The sunken area was a little under half a mile long, he judged. The road was narrow and steep, but many, many feet and hooves over the centuries had worn it down so that it was between eight and twelve feet below the stony embankments on each side.

"Joaquim, you know this country well. Are there any geographical features that might help us make our ambush successful?"

The boy thought. "A small dry arroyo goes up behind the embankment on the left. It comes out just ahead." He studied the ground as they continued along the road, then pointed. "Here. We can ride the first part, but not all the way to the top."

The route didn't look like much more than a goat track, but it ran in the right direction. They proceeded up the hillside a short distance before coming to a small meadow with a spring. The track beyond was much steeper, so they dismounted and tethered their mounts by the spring, then continued on foot.

Higher up, the shallow ditch ran roughly

parallel with the embankment above the road, but a couple of feet lower. "Perfect!" Will said. "We can lie low here until the French are reported coming, then move into position above the road."

Tom nodded agreement. "Do you want us stationed on one side or both sides?"

"Both sides so we can catch the French in a cross fire. But more men on this side, I think, because it will be easier to lie concealed until we're ready to attack."

"So I see the French and come galloping back to warn everyone," Joaquim said. "Where will you be, Colonel?"

Will stood on the embankment and studied the terrain. "Down at the lower end, farthest into the valley, on this side." He pointed out the location. "When the French are as enclosed as they're going to get, I'll fire the first shot as a signal for the attack. Tom, I'll want you at the upper end on the opposite side to help steady the militia, with Gilberto across from you, and the next most senior sergeant of the veterans opposite me."

"Makes sense, but you're at the point where the embankment is lowest. If any of the French devils are mounted and have their wits about them, they'll charge right up the embankment to your position."

Will shrugged. "Someone needs to be

there and I'm a good shot." He turned to their scout. "Joaquim, are you ready to set off into Spain to watch for the French?"

"Yes, sir." He gave a smart salute. "I have enough supplies for two or three days, which should be long enough if your pet Frenchman is telling the truth."

"I'm reasonably sure he's telling the truth as he knows it, but plans do change." Will held out his hand to the boy. "*Vaya con Dios,* Joaquim."

The boy grinned. "If I do a good job, can I keep the mule?"

Will laughed. "Indeed you can."

As Joaquim skittered down the hill to the meadow where his mule was tethered, Will said, "Tom, what's the best use of our limited supplies of black powder? I didn't expect a war, so much of what Ballard brought up has to be used for the firearms, and thank God we have it. What can we do with the rest?"

"How about if we pack it into a few wooden boxes and set them along the enemy's line of march? Then fire into the boxes when they come by. The times we've done that, it's been effective." Tom smiled. "Makes a fine great bang, it does."

Will considered. "That works well in some cases, but it uses a lot of gunpowder. Even if we try to disguise the boxes, they might call attention to themselves as being out of place on a reasonably clear road. Plus, shooting them will be difficult if the French come through in the dark, which seems likely."

"All good objections," Tom said with regret. "What about grenades?"

"I'm thinking they're our best choice." Will studied the sunken road again. "Wine bottles made out of the thinnest available glass with black powder inside, sealed with wax and a wick."

"They'd have to be thrown by the steady men who have been in combat before," Tom said. "They'll terrify the inexperienced militiamen."

"True. We don't want to put grenades into the hands of someone who will blow up the wrong people." Another thought struck. "We can create a form of shrapnel by putting pebbles or nails and scrap metal into the grenade bottles. When they go off, the pieces will shoot all over the road. It should be particularly effective in the dark."

"I *like* that idea!" Tom grinned. "We're a bloodthirsty lot, aren't we, sir?"

"Yes, but in a good cause." Will began walking along the embankment, studying the ground. "We'll survey up this side and come back down the other so we know where to position our men. Then off to the Alcantara winery to beg some bottles. First a test grenade. If it works, we have enough gunpowder to make a couple of dozen."

"Roughly one for each experienced soldier. We'll need covered lanterns to light the fuses from. I'll ask Señora Oliviera for some."

With plans and grenades in prospect, Will felt a little more hopeful. If he was really lucky, he might make it back to the castle tonight.

The castle courtyard was getting crowded as whole families moved in and set up camp. As the most defensible site in San Gabriel, the castle was the designated sanctuary for much of the town and the surrounding countryside. The elderly and unwell were sheltered in outbuildings, but the weather was pleasant enough that most people could stay outside comfortably. In fact, Athena guessed that a fiesta might start soon. The Gabrileños were a resilient lot.

With Sofia overseeing the refugees in the castle, Athena and Señor Oliviera rode to the town of Espirito Santo at the other end of the valley to put the evacuation wheels in motion. There was less urgency here, since the castle area was much closer to the Spanish road and this end of the valley would have more warning.

But if the French survived the ambush in good order and swept into the valley, no place would be safe.

If that happened, Will would probably be dead; he wouldn't run away in terror. He'd try to rally his men, but what if not enough of them stood their ground?

She shuddered at the thought. Though she'd accepted that their affair would be brief, she'd hoped for more than a single night. She *needed* more than a single night. She needed his understanding, his humor, his deep caring. And his passion, which made her feel desirable and . . . loved. Loved as she'd never been before.

She spent the long hours on the road praying that the French would be defeated, with no Gabrileño casualties. Most particularly, not to the commander in chief.

CHAPTER 30

It was late when Will returned to the castle. For form's sake, he debated whether he should go to Athena's room, but he already knew what he'd decided. After a brief washup in his room, he walked silently to the far end of the corridor.

Though the courtyard outside buzzed with people, the family quarters of the castle were silent. He was glad to find that Athena's door wasn't locked. He pushed the handle down and stepped inside. "Athena?" he asked softly. "Don't shoot, it's me."

"Will!" Athena leaped from the bed and closed the space between them in three long strides. She hurled herself into his arms, locking him in a rib-bruising embrace. "I'm so glad you came! I'd given up thinking you'd be back tonight."

The simmering emotions he'd felt all day flared, shooting through him like a rocket.

His lover, his beloved, his mate. "I almost didn't make it. I'm sorry it's so late."

For reply, she found his mouth and kissed him with fierce urgency. The world dissolved, leaving only his frantic need to make love to her. "Athena," he gasped. *"My goddess . . ."*

They stumbled over each other on the way to the bed, luckily landing on the mattress rather than the floor. He discovered that she wore nothing under her loose nightgown, and that she was extremely adept at undoing the buttons that secured the fall of his trousers.

They came together with a force that should have made the heavens shake. As their bodies clashed, their spirits melded. He hadn't known desire could be so intense, or so satisfying. Even better was knowing how well he satisfied Athena. She moaned with ecstasy, her nails digging into him as they fought for completion. His goddess, his little owl, who had never been loved as well as she should have been, and who deserved everything he could give her and more.

"Will . . ."

Her climax triggered his own and nearly melted his mind. Also his body, as the tension flowed away and he folded himself around her. When his brain began working again, he panted, "I didn't actually come here to ravish you. At least, not right away."

She gave a choke of laughter. "I don't think it's ravishing when I'm trying to tear your clothes off."

He rolled to his side and pulled her close against him, then tugged the coverlet over them. "As busy as I was all day, in the back of my mind was the fear that I wouldn't see you again. I feel as if we're just beginning to really know each other. I hate thinking this might end almost before we've begun."

"I feel the same way." Her voice half teasing, she added, "I've never known a man like you. I want to spend enough time with you to discover if you really are as wonderful as you seem. But everything is in limbo. I feel like the sword of Damocles is hanging over our heads."

He stroked her neck and shoulders, gently kneading the tight muscles. "Exactly, except that it's hundreds of swords."

"More likely muskets. Were you able to complete what needed to be done today?"

"Yes, by tonight we'll be as ready as we can be. Today we surveyed the ambush area, sent off a scout to look for Baudin and his forces, and I spent the afternoon making grenades out of wine bottles and black powder."

She stroked a hand from his neck to his waist, her fingers light and soothing. "That sounds like a more interesting day than mine. Did you know that you have a lovely back? All strong and touchable, even when you're wearing several layers of clothing."

"I haven't actually thought much about my back," he said with mild surprise. "Mostly, I take for granted that it will do what I want it to do. How was your day spent?"

"Señor Oliviera and I rode through the valley and encouraged everyone to withdraw to the safe houses and caves with enough water and food to hold out for at least a fortnight. People are anxious but not panicked. They're better prepared than last year."

"The weeks of planning and drilling haven't been wasted, though I didn't expect a full-scale assault on San Gabriel," he said wryly. "I feared a few dozen bandits, maybe, but not this."

"Now that you've surveyed the ambush grounds and made your grenades, do you have any better sense of what might happen?"

He frowned. "I really have no idea. Once

fighting begins, plans go out the window. The ambush ground is good. The scout Gilberto found us should be able to give us enough warning to position ourselves.

"But we're still dramatically outnumbered, perhaps two to one or worse, and only about one in ten of our militiamen have any combat experience. Most should be able to manage as long as they're on the high ground shooting down into the road, but when the French start fighting back — and they will — some of the raw militiamen will probably break and run. When that happens, usually more men follow."

"It sounds like you need as many experienced shooters as you can find," Athena said slowly. "I'm going to join the ambush."

"What!" Will jerked up and stared down at her, unable to read her expression in the dim light. "You can't do that!"

"Why not?" she said reasonably. "I'm quite a good shot, and you said yourself that my nerves are steadier in battle than those of many experienced soldiers."

"Yes, but I can't bear to think of you going into such danger," he said flatly.

"How is that worse than me seeing you go into battle?" Athena asked. "You need people who can shoot and not run away. I've proved I can stand my ground and do what is necessary."

He couldn't deny that, yet the idea of her engaging with the French in battle appalled him. "*No!* I'm the commander in chief and I give the orders, no matter how irrational I may be."

"I'm not a soldier under your command," she pointed out. "I really don't think you can stop me. The ambush is strung some distance along the road, isn't it? I can take a position and you won't even notice in the dark."

All the horrors of battle passed through Will's mind as he stared at Athena. "You don't belong on a battlefield."

She raised a hand and cupped his cheek, her gaze sad. "No woman ever born has been happy to see her husband or son or brother go to war, but sometimes, war can't be avoided. I am English in my bones, but San Gabriel has given me the best things in my life. A position, a home, a family." She smiled a little. "You. I have taken much, and now I must give back, even if it means risking my life."

"Surely, Sofia needs you. You've been her right hand for the last five years."

"This time she has Justin, and he can help her in ways that I can't." Athena's voice gentled. "It would be different if my going off to fight wouldn't make a difference, but in this case, it might. You need experienced fighters, and I have some experience. Can you deny that I might be of value? Or that I have no right to risk my life on behalf of those I love?"

"No, but . . ." He halted, not knowing how to express what was basically a primal scream of protectiveness.

Her voice even softer, she said, "You seem to think I'm an unusual woman, and you like that. My willingness to fight if needed is part and parcel of my uniqueness. You can't deny that without denying who and what I am."

Despairing, he realized that she was right. "I surrender, my brave, wise owl," he said with profound reluctance. "But if you're there, you'll be stationed at my left hand, where I can watch out for you."

"And vice versa." She drew him down in a long hug. "Thank you, Will. For knowing me well enough to let me be who I am. For caring enough to accept the possibilities of pain and danger."

"Apparently, women have been doing that from time immemorial," he said wryly. "But knowing that doesn't make it any easier to accept!"

■ ■ ■ ■

Sofia was aghast that Athena was going to join the militia. "You can't go! No woman belongs on a battlefield! I need you here!"

"Sofi, my love, you're going to run out of exclamation points," Athena said as she packed a blanket, a canteen of water, bread and cheese, ammunition, and a few basic medical supplies into a canvas sack she could sling across her back. "You also sound exactly like Will."

"I always knew he was a man of great good sense." Sofia bit her lip. "It's bad enough that so many male Gabrileños are risking their lives. You're the chief advisor of the royal princess of San Gabriel. I need you here!"

"No, you don't." Athena slung the sack over her shoulder. "You have the Olivieras, the mayor of the town, the priest, and Justin, and they are all people of great good sense."

"It's unnatural for women to fight like men," Sofia said stubbornly.

"May I remind you of your great-grandmother Queen Maria Mercedes de la Alcantara? When she was traveling here to wed your great-grandfather, her party was attacked and she led the charge that drove them away, spurring on her guards and waving a sword."

"She didn't have a choice." Sofia's gaze was stark. "You do."

"I don't." Athena's expression was grave. "You know that I have unladylike abilities because you've seen me in action. I don't seek out danger, but I can fight when it's needful, and now is one of those times."

Sofia sighed. "I know you're right, but I'm terrified for you. You're the only family I have left. Please, please, be careful! And don't let Will get killed, either."

"I'll do my best on both counts." Athena hugged her. "It's time for me to go. Will suggested that you and Justin keep an eye on Jean Marie. I don't think he's going to run off to warn Baudin, but best that he doesn't have the opportunity."

"We'll make sure he stays here." Sofia bit her lip. "I hope that by tomorrow afternoon, this will all be over and San Gabriel will be safe again. But that's not very likely, is it?"

"Will says it's impossible to predict. But I'm sure our militia will do serious damage to the invaders, and the sanctuaries and supplies we've arranged will protect most of the population. Will said that if the ambush goes badly, the militia will fall back to the castle and defend it. The Gabrileño army will be back in a fortnight or so. Your country will survive, your highness."

"But the sooner the French are stopped, the less San Gabriel will suffer." Sofia straightened. "I'll escort you down to the stables, then go to the castle chapel to pray. It's all I'm good for."

"That's not true!" Athena said sharply. "You are the soul of San Gabriel. Your courage, dignity, and compassion make you beloved, and raise everyone's morale tremendously. Don't ever discount that. Other people can shoot the enemy, but San Gabriel has only one royal princess."

Sofia supposed Athena was right, but as they went down to the courtyard together, she thought how much simpler her life had been when she was the pretty, frivolous princess with no responsibilities other than to marry well.

CHAPTER 31

By early evening, the members of the San Gabriel militia had gathered in the small meadow below the embankment, where they would wait in ambush. Counting Will and Athena, 198 defenders. He had hoped there would be a few more, but what they lacked in numbers, they made up in grim determination.

Will moved up the hill a little so he was above the crowd. Raising one arm, he called, "Men of San Gabriel, hear me!"

When he had everyone's attention, he said in a voice that carried through the meadow, "We all know why we are here. If our information is correct, a sizable force of renegade French soldiers under General Baudin will be invading the country in the next hours to finish what they started last summer."

His words triggered an angry murmur of voices. Will waited until that subsided, then continued, "The French are experienced soldiers. They know how to fight. But you have one huge advantage. San Gabriel is your home. You fight to protect your land, your families, your friends. That gives you a power the French cannot match."

His gaze swept the crowd. The ages ranged from very young boys to grizzled old men. Some carried muskets so old he hoped they wouldn't explode; the army veterans had rifles — the six French rifles they'd captured a few days before had been distributed to men most likely to get good use from them. He and Athena carried sleek, accurate carbines, which were lighter in weight and easier to reload, and he also carried a pistol. Not to mention the Royal Sword of San Gabriel.

What they had in common was commitment to preserving their country. "We will fight, side by side," he said more quietly. "If you're afraid, that's as it should be. You'd be fools not to be afraid. But stand your ground and fight together, and we will win!"

There was a great roar of approval. Then someone shouted, "What is Lady Athena doing here?"

"She will fight with the men of San Gabriel because she loves this country and your princess, and she shoots well," Will explained. "She has volunteered her rifle and her life to aid our cause."

"Why are you letting a woman fight with us?" another voice called doubtfully.

"Have you ever argued with an armed woman?" Will quipped.

As laughter rang out, Athena stepped up the hill to stand beside him. In truth, with the wind whipping her divided skirts and her carbine in hand, she looked like a warrior goddess.

"I have faced the French in Porto when they conquered the city, and just a few days ago when a scouting party attacked us as we surveyed the river," she called in a carrying voice. "I have shot and killed the enemy, and I have never fled in fear." She grinned. "If a mere woman can stand and fight, surely every man here can do the same!"

That produced good-natured comments and a few teasing remarks, but the mood was positive. Will said under his breath, "Well done. None of them would dare run when you're still holding the line."

"Use their male pride against them," Athena agreed with tart amusement.

Will raised his voice again. "You will be divided into squads of nine, each to be commanded by a veteran. You'll also be given the numbers one, two, or three for firing order. When I fire the shot to begin the attack, all of the number ones will fire, then the number twos, then the number threes. By then, the first group should be reloaded to fire again. The idea is to pour continuous fire into the French so they can't escape and so they think we have more men than we do. Does everyone understand?"

Most of the men nodded. They looked nervous and a few were visibly fearful, but his veterans were alert and ready. They wouldn't run when the shooting started, not when their homes were at stake. "Some of us will spend the night in ambush position," Will continued. "The rest of you can relax here for now. Hundreds of men on the march will make noise no matter how hard they try to move quietly.

"But with luck, our scout, Joaquim Cavaco, will come in advance to give us a better idea of how many men we face and how soon they'll arrive. That means that if you hear one young man and a mule coming down the road, hold your fire! After Joaquim reports, I'll pass on what he says." Will smiled, wanting to ease the mood. "Joaquim might show up and say the French have changed their minds."

"Not bloody likely!" Tom Murphy called.

"No," Will agreed. "Perhaps Joaquim will report that the French are moving more slowly than expected. Or maybe they're traveling faster. This is why we need scouts. But whenever the French come, we will be ready. We will fight, and we will *win*!" He pulled the Royal Sword of San Gabriel from the scabbard at his side and raised it above his head, the shimmering Damascus steel blazing in the afternoon sunshine. "For San Gabriel, for Princess Maria Sofia, and for victory!"

The roar that sounded from his troops must have been audible from one end of the valley to the other. Then the crowd broke up with the captains and lead sergeants heading up the hill to their positions and the other men finding places to get comfortable.

Will said, "Time to take our stations, Lady Athena. And if you have any special goddess-of-war magic, feel free to exercise it."

She chuckled as she climbed the hill by his side. She wore her split riding skirt, sturdy boots, a loose jacket with many pockets, and her gleaming carbine. At her waist was a sheathed knife and slung over her shoulder was a canvas bag of supplies that probably included bandages and other useful things. He might worry about Athena's safety, but she was certainly ready.

"How far apart will we be stationed?" she asked.

"Every twenty feet or so. The grenadiers are distributed fairly evenly along the lines."

"Twenty feet from you," she murmured wickedly. "Too far."

"Behave yourself, wench," he ordered. "We have a battle to fight!"

"After that speech you gave, I feel invincible," she said.

Will wished that he were equally confident.

Hours passed with nothing much happening, so Athena moved fifteen feet to her right so that she was within easy talking distance of Will, though regrettably out of touching distance. "I've just learned something truly terrible about going to war," she said in a voice barely above a whisper. "It's really boring."

There was enough moonlight to show Will's grin. "Long periods of boredom and discomfort punctuated by brief bursts of noise and terror. The soldier's life."

"I'm realizing that when I've faced danger before, it happened swiftly and I had to react. I'm not so good at waiting."

"Go back to your position and roll up in your blanket and get some sleep," Will suggested. "We're not likely to see much happen for a few hours yet."

"I don't know if I can sleep, but I'll try to rest." Her voice became even softer. "I wish I could curl up next to you, but I expect that would be counter to good discipline."

"Especially mine." He made a shooing motion with his hand. "But at least we both have excellent motivation to survive."

Chuckling, she returned to her position. Oddly, despite the discomfort of sleeping on the ground and the threat of danger, she dozed off. She felt safe with Will near. . . .

In a silent night broken only by the rustling of a breeze in the bushes and the sounds of night creatures, hasty hoofbeats sounded very clearly. As Will skidded down the embankment, he sensed his fellow soldiers coming alert.

When the mule approached, he recognized the small form of Joaquim. He waved the boy down, asking, "What news, Scout Cavaco?"

Joaquim pulled up the mule, both of them panting for breath. "The French are not far behind! Maybe half an hour, no more. I was delayed because they blocked my route and

I had to go around." The boy pulled off his hat and wiped his face tiredly.

"Do you have an idea of the numbers?"

"My guess is closer to six hundred than five hundred, but I'm not sure. Many. They march in a column, keeping good order, a few supply wagons behind, but most of their supplies on their backs or on mules."

"Do they look alert and ready for battle?"

"They look . . . hungry," the boy said slowly. "Desperate, even."

So they would go into battle as motivated as the Gabrileños. Not good. But with luck, they'd be worn out by the long march and not expecting attack here and now. "Anything else you can think of that might be useful to know?"

Even in the dim light, Joaquim's snarl could be seen. "Their general, Baudin, rides at the head with several of his officers on fine horses."

"Probably he stole them from Napoleon's stable," Will said easily. "Continue on to the castle and give the news to Princess Sofia. After you get some rest, you can join the castle guards."

"I'll get to meet the princess?" Joaquim said, brightening.

"Yes, and she'll be well pleased with your work."

As Joaquim proceeded along the road at a slower pace, Will climbed the embankment on the other side and passed on the news to Ramos, the army veteran stationed opposite him.

"Time to move everyone into position. I'm thinking that if we can take out Baudin, it might break the nerve of his men," Will said. "You and I both hold grenades. After I fire the first shot and the fusillade begins, shall we aim our grenades at Baudin?"

Ramos's teeth flashed white in the darkness. "With pleasure. May the Blessed Mother grant me the honor of being the one to blow him to hell."

"You'll have competition for that," Will said with a friendly clap on the shoulder. "And now, battle stations!"

The next minutes were a blaze of activity as the sergeants got their men into position. When Will passed Athena, he said softly, "Hold steady, little owl. And aim for the officers leading the column on horseback. One of them should be Baudin."

"Worth a try. The man is evil." Athena swallowed hard. "Go with God, Will."

He touched her cheek, then moved on down the line. The veterans did a good job positioning the militiamen. While there was anxiety and a few had lost their suppers, no one had deserted. They appreciated Will's comments and jokes.

When he reached Gilberto, Will said, "Years from now, old men will be telling their grandsons that they were here this day, defending San Gabriel."

Gilberto snorted. "Remembering the glory and forgetting the blood!"

"Glory grows in proportion to how long ago the battle took place. Go with God, Captain." Will shook Gilberto's hand, then turned and trotted back to his own position.

Then, they waited.

CHAPTER 32

As the first faint light appeared along the eastern horizon, the distant sounds of marching men could be heard. Heavy feet, the clink of harnesses, the occasional barked order of a sergeant. The noise intensified when the column entered the sunken road and was contained between the embankments.

The back of Will's neck tingled with nerves and anticipation. To his left, Athena was a dark, quiet form as she waited, carbine ready. He imagined that the inexperienced militiamen were ready to jump out of their skins with the French marching just feet below them, but they held their fire. The light had increased enough to see men and horses as individual shapes, though details were still unclear.

The half-dozen mounted officers in the lead came level with Will. He took careful aim at the first rider, hoping it was Baudin, and fired. As the crack of his carbine echoed from the stony hills, his bullet struck his target.

Before the man hit the ground, the first rank of Gabrileños fired. Cacophony, a screaming horse, sergeants shouting orders to their men.

Second rank fired. Third rank fired. The first again. The volleys became more ragged as reloading time varied, but the bullets were taking effect and the French troops were breaking from their regular marching formation.

The sunken road filled with clouds of stinging smoke and Will saw that dozens of French soldiers had fallen. Others had dropped into firing position and were returning fire whenever they caught a glimpse of a defender, but they were at a great disadvantage.

Will lit the first of his grenades and hurled it among the leading horsemen, then ducked. The grenade exploded and shrapnel flew in all directions. Furious curses split the air from the French soldiers.

Athena had flattened herself on the edge of the embankment and coolly fired down at her targets. *What a woman!* Will thought.

The chaos of battle roared around Will as he fired, reloaded, fired again, all while keeping mental track of how many volleys of bullets he heard, how his militia was holding, how well the French were starting to fight back.

So far the Gabrileños were performing admirably, but the longer the battle continued, the more the advantage would shift to the seasoned French troops. Already some were starting to scramble up the embankments, cursing and shouting death threats. Most were shot, bayoneted, or clubbed as they crested the banks, but they had numbers on their side and more and more of them were scrambling upward.

His heart almost stopped when he saw that one damnable soldier was clawing his way up the bank toward Athena. She was reloading, so Will clamped down his fear and shot the man in the chest. As the soldier tumbled backward, Will lit his second grenade and hurled it into the turmoil on the road. The riders in the lead had spread out so one blast wouldn't catch them all, but there was no shortage of targets.

More grenades were exploding along the road, yet in the face of raking gunfire and cacophony, bellowing French officers and sergeants were beginning to successfully rally their troops. Will realized that the battle had reached a critical point. If the fighting didn't end very soon, the Gabrilenos would be overwhelmed and the French would have a clear path to invade the valley.

His jaw tightened as his well honed battle instincts recognized the best and only hope for ending this quickly. *Cut off the head and the snake dies.*

If Will could take Baudin down, this battle would be over. Baudin was the inspiration and charismatic leader who had persuaded these men to cross the whole of Spain to conquer a small, weak nation. His men hadn't expected this stiff, bloody resistance. Without their general, the invasion force would collapse into a demoralized mob. In the face of continuing Gabrileño fire, the surviving French troops would withdraw and likely look for easier prey, or even return home to lay down their arms.

The light had increased, so Will narrowed his eyes and studied the men on horseback who had led the column. The fighting had drawn them back along the road, but they were still within shooting range. Yes, that broad man who was shouting orders at the top of his lungs was surely Baudin.

Will took careful aim and fired, but Baudin was in constant motion. The number of other men and horses thrashing about around the general made it impossible to get a clear shot. Will's bullet wounded one of the general's aides, leaving Baudin unscathed.

Will reloaded swiftly but his second shot also went amiss. He swore under his breath, recognizing that Baudin had the warrior luck that seemed to make many battle leaders immune to bullets. Such luck had kept Wellington alive throughout his career, not to mention Will himself. A damned shame that Baudin had it, too. Maybe those without the luck died young.

But no man was immune to a bullet at close range. If Will couldn't take the devil down from up here, he must descend to Baudin's level.

Knowing he was signing his death warrant, he leaped over the edge of the embankment and skidded down the rough slope in a cloud of dust and pebbles, his carbine in hand and his pistol holstered at his side. As soon as his feet hit the road, he sprinted toward the mounted officers. Bullets whistled by, but missed. His own battlefield luck was holding. He halted a dozen feet from Baudin. The insignia of the general's rank was now clearly visible.

Ignoring the churning horses and men around him, Will raised his carbine and aimed. At the last moment, Baudin saw him and jerked his reins back, causing his mount to rear up. Will's bullet struck the beast instead of the man.

The thrashing horse went down hard, but Baudin skillfully freed himself from the saddle and rolled to his feet. The sky was bright enough now to see faces, and for an instant Baudin stared at Will. In the midst of chaos, the two men might have been alone.

"You!" the Frenchman snarled. "Surely, you are that great hulking English spy, one of the ones who escaped my execution in Gaia!"

So Baudin was the officer who had condemned five men out of hand. Somehow it wasn't a surprise. "Not a spy," Will said in cool, sharp-edged French as he yanked his pistol from its holster. "A soldier."

He held the pistol in both hands so he wouldn't miss, but as he fired, Baudin drew his sword and lunged forward, the sweep of his blade knocking the pistol from Will's grip and sending the bullet awry.

Will had chosen to lay down his life to end this battle, and he damned well wasn't going to fail! With a fatalistic feeling of rightness, he drew his last weapon, the Royal Sword of San Gabriel, and balanced himself to react to the general's attack. He must end this now, before Baudin's aides had time to shoot him in the back.

Sword fights in the midst of battle were quick, dirty, and deadly. Will's weapon was light and sure in his grasp, but Baudin's was longer and heavier. The Frenchman took advantage of that as he tested Will's skill with a flurry of swift thrusts and parries, filling the air with the shriek of metal scraping metal.

Will responded clumsily, taking advantage of the fact that French officers prided themselves on being better swordsmen than their British counterparts. Baudin clearly believed that, for when Will feinted a stumble on the rough road, the general moved in recklessly for the kill.

Will stepped to one side and stabbed his Damascus steel blade through the French general's brutal heart. Baudin's pale eyes widened with shock before he collapsed in his own blood, the weight of his body pulling free of the blade that had killed him. Their struggle, from Will's first shot to this end, had lasted only a handful of moments.

He'd known that taking the fight to the enemy would be a one-way trip, and now he paid the price for his audacity. The first ball crashed into Will's shoulder, the second into his leg.

As the next shot pitched Will into darkness, he prayed that now the battle and the invasion were over.

Athena watched in horror as Will vaulted from his safe spot on the embankment and charged into the middle of the fray. Time seemed to stretch as he shot, brought down Baudin's horse, then crossed swords with the general. Her heart almost stopped when Will stumbled. Then Will struck, killing Baudin, and she realized that his stumble had been deliberate and lethally effective.

Even before she could scream, *"Run!"* Baudin's aides were aiming their weapons and shooting at their leader's assassin. Will went down only a yard from the general, his bloodstained sword still in his hand.

Faces twisted with rage, three of the general's aides were busily reloading so they could ensure that Will was dead. Athena aimed with bitter efficiency and took one down. While she reloaded, Ramos, the veteran on the opposite side of the road, shot another. Athena aimed her carbine again and fired at the third.

The last of the general's avenging aides fell from his mount and lay motionless. As his horse galloped off, Athena slung her canvas bag around her shoulder and scrambled down the embankment, shouting in French, "*Baudin is dead!* Your leader, your general, is *dead*! Retreat before you die beside him!"

Her cry was picked up by other voices and news of the general's death blazed along the sunken road. As Athena dropped beside Will, she heard a French bugle sound the call for retreat and the soldiers in blue began scrambling back toward Spain.

Ignoring the risk of Frenchmen who might still be inclined to fight, Athena began to examine Will's wounds. He was bleeding in multiple places, but still he breathed.

She'd packed her bag with clean rags and folded bandages, as well as two sizable canteens, one filled with water and the other with strong, cheap brandy for cleaning wounds. As she used a rag to blot blood from the graze on Will's head, his eyes opened and he asked in a barely audible voice, "It's over?"

"Yes, the retreat has sounded and I can no longer see French soldiers along the road," she said unsteadily. "They're heading back to Spain."

"Good." He managed a smile. "It's been a fine thing to know you, little owl." As his eyes closed again, he said so faintly that she could hardly hear the words, "I love you,

you know."

"We can discuss the issue when you're better." As she fought to control the bleeding, Athena told herself, over and over, that while Will lived, there was hope. He wasn't going to die; *she wouldn't let him die.*

She wasn't sure how much time passed before Tom Murphy knelt on Will's other side. He was dusty and there was a smear of blood on his cheek, but it didn't seem to be his. "The French are flying the hell back into Spain and our casualties are fairly light. How is Major Masterson?"

"Alive, barely," she said in a choked voice. "Find a French wagon to take Will and other seriously wounded men back to the castle."

"One is on the way," he said tersely. "I'll go speed it up."

Not looking up, she nodded and used the knife she had sheathed at her waist to cut fabric away from the wound on Will's thigh. The bullet didn't seem to have shattered the bone, thank God.

She continued working until a wagon pulled up beside her. The last bandage had been tied off and Will was still breathing. She looked up to see a Gabrileño driving the wagon and Tom approaching with a litter and several other men behind him.

"We'll take him now, Lady Athena," Tom said quietly.

She stood and might have fallen if Tom hadn't put out a hand to steady her. "His condition is . . . very grave," she whispered.

"The major is the strongest man I know," Tom said fiercely, as if he was trying to convince himself as much as Athena. *"He'll survive this!* We'll get him down to the castle and into the hands of the surgeon as soon as possible."

He and the other men carefully transferred Will's considerable weight onto the litter, then carried him around to the back of the wagon. Athena followed and saw that the wagon was full of wounded, except for the space left for Will.

After the litter bearers transferred him into the wagon, Tom turned to Athena, his expression set. "I know you want to go with him, but there are other men here who need your help." His mouth twisted and he no longer looked young. "Cleaning up after a battle generally takes longer than the actual fighting."

She bit her lip. "I'm no surgeon."

"You're better at treating wounds in the field than anyone else available," Tom said flatly. "The sooner injuries are treated, the better the chances of survival."

Athena wanted to say to hell with everyone else, she needed to be with Will. But she'd done her best for him, and now there were other men, sons and husbands and fathers, who were also in need. She knew many of them. With a sigh, she yielded. "Very well, I'll do what I can."

Tom smiled and touched her shoulder. "Thank you. If I ever have a daughter, I'm going to name her Athena."

"She won't thank you for that," Athena said dryly. "Now where are these men who need treatment?"

As Tom escorted her back along the road, she gave thanks that the battle for San Gabriel was won. But what mattered most to her was the battle for Will Masterson's life.

CHAPTER 33

It was dark by the time Athena returned to Castelo Blanco, and she was beyond fatigue and wore the blood of multiple men. Ignoring both fatigue and blood, she headed directly to Will's bedroom on the far end of the family floor.

"How is he?" she asked Sofia, who sat outside Will's room, her face drawn.

"Athena!" Sofia went into Athena's arms, not crying but shaking.

Athena went cold to the bone. "Dear God, is he . . . ?"

"No! No, Will is still alive." Sofia collected herself. "Alive and coherent, but very, very weak. The surgeon said he wouldn't have survived long enough to reach the castle if not for your bandaging him up, but he's lost so much blood!"

She studied Athena's face before saying softly, "If you have anything you want to say to Will, say it now. Dr. de Ataide couldn't say how much time he has left. San Gabriel won, but at what price?"

Athena closed her eyes, feeling like her heart was being cut from her breast with a dull blade. She'd prayed for a miracle, and it wasn't going to happen. Or perhaps the big miracle of defeating the French renegades meant there could be no smaller miracles.

She opened her eyes and said starkly, "Will deliberately chose to sacrifice his life to end the battle before it could be lost. Yes, the price was too high, but Will and the others who fell today paid it willingly." Reminding herself of that, she opened the door and moved quietly into Will's bedroom.

A single lamp showed him as a broad, still shape in his bed. The bed where they had become joyous lovers for a few brief hours.

Though he was a mass of bloodstained bandages, his face was peaceful. "Will?" she asked in a low voice.

His eyes opened and he turned his head toward her and said in a rasping voice, "Little owl! I'm so glad you made it here in time. The French haven't regrouped and returned?"

"No, with Baudin dead and so many wounded, they lost the will to fight. When last seen, the survivors were fleeing back into Spain. We had surprisingly few casualties on our side. Your ambush was brilliantly successful." It seemed damnably unfair that Will should be one of its casualties.

"I presume my captains are maintaining a guard on the road." When Athena nodded, he said weakly, "Will you lie down beside me?"

She hesitated. "I don't want to hurt you."

"The surgeon was very free with the laudanum, so I'm feeling surprisingly little pain." He patted the mattress beside him. "Please?"

The bed was wide and there was room, so she stretched out on her side, very carefully, and took his hand. Lying there, touching him . . . such peace as she'd never know again. But she mustn't cry, she *mustn't*. "Do you have any last messages you want me to send?"

"Before we headed out, I wrote several letters to friends." He paused for an alarming fit of coughs. "Over there on my desk. Can you see they get back to England?"

"Of course."

He clasped her hand without much strength. "I have one other request, Athena."

"Anything," she said simply.

"Don't be too sure," he said with a ghost of humor. "Will you marry me before it's too late?"

She jerked up on her elbow and stared at him. "You don't have to do that!"

"Perhaps not, but I want to." His gray eyes were clear and determined despite his weakness. "Not just so that you and any possible child will be taken care of, but because I want to have you for my wife, even if only for a few hours."

Her throat hurt so much that at first she couldn't talk, so she just nodded her head. "I'll have Sofia call in the priest," she managed. "I expect he'll be willing to waive the usual formalities and banns for the hero of San Gabriel."

"Heroes. Plural." His smile was radiant before his eyes drifted shut. "You were magnificent, my lovely little owl."

Terrified he might not have enough time for her to fulfill his last request, Athena rolled from the bed and darted into the corridor. She found Justin holding Sofia in his arms for mutual comfort. His face was stricken, for he and Will had been friends for most of their lives.

Not wasting words, Athena said, "Sofia, Will wants to marry me. How quickly can you get the priest up to the castle?"

Startled, she said, "Father Anselmo is already in the castle. He came to perform the last rites for several of the other soldiers. He'll probably welcome a different task."

Athena sighed. "The reasons for a swift ceremony aren't happy, but at least he won't have to perform the last rites for an English Protestant. Will you and Justin stand witness for us?"

"Of course."

While Sofia sent for the priest, Athena returned to Will's room and sat beside the bed, holding his hand. "The priest is on his way."

"Good," he murmured without opening his eyes.

She studied his face, wanting to memorize every detail. The lines of humor around his mouth, a faint scar on his temple, the whiskers that hadn't been shaved. His dear, dear face.

Father Anselmo arrived with Sofia and Justin behind him. He was a tall, lean man, and his kind face reflected the gravity of the occasion. Sofia brought a small bouquet of wildflowers from the castle garden for Athena to hold.

With her other hand, Athena gripped Will's hand as if she could hold him back from the night. She whispered her vows, but Will's voice was surprisingly strong as he said his. " 'Till death do us part. . . .' "

When the time came for the ring, he said, "Athena, take the signet right off my hand. It's all I have to offer."

Tears stinging her eyes, she carefully worked it off the third finger of his left hand and let him slide it onto her finger. " 'With this ring, I thee wed.' " She wanted to howl. Instead, she bent and touched her lips to his. "I never thought I'd ever have a husband, Will, much less a man as splendid as you."

He smiled up at her. "And you have the advantage of not having to put up with my bad temper when I have to get up too early."

Her tears threatened to overflow. "Please don't joke. I can't bear it."

He patted her hand. "Sorry. Now that we're officially married, the rest of you can go away. I want to sleep with my wife."

Sofia wordlessly kissed his cheek; Justin shook his hand; then they followed the priest out, leaving the newlyweds alone together. "A good thing we anticipated our vows, or you wouldn't have much in the way of memories," Will observed.

This time Athena did cry. "I'm sorry," she said as she dabbed at her eyes. "I never thought to be wedded and widowed within a day."

"Better than not to be wedded at all." He

patted the bed beside him again. "Let's not waste what time we have."

She stretched out beside him and inched up against his side. "Strange how even in these circumstances you bring me peace."

"And you bring me joy," he whispered. "Sleep well, little owl."

She didn't mean to sleep, but she was so exhausted that consciousness slipped away. She drifted off with her palm resting over his heart. The slow, steady beat was reassuring. *Still alive, still alive, still alive . . .*

She awoke to find the sun had risen and Will was still alive. In fact, he was propped up on one elbow watching her. "You sleep very charmingly," he said.

She blinked, startled. "You look much stronger than you did last night."

"I feel much stronger. In fact, I don't feel at all like dying," he said thoughtfully. "I believe you're going to be stuck with me for longer than you anticipated."

Sputtering, she shot up to a sitting position. "Were you pretending to die so I'd marry you?"

His brow furrowed as he thought about it. "No, several people said that I was dying, and I thought they probably knew more about it than I did," he said seriously. "I think I'd had so much laudanum that I was willing to believe anything I heard."

"But what about the bullet wounds?" she asked, balanced between delight at his survival and a suspicion that he'd deceived her. "You were hit several times, and I had trouble stopping the bleeding."

Will grimaced. "The wounds are real, and painful now that the laudanum has worn off, but I vaguely recall the surgeon saying that I was lucky to have received just flesh wounds. I lost so much blood I feel weak as a kitten, but I don't feel that death is imminent and I've never been prone to having wounds become inflamed." He smiled down at her. "I certainly hope I'm recovering, my lovely bride!"

He'd always been so honest that she couldn't believe he was lying now, but a certain wariness remained. "I believe you did think you were dying, but would you have lied to persuade me to marry you?"

"That's an interesting question. I think of myself as an honest man, but where you're concerned, I suspect I could be rather deceitful." He smiled at her with deep affection. "Because I do love you so very much, little owl. You enchant and delight and awe me. Are you at least a little glad I'm not going to die this time?"

Having recovered from her shock and

confusion, she felt a rush of joy. "Yes!" She rolled across the bed and hugged him exuberantly.

"Ouch!" he said as he hugged her back. "With the laudanum worn off, that hurt!"

"You deserve it," she said unfeelingly. She nuzzled her face into his whiskery neck. "Thinking you were about to die tore holes in my heart." She sighed, some of her exuberance fading. "Part of me adores the idea of being married to you, but I'm still worried about London and society and that whole world that is yours, which never had a place for me."

"Will you trust me, little owl?" He cupped her head with a large, gentle hand. "My friends will love you because I love you. Together we will find or create a place where we can be happy. Even if that means returning to San Gabriel, where we can both be honored as heroes of the French invasion."

"Since we've made our vows, I must trust that you're right." She let go of her fears and allowed herself to rejoice and share his confidence that they could make their marriage work. "If your friends and family accept me, that will be enough. For now, I just want to lie here with you and be happy, even if it wasn't a very satisfactory wedding night."

He laughed and hugged her to him. "I'll make it up to you soon, my dear girl. 'Till death do we part.' "

Those words were no longer heartbreaking, but a promise of joy. With a sigh of pure pleasure, she settled closer and draped her arm over Will's waist, careful to avoid any of his bandages. He might be somewhat damaged now, but he was still warm and strong and deliciously male. Her husband.

With any luck, it would be hours before anyone disturbed them.

CHAPTER 34

Exercising her royal prerogative, Sofia invited Justin to a private breakfast with her in the family room. He arrived to find her cat, Sombra, sitting politely on a third chair, while expressing keen interest in the breakfast food on the table.

He scratched the cat's furry head and brushed a light kiss on Sofia's forehead. She looked lovely and composed after the stress of the last days. Her dark hair was shining and she wore mourning black as a mark of respect for those who had died fighting the French. With her fair complexion and delicate coloring, she was beautiful in black.

Resisting his desire to kiss her seriously, he rounded the table to the other side. "This feels wonderfully domestic. Not to mention quiet."

She smiled up at him. "I could not face the noisy celebrations of the Olivieras, may God bless and keep them."

"Nor could I." He seated himself opposite Sofia. The knife wound across his chest still hurt if he wasn't careful, but he was healing well. His smile faded. "Knowing that Will is dying takes much of the pleasure from the celebration. I suppose we would have heard by now if . . . if he'd passed away during the night."

"Athena would have told us if his condition had worsened," Sofia assured him.

Justin's face eased. "I'm glad Will got to marry Athena. He wanted that so much."

Sofia poured coffee for them both. "It wouldn't surprise me if he's feeling much better today. Dr. de Ataide tends to take a dire view of what might happen. I think he feels that if he predicts the worst and the patient dies, he won't be blamed, and if he predicts the worst and the patient recovers, people will say what a fine doctor he is. He did admit that while Will had lost a lot of blood, none of his injuries were critical as long as they didn't become inflamed."

Justin's wave of relief was immediately followed by suspicion. "Did you deliberately make it sound as though Will was dying so Athena would marry him?"

Sofia's dark eyes were round and guileless. "I may have exaggerated a bit," she admitted. "I was so very worried and I'm very fond of your major."

Not fooled, Justin said severely, "That was very bad of you, Princess."

"Was it? Athena and Will are so perfectly suited, but she was holding back and it was hurting both of them." Sofia's wistful gaze caught his. "I thought that at least one couple should be happy, even if we can't be."

Touched, he reached across the table and took her hand. "You make it very hard to argue with you!"

"I prefer not to manipulate people," she said seriously, "but to be raised royal is to have a certain pragmatism. Athena will not regret marrying Will, and I will not regret encouraging them in that direction."

"You're dangerous!" he said feelingly.

She bit her lip. "Are you angry with me for deceiving your friends?"

He thought, then shook his head. "Not really. I agree that they're perfect for each other, but Athena's background made it hard for her to accept him. Now that they're married, her new husband will make sure she has no regrets." He fixed Sofia with a stern glance. "But do not *ever* do such a thing to me!"

"I don't think I'll have the opportunity, Justin. Besides, you see through me," she said candidly. After several bites of baked egg, she paused with her fork in the air. "I just realized I haven't seen Jean Marie since yesterday. Has he been with you?"

"No, he said something about going outside to help. I thought he meant helping with the wounded being brought into the courtyard." Justin frowned. "Do you think he took the opportunity to escape and return to his French comrades?"

Sofia shook her head, bewildered. "If so, he can't have warned them of the ambush because they walked right into it."

"Perhaps when he said he wanted to help, he meant to go up to the battlefield? He'd be able to translate for the wounded French, since he's been picking up the Gabrileño dialect very quickly."

"I thought he meant the oath of loyalty he swore." Sofia bit her lip. "I suppose we'll find out whether he meant it if he returns."

"If he doesn't . . ." Justin shrugged eloquently. "At least he didn't betray Will's plans to Baudin."

In the silence that followed, distant music could be heard. Sofia stiffened and set her cup down so hard the coffee splashed. "That's the Gabrileño Army marching song! It must be Colonel da Silva!" She dashed to the window and looked out. "Yes, our troops are marching up the road to the castle!"

She tore out the door like a five-year-old rather than a royal princess. Justin followed more slowly, not just because he hadn't fully recovered. Greeting the returning veterans was Sofia's job and he'd only be in the way.

The army's return was bittersweet for him. Now life in San Gabriel would return to normal, or rather, a new normal based on how the world had changed in the last years. But high on the country's agenda would be finding a suitable husband for the royal princess, and that did not include a Scottish wine shipper.

Sofia reached the courtyard as the gates opened. The marching music was booming now, triumphant pipes and drums echoing from the stone walls.

Most of the people who had sheltered within the castle walls had gone home now that it was safe, but every Gabrileño within hearing had gathered to watch. Some jumped with joy; others wept with equal joy.

Leading the procession were two men on horseback with huge grins on their faces as they waved to their countrymen. The Army of San Gabriel had returned, all banners flying. Sofia was too short to see the colonel clearly, so she ruthlessly shoved her way through the gathering crowd.

She reached the front, then stopped dead in her tracks, hardly able to breathe as she recognized the men leading the march. She closed her eyes for a moment, wondering if she was hallucinating, but when she opened them again, the vision hadn't changed. She shrieked, *"Papá! Alexandre!"* as she raced to the horsemen.

His Royal Majesty King Carlos Miguel Emmanuel de la Alcantara leaped from his mount and swept her up in his arms, tears running down his face. "My little Sofi! God in heaven, how you've grown!"

Her brother was only an instant behind and he joined in the three-way hug. "No, she hasn't," Alexandre said with a laugh. "She's still tiny, but she looks much bossier."

Sofia stepped back, studying their beloved faces. They looked thin but otherwise healthy enough. "What happened? There was no word, no report of any kind. We were all sure you were dead!"

"It's a long story, but the short version is that your brother was so obnoxious and difficult that General Baudin slammed us into a French dungeon under false names, told the keepers to allow no outside contact of any sort, and left us to rot," her father explained. "The blasted jailor was incorruptible, so we couldn't get any messages out."

"Be fair, sir!" Alexi protested. "You were every bit as obnoxious."

Sofia supposed that both of them had infuriated Baudin — it was an Alcantara talent — but no doubt the general was too cautious to kill royal prisoners outright, since they might prove valuable later. "Were you freed when the emperor abdicated?"

"Not right away." Her father waved at a man sitting quietly on a horse behind him. "This British colonel, Duval, came looking for us. A very persistent man. With Napoleon off the throne, he was eventually able to bully the truth out of enough people to locate us."

Duval inclined his head in acknowledgment. "I expect you would have been released eventually, but sooner is better than later."

Alexi gave an elaborate shudder. "An understatement! I also give thanks that you were able to bring us to Colonel da Silva for the journey across Spain. The colonel is well, Sofi, but he went directly home once we reached the town. He has been talking about his wife and daughter for the last hundred miles."

"Of course," Sofia said. "No need for him to waste a moment before returning to them." All around her, other reunions were taking place as the returning soldiers were hugged by friends and family. The happiness was contagious, and it also created privacy for Sofia and her family.

Her father said, "I'd like to know more about the fleeing French soldiers we met as we headed up the road to San Gabriel. They were exhausted and demoralized and not inclined to talk, and I didn't want to wait for them to become more communicative."

"General Baudin collected six hundred or so French soldiers and promised them a sweet life if they helped him conquer San Gabriel," Sofia said succinctly. "He planned to force me into marriage and take the crown for himself."

Her father, brother, and Duval all stared at her with horror. Duval recovered first. "Obviously, they didn't succeed. What happened? Baudin wasn't with the men."

"He's dead and his invasion was repelled by ambushing his men in the sunken section of the road into San Gabriel. It was led by your Major Masterson, Colonel Duval, and thank God for him!" Sofia explained.

"What did you do with the French soldiers?"

"We captured and disarmed them and left a company of Gabrileños to guard the captives until we decide what to do," Duval said. "As renegades, they could be shot, but we were all inclined to think that enough blood has been shed."

"If Baudin had been with his men, I'd have cut his liver out with a dull razor!" her father exclaimed, his eyes still furious. "To think he wanted to force you into marriage to gain control of San Gabriel! He died too quickly."

"He is gone, and we can't spare enough food to feed so many captives," Sofia said after a moment's thought. "Escort them back to France and say that they were misled by their renegade leader, General Baudin, and thought they were still fighting under orders."

"See, she's become much bossier," Alexi said. "But it's a good plan."

"I agree," her father said. "Colonel Duval, will you be able to arrange that after you've had a chance to rest?"

"Of course. As you say, it's a good plan," Duval agreed. "Where is my Major Masterson? Surely, he hasn't left for Porto already?"

"He personally took down Baudin and was gravely wounded in the act, but he's now recovering here in the castle," Sofia said. "In fact, he got married last night."

Her father's brows arched. "He fell in love with a local girl?"

"Not exactly. His bride is Athena Markham, and they shall suit very well," Sofia assured him. Thinking that the general spirit of celebration was a good time to ask for favors, Sofia stated, "She has been a treasure beyond price this year, Papá. I don't know how San Gabriel would have managed without her. Will you make her a contessa?"

He blinked. "I suppose I could. She has been a great blessing to San Gabriel and the Alcantaras. I'll draw up the formal paperwork when things have settled down a bit."

"Thank you!" Now for the really great favor. Sofia glanced over her shoulder and saw Justin, quietly waiting with a warm smile for her happiness. She beckoned him forward and took his hand. "Now I would like you to meet my affianced husband, Justin Ballard of Scotland and Porto."

Her father's expression turned briefly thunderous. Then curiosity displaced anger. "Ballard Port?"

"Yes, your highness." Justin bowed re-

428

spectfully. "I brought supplies up from Porto at Major Masterson's request. While here, we did a survey along the river valley, and I believe we have found a way to transport your superb wines to Porto for export."

"Have you now!" Carlos's eyes gleamed. "Speaking of which, I must have some Gabrileño wine instantly. Only then will I know I am really home. Mr. Ballard, we must talk later at greater length. Now, let us go inside. I am anxious to see my home and Uncle Alfonso. Is he still among us, Sofia?"

"Yes, he never believed that you were dead." Sofia took Justin's arm and prepared to climb the steps that led into the castle.

She paused as a different note sounded in the crowd. "She's here! She's here!" a woman cried ecstatically. "The Queen of Heaven has returned!" Other voices took up the cry. *"The Queen of Heaven has returned!"*

"I beg your pardon?" Alexi said, bemused. "A divine visitation? I didn't think the Blessed Mother was *that* interested in our return!"

"The sacred statue was stolen from the church by Baudin's men," Sofia explained as she climbed up two steps to get a better view of what was happening. "Yes, *yes*! The statue is brought through the gates in a donkey cart!"

She plunged back into the crowd. People were falling on their knees and crossing themselves as the ancient, beloved statue approached. And to Sofia's bemusement, the cart was being driven by Jean Marie Paget and another man, who wore what looked like a French uniform with the distinctive blue coat removed.

Justin was right behind Sofia. When the cart stopped, he said, "I'm glad to see you, Jean Marie! How did you find the statue?"

"It was a miracle," the Frenchman explained as he and his companion climbed from the cart and then carefully lifted the statue to the ground.

"A miracle indeed," Sofia said reverently as she crossed herself. Others in the crowd approached to touch the statue, their expressions awed.

Carved of wood and hundreds of years old, the graceful image of the Holy Mother was almost six feet tall and she wore an expression of serene love and compassion. Her jeweled gold crown had been stolen, but otherwise the holy image was undamaged. The crown could be replaced.

Interested in more worldly details, Justin asked, "How did you find the statue? Surely,

Baudin's men haven't carried her clear across Spain twice!"

"I went up to the site of the battle to help translate for the injured and serve in whatever other way I could," Jean Marie explained. "One of the prisoners was my friend Claude Fontaine, who had been knocked unconscious but was not badly hurt." He gestured to the other young man, who bowed deeply.

"Your royal highness, sir," Claude said nervously. "I was part of Baudin's force that came through your country last year. The statue was stolen because of the jewels, but halfway over the mountains, the general said it was too heavy, he would take the jewels and burn the statue."

When Sofia gasped in horror, Claude continued, "I am a good Catholic and felt the same way, your highness. To burn the Blessed Mother would have been sacrilege! So I and another man hid her in a cave not far from the road. Ever since, I have been troubled by the knowledge that she was there alone, stolen from those who love her. So when I saw Jean Marie, I told him of the statue and begged that he rescue her so she could come home."

Taking up the story, Jean Marie said, "I found Captain Oliviera and asked him for permission to release Claude so he could lead me to the cave where Our Lady waited. He agreed and even gave us a cart to bring the statue back."

"You have done a great service for San Gabriel, Jean Marie," Sofia said warmly.

Jean Marie glanced at his friend. "Claude would like to ask for the same sanctuary you offered me, your highness."

Claude bobbed his head. "Your country is very beautiful and I feel that the Blessed Mother led me back here."

Sofia smiled. "Then welcome to your new home, Claude Fontaine." She took Justin's arm, thinking that truly, it was a day of miracles.

As they followed her father, brother, and Colonel Duval into the castle, Justin said under his breath, "I'm your affianced husband?"

Suddenly worried, she said, "Are you not? We had discussed marriage. Do you not wish that anymore?"

"Of course I do!" Justin grinned. "But I think we need to make sure our stories match before your father interrogates me. I'm hoping that he will consider an alliance with the Ballard shipping empire to be worthy of his only daughter."

"He will," Sofia said confidently. "You saw

his interest when you said you had found a route for exporting our wines. San Gabriel must become more involved with the world beyond our borders." Her brow furrowed. "Because I thought marriage impossible, I haven't considered how we would live. Where we would live. What might I expect?" She pulled Justin into the alcove below the steps that led up to the family floor so they could talk in private. "I wish to see more of the world, but . . . but I can't imagine leaving San Gabriel forever."

"You won't have to," Justin assured her. "We would travel regularly. To Edinburgh, to meet my family. Homes in London and Porto. And we would come here, because there will be strong business reasons, as well as family ones. Do you think you will like that? I hope so!"

A slow smile spread over her face as she contemplated her future. "I will love such a life! Most of all because you will be at my side."

"Mi querida!" Justin pulled her into a kiss that lifted her toes from the floor.

She kissed him back, and for the first time she released the full force of her love. By the time the kiss ended, they were both reeling. "We'd better go upstairs," Justin said huskily. "Or we risk behaving very badly!"

433

"We had best marry quickly!" Sofia agreed as she took his arm. They were halfway up the stairs when she said in a low voice, "I had become used to the idea that I would ascend to the throne next year. Now that has changed again. But I think I would have served my country well, wouldn't I?"

"You would," Justin agreed instantly. "You would have been remembered as Queen Sofia the Great and Wise. But you will still serve your country, *querida.*" He raised her hand and kissed her fingers. "We will serve San Gabriel together."

CHAPTER 35

"How does it feel to be back in England?" Will asked.

Athena couldn't tear herself away from the window of the carriage that was taking them through the countryside to London after their early-morning disembarkation. "Wonderful. Strange. *Green!*"

He laughed. "Definitely green. Our reward for enduring English rain."

She settled back in the seat and took Will's hand. Life had changed so much in the last weeks, not least because she and Sofia were both married women now. After grilling Justin Ballard on his family, wealth, and business prospects, King Carlos had given his blessing to his daughter's marriage. The wedding had followed quickly because Athena and Will would be leaving when he recovered enough to travel, and Sofia said it was unthinkable that she marry without Athena by her side.

A royal wedding was just what San Gabriel needed to celebrate the end of the wars and the return of the king and prince, so it had been a very grand affair. Sofia and Justin had both blazed with happiness.

During the feast that followed, Uncle Carlos summoned Athena to the head of the royal table and made her a contessa and a hero of San Gabriel, complete with impressively sealed letters of patent and a bejeweled badge of rank that hung from a gold chain. She could wear it on grand occasions.

Carlos had made the presentation with laughter, but also sincere thanks for her services to his kingdom. He'd added that the title could be passed down through the female line, as well as the male. Athena suspected Sofia's hand in that.

When she returned to her seat, Will grinned and said, "I've always wanted to kiss a countess." And then he had done so, to the cheers of the other wedding guests.

The wedding of Tom Murphy and Maria Cristina Oliviera had been smaller but equally joyous. Tom had bought a handsome villa on the edge of the town, and had carried his bride over the threshold with hoots and laughter.

They were both fine weddings, but as

Athena told Will that night, neither could match the drama of marrying a man on his deathbed. After which he'd taken her to their bed and proved how thoroughly he'd recovered.

The thought made Athena blush and turn her gaze out the window again. Though she'd learned she wasn't with child yet, her female intuition said it wouldn't be long.

She'd never been happier in her life. With Will, she had passion and trust and a deep intimacy that belonged to the two of them alone. With him beside her, she could face anything. "What time do you think we'll reach your brother's house?"

"Just as the midday meal is served, I hope," Will said cheerfully. "Arriving in time for meals is an old joke between us."

She saw the fondness on his face and squeezed his hand. "You are going to like being in the same country with your brother, aren't you?"

"Enormously. And he'll be glad not to have to worry about me so much." Will slid his arm around her shoulders. "We have hours to go. Why not take a nice nap against me?"

"That shouldn't sound appealing when we've been cooped up together on a small packet ship for days, yet oddly, it does." She stretched her legs out and settled down so that her head was on his shoulder and her arm draped across his waist. "Though if we get bored, there is something that I've always wanted to try in a carriage."

Will gave a shout of laughter. "Now that I've recovered from my wounds, you've developed a wicked imagination." He kissed her temple. "Wickedly good."

She dozed off, smiling. She had good reason to fear London's society, but Will she trusted for anything.

"We're almost there." Will pointed at the grand building ahead on the right. "That's Damian's. The club is busiest in the evening, but some members gamble through the night and a fair number come by for a midday meal and a hand or two of cards."

"Impressive! You'll have to take me inside while we're in London." Athena gave him a teasing glance. "Or is that one of those things that women shouldn't do?"

"Mac will be delighted to take you for a tour. Damian's makes a point of being a safe, respectable place for women to visit. A bit fast, but appealingly so. Mac's wife has a lovely little perfume boutique for the customers and she does very well with it, too."

"She's a perfumer?"

"Yes, it's been a tradition among the women of her family for generations." The carriage rumbled to a stop in front of the house just beyond the club. "Here's Mac's house. I hope they're in residence. If they aren't at their country place, he'll probably be over at Damian's."

The guard opened the passenger door and let down the steps. Will exited, then offered his hand to Athena. She didn't need help to get out of a carriage, but she loved his little courtesies. Plus, it was an opportunity to touch her husband, and she would never have too many of those.

She took Will's arm and they were moving toward the entrance to the house when a portly, fashionable, and clearly foxed older man emerged from Damian's. He glanced around as if trying to get his bearings.

His gaze locked on Athena. "Lady Whore!" he cried with delight as he walked unsteadily toward her. "So glad you're back in London! I heard a rumor that you'd died, but damn me if I'm not happy to see you again!"

Athena froze as solid as if ice water had been poured over her. She'd barely set foot on a London street and already her worst fear had been thrown in her face. She wanted to run. Or hide. Or vomit.

As she struggled to breathe, Will barked,

"Sir!" in a voice that would terrify even the most hardened soldier.

He laid a warm, protective palm on the small of Athena's back and continued, "You quite mistake the matter. My wife is the Contessa de la Alcantara and I assume you did not intend to offer her insult. *Did you?*" His tone promised that any insult would be followed by swift and painful consequences.

The drunk's eyes widened and he stammered, "N-no, no, not at all!" He swallowed hard, his Adam's apple bobbing. "A mistake, made a mistake. My sincere apologies, my lady. Contessa."

He bowed so deeply that he almost toppled over. "It's just that you have such a look of a woman I remember, damn me if you don't." He straightened and blinked at her. "You're much younger, though, and now I see your features aren't hers. But her height and grace and presence . . . !"

He looked wistful with memory. "Very sorry to have upset you, but I was so delighted to see you. Her. *Hoped* you were her. Most beautiful woman I ever saw, and the most charming." Muttering to himself, he moved away.

Will wrapped an arm around Athena's shoulders. "Please don't faint here. It will be much more comfortable to do inside."

Shaking and grateful for Will's support, Athena slid her arm around his waist and together they resumed walking toward the entrance of his brother's house. "I don't know if that incident was a sign that I should leave London forever," she said in a shaky voice, "or that it means that things can only get better."

"The latter," he said reassuringly. "That fellow was a horrid introduction to your homeland. But remember that he was delighted and complimentary about your mother's beauty and charm, so it wasn't all bad."

"You're very good at finding silver linings, my lord," she said wryly as they climbed the steps and Will wielded the heavy knocker. Collecting her shaken nerves, she added, "I'll try to see his words as a compliment."

The door was opened by a rugged-looking male servant. He smiled with unprofessional enthusiasm and announced in a stentorian voice, "Lord Masterson! Welcome home!" He stood aside and made a grand gesture for them to enter.

The entryway was well proportioned and elegantly furnished, though a strange statue of a man with an elephant head lent a touch of the exotic. Before Athena could study the stone image more closely, the door at the opposite end of the foyer swung open and a man bounded through. "Will, *finally*!"

He was as tall and broad as Will, and he grabbed his visitor in a crushing and very un-English bear hug. His hair was a slightly warmer shade of brown and his eyes were of two different colors, but no one would ever mistake them for anything but brothers. Without another word being spoken, Athena could see the bond between them, and how they had been each other's salvation.

"Easy, Mac, easy!" Will laughed as he hugged his brother back. "I was on my deathbed a few weeks ago, so show some respect for my aging bones!"

"Sorry!" Mackenzie stepped back, alarmed. "Your deathbed?"

"It could have been worse. I'll explain later." Will took Athena's arm and brought her to his side. "Athena, you'll have guessed that this reprobate is my brother, Sir Damian Mackenzie. Mac, meet Athena, Lady Masterson and Contessa de la Alcantara."

Athena braced herself for shock and perhaps disapproval, but Mackenzie beamed at her with real delight. "What a pleasure this is, my new sister-in-law! Justin Ballard wrote that Will might return with a most magnificent woman at his side. I'm glad you got her to the altar before she knew you well enough to escape, Will."

Laughing, Athena offered her hand. "The pleasure is mine, Sir Damian. Will tried to explain his little brother, but he did you less than justice."

"Call me Mac or Mackenzie." Her brother-in-law clasped her hand warmly between both of his. "Will has been trying to explain me for years, but it's an uphill task."

Athena noticed the heavy gold ring Mackenzie wore. She looked closer. "That looks like Will's signet, but there's a black bar across it?"

"The bar sinister, the mark of illegitimacy in heraldry," Mackenzie explained. "Will gave it to me for a birthday present one year. Sort of a private joke."

Athena said thoughtfully, "Perhaps you should have one made for me, Will."

Her husband chuckled. "Isn't the wedding ring I gave you when I recovered sufficient?"

"It is." They smiled at each other in what she suspected was a ridiculously sentimental way.

"My brother Will, you have returned intact from the field of battle!" This voice was female with a very faint musical accent, and belonged to a dark, spectacularly beautiful woman who flowed across the room to give Will a hug.

"You look splendid, Kiri!" After hugging her in return, Will put his hands on her shoulders and studied her. "Clearly, the baby has arrived. A godson or goddaughter?"

"A most lovely little girl. Damian dotes on her madly and says that she looks just like me. My brother Adam agrees and says she'll likely be a hellion. You shall meet our little Caroline later, but she sleeps now. Pray present me to your fortunate wife!"

"Athena, this is Lady Kiri, my sister-in-law, the perfumer," Will said. "I haven't said much about her because mere words can't do her justice."

Kiri laughed. "Flatterer. Lady Masterson, may I call you Athena since we are now sisters?"

"Of course." Again, Athena offered her hand and the other woman clasped it.

Athena realized how little Will had said about his brother's wife other than that she was adventurous and had interesting ideas. Though not as tall as Athena, Kiri was tall, and she was lovely in an exotic and un-English way, with glossy dark hair and striking green eyes. "Do you prefer Kiri or Lady Kiri?"

"Kiri, please. My father was the Duke of Ashton, my mother a Hindu lady, which is why I am shockingly un-English," she said with a smile. "But come, we were about to sit down to our luncheon. After you have refreshed yourselves, you must join us."

"I see my timing hasn't failed," Will said with a laugh.

Athena studied Kiri thoughtfully. So a duke's daughter had married the illegitimate Mackenzie. No woman would blame her — Will's brother was almost as attractive as Will — but it did explain why Will's attitude to Athena's parentage was so casual.

As Kiri escorted them upstairs to Will's usual rooms, Athena gave thanks that Will had been right that she'd be welcomed by his family. But she couldn't help but wonder how much wider a welcome she would receive.

Over a fine luncheon, Mackenzie said, "Several of the Westerfield Academy old boys and their wives are in town, Will. Shall I invite them for an informal dinner to see you and meet Athena? They'll all want assurance that you've survived the wars intact."

Will glanced at Athena. "Are you willing? I'd like to see my friends, and they'll all want to meet you. I think they feared I was becoming a dour old bachelor." When she hesitated, he said, "Think of it as getting the worst of London over quickly."

"Of course you must see your friends, but I have nothing suitable to wear," she pointed out, glad she had an excuse. "Even when the rest of our luggage arrives, I have nothing that isn't old and unfashionable."

Kiri leaned forward, her eyes bright. "Athena, I have something of a reputation for making friends look their most beautiful on short notice. Will you allow me to turn you out in style? Though you are taller, we are not dissimilar in build, and I have a gown that will suit you very well, with a few minor modifications. Please?"

"She's not exaggerating," Mackenzie said. "Give Kiri a few hours and you'll be fit for the finest society in London."

Athena hesitated, feeling awkward and out of place. Meet so many of Will's grand friends with no time to prepare mentally? Reminding herself that she could face anything with him at her side, she said, "I shall place myself in your hands, Kiri. It will be interesting to see what you can do with such unpromising material!"

CHAPTER 36

Five hours later, Athena stared into the full-length mirror, stunned. "Kiri, you are wasted as a duke's daughter. You could become the most expensive modiste in London if you wished."

Kiri laughed. "I prefer to work with friends. They are less critical than paying customers would be. But you're a very fine advertisement for my skills!"

Athena nodded, admiring the rich burgundy brocade of her gown, which brought out the red tones in her hair. No one would guess that the magnificent gold-embroidered band of material that Kiri had added to the hem wasn't part of the original design. Athena's elegantly upswept hair made her even taller, but not too tall for Will. "Thank you, Kiri! Now I have confidence enough for anything."

"The last touch." Kiri handed her a tiny gilded bottle. "One of my perfumes. Wear it if you approve."

Athena opened the bottle and sniffed, then smiled. "Lovely! It makes me think of earth and sunshine."

"I shall blend a custom perfume when I know you better, but I thought this would suit on short notice."

"No wonder your boutique at Damian's does well." Athena dabbed the perfume on her wrists, then behind her ears. "Who will be coming tonight?"

"Mostly classmates of Will's. My brother Adam, the current Duke of Ashton, and his wife, Mariah. Lord and Lady Kirkland. They both play the piano superbly and I shall try to persuade them to perform for us. The Randalls. Besides being a classmate of Will's, Randall also served in the same regiment for years."

Kiri cocked her head to one side as she considered. "I think that's all, but Will and Damian went out together this afternoon, so I have no idea whom they might bring home. Perhaps they'll find another guest or five."

Athena laughed. "You're very relaxed about that."

"As I said, an informal dinner of friends. What matters is the company." Kiri chuckled. "Though it helps to have a really superior chef, of course."

Athena was about to ask if it was time to go down, when a knock sounded on the door, followed by Will calling, "Are you ready to be admired?"

"Indeed she is," Kiri called back.

The door opened and Will stepped into the dressing room. Athena's jaw dropped at how shockingly handsome and fashionable her husband looked in his dark, superbly tailored evening wear. "You said that a superior valet informed you that a man with your build could never be fashionable! You have proved him wrong."

"It helps when I borrow Mac's clothing," Will explained. "He's much more fashionable than I, and the effect carries over. But look at you, my dear girl! An owl in the finest of feathers!"

Athena blushed. She knew that Will liked her in anything, and best when she wore nothing at all, but the admiration in his gaze was silent proof that he would never be ashamed to have her on his arm.

He came forward and gave her a light kiss before he produced a velvet-covered box. "We visited a jewelry store because Kiri ordered me to buy you garnets. I hope you like garnets? They'll look good with that gown."

Athena opened the box and gasped at the splendor of the intricate necklace and earrings. "These are beautiful!"

No one had ever given her jewelry before. She tilted her head up and gave Will a kiss that was a good deal more than casual. "You are the best of husbands. Will you fasten the necklace for me?"

"With pleasure." Will moved behind her and fastened the catch while she removed the simple gold hoops from her ears, then inserted the lovely dangly garnet earrings. Sliding his hands to her shoulders, he gazed into the mirror as she studied her reflection. "My friends will be dazzled by my good fortune."

"I'll settle for their not being shocked by your error of judgment," Athena said wryly. "And now into battle, my comrades!"

Laughing, Kiri led the way downstairs to where Mackenzie was greeting guests. Introductions were made over sherry glasses, and Will's friends were as welcoming as he'd promised. She knew that not everyone would approve of her heritage, but good friends like these would be enough.

All were profoundly happy to have Will home and safe, and they greeted Athena with enthusiasm. Kiri's brother, Ashton, shared her exotic, mixed-blood good looks, but his wife, Mariah, was a warm and charming English blonde. Lord Kirkland was dark and contained, but clearly delighted to greet Will, and his blond wife had a quiet warmth that made Athena want to purr like a cat.

Last to arrive were the Randalls. He was a tall blond man who matched Will in military bearing, while his wife was a petite brunette who made Athena think of Sofia, though she was older and she radiated calm serenity rather than Sofia's bright charm. With the couple was a handsome dark-haired man who looked like he might be Mrs. Randall's brother.

Mackenzie escorted the newcomers over. Randall caught Will's hand in a hard grip, saying, "There were times I thought we'd never both leave the Peninsula alive!"

"I thought the same," Will said with a laugh. "And quite recently, too!"

As the two men drifted off to talk privately, Mackenzie added, "Athena, this is Lady Julia Randall and her brother."

Another highborn lady, and this one was staring at Athena with disquieting intensity. Perhaps not all of Will's friends would approve of her?

Lady Julia said, tension vibrating in her voice, "Forgive me, Lady Masterson, but was your father the Duke of Castleton?"

Athena flinched back, shocked. How could this woman possibly know . . . ?

Understanding came in an instant. Lady Julia and her brother looked like Athena. The shape of the features, the coloring, were reflections of what Athena saw in the mirror every morning. She swallowed hard, then nodded numbly. "I was never, ever supposed to tell anyone of the connection."

"How very like him!" Lady Julia said with exasperation as she reached out to clasp Athena's hand. "I'm so happy to meet you. I've always wanted a sister, and from what Will wrote about you, you've led a fascinating life."

Athena's eyes filled with tears. "You don't despise me?" she whispered.

"Why on earth would we want to do that?" her brother said as he offered his hand. "It's more likely that you would want to give us the cut. My father died several months ago and he was a *most* difficult man. I'm Castleton now and I learned of the existence of a half sister when I met with my father's lawyers." The new duke shook his head. "He treated you abominably! I hope you won't hold his behavior against Julia and me."

Dazed, Athena said, "I shall forgive the

sins of your father if you'll do the same for the sins of my mother. I'm sure she was no blameless innocent in their affair."

"Then we are free to become friends." He gave her a warm smile very like his sister's. "I'm quite fond of the sister I knew about, so I welcome having another one."

"I never had a brother, but I seem to be acquiring several, your grace!" She nodded toward Mackenzie, who was watching with quiet satisfaction.

"Please call me Anthony," her brother said. "Since you're family."

"You're being so kind!" Athena lost the battle with her tears and gratefully accepted the handkerchief Mackenzie handed her.

"That's because we take after our mother, who was a very kind woman," Julia said with a laugh. "You must resemble your mother also, since Will never would have married a woman who had a temperament like that of my late father." She touched Athena's hand. "I must talk to Kiri because I want to see the baby, but may Anthony and I call again tomorrow? We have so much to learn about each other!"

Athena whispered, "I look forward to your call. I hope I don't prove disappointing on further acquaintance."

"You won't," Anthony said confidently

before he followed his sister and brother-in-law across the room.

Will materialized beside her and slipped his arm around her waist. "Am I permitted to say 'I told you so' about your welcome by my friends?"

She laughed. "You're permitted. I never could have imagined that my father's other children would actually welcome me! How did that come to pass?"

"Justin saw the resemblance, and from what we knew of the late Castleton, the story was a good fit," Will explained. "I wrote Randall and asked him to discuss your possible relationship with Julia. She and her brother had already learned that they had a half sister, so they were delighted to locate you. Neither of them has much reason to be fond of their father, and I've noticed that difficult parents tend to make the children draw closer together."

"How very wise you are." She tilted her head against his, sure that his friends would forgive the impropriety of the gesture on the grounds that she and Will were newly-weds. "Wise and kind and handsome and very, *very* patient! Have I mentioned lately how much I love you?"

Will caught his breath. "No, I don't believe you have."

Startled, she looked into his eyes and realized that in her fear and defensiveness, she'd never actually said that she loved him. "I'm sorry it has taken me so long to find the words, beloved," she whispered. "I love you, body and soul, now and forever, till death do us part. And may that be at least fifty years in the future!"

Will gave her a smile that took her breath away. "Welcome home, my darling little owl. Finally you are where you belong."

And with a flagrant lack of propriety, he kissed her.

AUTHOR'S NOTE

Several years ago, I cruised the Douro River in Northern Portugal from Porto on the Atlantic Coast to the border with Spain, plus an excursion to Salamanca, the great Spanish university town. I saw the terraced vineyards stepping down the steep hills to the river, and was walloped with the impact of concentrated port wine scents when we visited a wine shipper warehouse in Gaia, on the opposite bank of the Douro River from Porto.

This part of the country was heavily involved in the Peninsular Wars, with French, Portuguese, British, and Spanish troops engaging. I learned of the bridge of boats catastrophe when the French invaded Porto, and I stood in the picturesque ruins of Castelo Rodrigo, a medieval hill fortress that has been restored as a market for arts and crafts. The guide on our cruise knew I was a historical writer, and she pointed down the hill and said, "That building is a convent. Wellington used it as a hospital for his men after the battle." Is it any wonder that I've wanted to set a story in that part of the world?

The hero had to be Will Masterson, who was in my Lost Lords series from the beginning, but as a serving officer in the Peninsula, he was usually off stage and he only made appearances in *Loving a Lost Lord* and his half brother's book, *Nowhere Near Respectable.*

But in April 1814, Napoleon abdicated and the long wars were over. (Or so everyone thought. The emperor's escape from Elba and his hundred days of ruling France, culminating in the Battle of Waterloo, were in the future.) Will was ready to go home, and I was ready to complicate his life enormously.

The very small kingdom of San Gabriel is fictional, and I deliberately gave it language and characteristics from both Portugal and Spain. Interestingly, there was a real microstate called Couto Misto on the border between those two countries, and it lasted until the Treaty of Lisbon in 1864 divided the land between Spain and Portugal.

I couldn't use Couto Misto because it had its own history, and also because it was on the northern border of Portugal while I needed a setting on the eastern border. But I did borrow the country's myth of the fugitive pregnant princess (Saint) Ilduara Eriz, who found refuge in Couto Misto and gave birth to (Saint) Rudesind Guterrie. What a great backstory for my fictional San Gabriel!

None of the events in *Once a Soldier* happened. But perhaps they could have.